I0777108

Witch Bottle

Also by J.E. Marriott

The Witch Books:
Witch Tree

The Chameleon Sagas:
Chameleon
Castrum Lucis

The Witchlets of Witches Brew

Magic, Tea & Witches:
Maud and the Tea of Dume

Witch Bottle

J.E. Marriott

Wyrdwood Publications
Canada

THIS BOOK IS PUBLISHED BY WYRDWOOD
PUBLICATIONS, OTTAWA, ON, CANADA

Printed in the United States of America

Issued in print and electronic formats.

ISBN 978-1-988332-12-3 (pbk.)
ISBN 978-1-988332-13-0 (ebook)

First trade paperback edition November 2014
Second trade paperback edition November 2023

Dedication

This book is dedicated to all my wonderful and enthusiastic readers, without whom I would not have written it.

Special mention goes out to the indomitable Lee A. Farruga for her constant encouragement and willingness to help guide me into the limelight.

Also, huge thanks go to Heidi O'Brien for her reliable, strong shoulders and her undying enthusiasm for my stories.

Chapter One

June 1625, London, England.

Again she heard the noise, it was a small squeak, and scratching, so close to her ear it made her twitch and twitching hurt. In fact, the slightest movement of her bruised body made her hurt. She tried to open her eyes but only the right one would open, the left was not only hindered by the bare earth it was resting on, but also by how swollen it was from the beating she'd recently received.

Her tongue roamed carefully around her teeth, probing the loose ones, she gently spat out blood and winced at her split lip. She tried to move, to get away from the irritating noise, she wanted to sit up against the rough stone wall behind her, but, when she tried, the pain in her arm and her side almost made her pass out. She paused mid-movement and breathed deeply as she wavered on the edge of unconsciousness. Laying back down, on the damp, cold floor, she came fully back to her senses and realised the bothersome sounds must be coming from a mouse or a rat nearby.

"'Tis nowt but a critter belonging to thy Mother. Come now, Erda. Thy still be alive." She said, feeling the need to both comfort and chide herself in the gloom.

She looked about her, the best she could with her one properly functioning eye. The small room was very dark, except for a single tallow candle which sat in a pewter holder, placed upon the ground. Its stink fought with the smell of mold and the rank stench of stale urine, which swirled around the room in the cold draught from under the wooden door that made the candle flicker. The old stone walls were damp and slimy, the cold and wet soaked into Erda's clothing chilling her to the bone. She could hear water trickling down the walls somewhere and presumed it was soaking away into the mud floor or perhaps a small drainage grate. There were no shackles attached to the walls or iron rings from what she could see. She breathed a small sigh of relief, at least she was not in the town gaol, very few people come out of there alive.

Her small measure of relief was short lived, however, as she could hear voices and they were getting closer and becoming more distinct.

A light appeared and seemed to grow beneath the door. Erda froze and listened, her stomach dropped with fear when she heard the sound of steel scraping against steel as the door was unbolted. She was in no position to fight or run, so she did the only thing in her power; she closed her good eye and prayed.

As the heavy wooden door opened, light burst into the room, Erda could see the red of it through her eyelids. By sheer force of will alone, she stilled her trembling body so she would appear unconscious. She was now grateful her face was laying in the dirt, hiding her fear.

The footsteps came closer and stopped.

"Thy lazy bitch sleeps still, Doctor." The gruff, uneducated voice called out as he roughly nudged her leg with his foot a couple of times.

"Bring her hence." An educated voice replied from the depths of the dark corridor outside the room.

Erda was roughly grabbed, picked up and thrown over a large man's shoulder making her groan from the pain in her ribs, unfortunately, the sound was out before she could stop it. The man stank of rancid sweat and pitch, the smell was acrid in Erda's nostrils. She fought not to pull away from the stench, careful not to reveal herself as fully awake. Her hair, now messily unbound, fell over her face affording her the opportunity to see where she was going without being seen, or rather, where she had been as she was looking away from the direction they were actually going.

She peered carefully through the curtain of her hair, which only partially obscured her view as the man carried her up rough stone steps, through the richly decorated hallway, out through a large kitchen and into the garden and the fresh night air. She recognised the house, of course, after all it was where she had been giving lessons to the Doctor in the art of Cunning for the last three years and where he had seduced her that first summer. Erda's heart ached deeply, she had loved John and at first he had treated her well, considering she was low-born and she could never be more than a bed mate to him. Over time, she had found out more about the good Doctor than she had truly wanted. Some of the things she'd learnt made her blood boil and they were the reasons why she withheld certain knowledge from him and why she was here now, much to her regret.

The large man carried her past the ornamental garden and down a secluded path to the Doctor's walled herb garden. It only had one low gated entrance, the big man stooped to enter and marched forward to what seemed like the middle of the garden from her vantage point, presumably following his master.

Erda suddenly found herself on the ground, the air forced out of her lungs by the speed of the drop. She groaned as her ribs stabbed pain into her bruised side and she tried desperately to gain her breath once more.

"Ah, my whore with serpent's tongue dost awaken." John said close to her face, while he gently brushed a finger over her unbruised cheek. He seemed reluctant to touch the damage he had created by his very own fist, almost as if it would soil him to do so.

Erda turned her face away and tried to speak but her mouth was dry and her split lip opened again and it began to bleed anew.

"Take her, Baldwin." He said quietly.

Again she was lifted, but this time like a sack of turnips. His hands grabbed her under her arm pits and Baldwin began to drag her backwards. Roughly, she was stood up and set against something hard and her mind faded dizzily for a few moments. When she could focus again she realised she was now bound tightly against the hard thing, no matter how much she tried, she couldn't move an inch. The rope holding her burned her bare flesh where it touched it and crushed against her where it pressed against her clothing. She felt the warm breeze of the late evening and smelled the herbs and flowers upon that welcome breeze. The wind gently stroked her face like a lover's caress. See, thy Mother comforts thee, she thought and breathed in deeply the fragrant and welcoming scent of the garden.

She finally managed to clear her dry throat, "Shalt nay reveal it. It matters nay what thou doest to me." She said bravely, feeling her courage return to her as if the warm breeze had revitalized her.

"Afford me thy place name and death shalt be swift." John said, his voice calm and even.

Erda's spine tingled, she had never heard him sound so calm and yet so evil. "Thwarted shalt thy evil doings be. She is safe, she is safe!" Erda looked away, unable to see him this way after all the moments they had shared as lovers.

"Baldwin make thy start." John said. His face was impassive but his eyes shone with triumph, he knew she would reveal the hiding place before her end.

Baldwin was out of Erda's sight, she tilted her head this way and that to see what he was doing, but she still could not see him. She soon realised she had been tied to a large wooden post and it was too large to see around.

"Doctor Lambe, Doctor Lambe!" An old, male servant called from the garden path, "Thy agent hath arrived, Doctor."

"Now shalt we knowest of thy safe place." John gave a smirk and marched off toward the servant and the house.

Erda tried to wriggle against the ropes again, but they were bound tight and held fast. The movement also caused much pain to rush up her damaged arm and through her ribs, which made the blackness swallow her whole again.

Her eyes shot open as the cold water hit her face, she gasped and blinked away the water. John had now returned from the house and was leaning in really close to sneer at her. She tried to move away from him but she had nowhere to move to.

"Thy destiny is decided, nay struggle thee." He said as he took a step back and began toying disinterestedly with his sleeve cuff.

"Thou shalt rue this day, John." Erda said.

"Nay as thy wilt." He smiled and nodded to Baldwin.

The smell of burning pitch met Erda's nostrils, it made her gag and her eyes stream as Baldwin placed the lit torch onto the bundle of sticks he had already placed by her feet. With a rush of heat, the pitch on the branches caught alight and the cruel fire began to rage toward her. She could feel the unbearable heat getting nearer and nearer to her feet, the smoke blocked almost all her vision as she struggled painfully and desperately against the rope that bound her.

"Before thy fate takes thee, knowest verily thy secret is loose. Dwell thy last stretch of time and lack thy joy. Thy daughter is found." The maniacal joy in John's voice could not be mistaken.

Erda felt her hate for him rise within her and she despised him, in that moment, more than she had ever loathed anything in her life before.

"Nay!" Erda shouted again and again until the smoke dried and burnt her throat making her cough. At last, a scream burst forth from her. She felt her feet blister and the flesh begin to burn away, her skirts caught fire and the flames began to lick up her legs. With a massive effort, she breathed in what little air she could and with the last of her strength she cried, "Thy life shalt be crushed from thee, thee shalt nay rest. Thy body and Soul shall rot in thy own mess akin to the cabbages upon a wet field. I hex thee, John Lambe, I hex thee!"

Before John could ward against Erda's words, she gave her last agonising breath and died, sealing the curse forever as her flesh blacked and the fire roared over her, burning her to naught but ash.

Chapter Two

October, present day, Canada.

The tired woman stood on the gravel road and leant on her large black suitcase, which stood against her leg. The misty rain whirled around her, almost like it was trying to hold her in its wet, wraith-like arms. She was still getting wet, despite the protection of her cheap plastic umbrella and the wind kept trying to steal it from her grasp, but she didn't care. Caring only let her feel the sadness, which lay deep in her heart and that was the last thing she wanted to do right now.

She watched the dark blue cab pull slowly away as it travelled back up the dark, unkempt gravel driveway. She continued to watch as the rain gradually enveloped it, the taillights slowly vanished.

Silence gently fell around her like the mist.

She turned and looked at the reason why she was stood on a gravel road, in a foreign country on a windy, rainy night. She took a deep breath in and slowly let it out.

The stone cottage sat, squat and grey in the intermittent moonlight, the dark windows on each side of the old door appeared as soulless eyes looking out upon the night. The tall maple trees, close to the cottage on the right hand side, cast dark shadows across the roof like claws of an unseen beast. The claws moved in the wind, as if scrapping their talons across the wooden roof shingles, trying to break them and crawl inside. Through the other trees, to the left of the cottage, she could just make out the three quarter moon glinting off the huge lake. The rest of the lake looked dark and inky. In the sky, however, the moon looked pristine and glowed until the clouds quickly moved over it again, seemingly forever hiding its joy. She felt like that moon, all her joy had been covered over and hidden by dark sad clouds.

Sighing heavily, she reached into her handbag for the keys and a small pocket torch she'd brought for just this purpose. She was tired and did not want to be here, she wanted to be at home in her cosy flat in London with Bilsby, her grey coated cat, by a warm fire, albeit an electric one, and a good book, maybe even a glass or two of red wine. She knew she was thinking about home in an effort to put off what she had to do here, but there was just no escaping it, not now as she was finally standing in front of the cottage. She took another deep breath and slowly let it out, "You can do this, Amy." She said to herself and forced her legs to move forward.

Gravel crunched underfoot, and echoed around the empty woods surrounding the cottage. With an effort she managed to drag her heavy suitcase behind her. She tried really hard to ignore the breathless butterflies flying around in her stomach as she anticipated what she was going to see within. Stepping from the rough gravel road onto the old stone path, she brushed past the overgrown weeds, shrubs and bushes that lined the pathway to the front door. It had been so long since she'd been here that seeing the old wooden door, even by torchlight, gave her a weird sense of déjà vu rather than any particular childhood memory.

She closed the useless umbrella to free her hand and placed it on top of the suitcase, then picked the largest and oldest key of the bunch, unlocked the old oak door and pushed. It didn't move. The door was reluctant to open from years of being unused and had warped with the rain. It was obvious that she would need to get it fixed and she put it on her mental 'to do' list. She shoved it harder with her shoulder, it moved more freely and she was finally able to swing it open fully. Scrambling inside, hauling in her belongings and closing the solid door hard behind her, she quickly shut out the wind and rain.

Leaning against the door and straining to see inside the cottage with her little torch, she spotted an old fashioned oil lamp on a small table in the hallway, thankfully with a box of matches sat next to it. Relieved, she lit it and a warm, amber light filled the hallway, reflecting in the mirror that hung above the small table. The lamp was the only warmth in the cottage, in fact it felt warmer outside than it did inside. Amy shivered and kept her coat zipped up against the chill. She noticed her long brown hair dripped onto her coat as if she'd had no protection from the rain at all. Lifting the lamp from the table Amy decided to check around the old cottage. She remembered it had been built from local stone on the outside and all the internal walls were clad with wooden boards and they were coated with a warm wood coloured varnish, the light from the lamp made the walls seem warmer than they actually were. The cottage was very old and had been in her family for many generations and now, she was the new owner. It felt strange for her to own a home of her own, she had only ever rented apartments in London before now.

Without warning, the bone deep sadness of the recent loss of her parents hit Amy. She gasped as the still raw pain ripped through her chest. She gave it a moment to wash over her before she clamped the lid shut again on her broken heart and sealed the hurt back in. This was now a familiar thing she had to do quite often just to function properly. One day she would let it out, but not today. No, not today.

This loss was the reason for her trip here, to this empty place full of her parents' belongings. The plan was to sort it out and sell the cottage, then return back to her life in London, as a successful writer of children's fiction. She took a couple of steadying breaths and looked around her. She hadn't been here for many, many years and she dreaded seeing all her parents belongings.

Amy walked the length of the hall carrying the lamp, the warm light showing her a glimpse of the four rooms off the hallway; a kitchen, lounge and two bedrooms, all with lower than normal sized doorways. She peeked into each bedroom and saw the furniture was covered with dust sheets. The bedrooms were quite sparse with only a bed in each, a nightstand and a wooden wardrobe. Both of the bedrooms had a large plaited rug, in the old homesteading style, on the bare wooden floor.

She walked back through the hallway into the lounge, a small cosy room with a huge fireplace dominating it. The wooden mantle was covered in dusty old photographs and ornaments. The wide stone chimney climbed up the wall behind it like a creeping vine that had been turned to stone in some bizarre fairytale. There was a three-piece sofa, again covered in dust sheets, and what looked like a wooden table under a sheet by the front window. The small windows were set deep, due to the thickness of the walls and they held nothing but dead plants, dusty ornaments and darkness. There was a wooden cabinet against one wall mostly hidden under another cover. Once again, the old fashioned rugs covered the bare wooden floor boards.

Amy knelt by the empty fireplace, grabbed some kindling from the brass bucket that sat to one side of the grate and quickly lit a fire and added larger logs from the pile left there. Within minutes the fire was roaring away and began to spread its warmth and light into the room, it started to make the place feel more welcoming. She stood and dusted off her hands, pleased to be able to do something positive and glad the chimney wasn't blocked after all these years. Although, it probably needed a good clean.

Picking up the lamp again, she walked through the low doorway into the simple kitchen. It had been remodeled at some time in the past, probably the 1970's, but was a perfectly usable kitchen for her short stay. She wiped away a substantial cobweb and, with the lamp against the glass, she peered through the small kitchen window and looked into the solarium beyond, a modern addition her parents had built, along with the modern bathroom.

Just beside the doorway that led to the solarium and bathroom, was a tall cupboard. Amy opened it, reached in and flicked on the main power switch. She clicked on the kitchen light and was pleased to see it all still worked. She turned off the oil lamp and placed it onto the old wooden kitchen table next to the empty fruit bowl.

Her parents had also constructed an access panel to the old attic just inside the kitchen doorway when they had become the owners of the cottage when Amy's Grandfather had died. Amy opened the hatch door, then pulled down and unfolded the aluminium ladder and climbed up. Turning on the light just inside the attic, she figured she'd better check for leaks while it was raining.

The attic space ran the entire length of the house and was unused except for storage, however, it had been fully boarded out as a usable room. The attic had two small windows, one at each end of the house, and it was filled with old furniture, mirrors, trunks, boxes and toys. It overflowed with the memories of a happy past with people now lost and gone forever. Tears prickled Amy's eyes and threatened to overflow. She gritted her teeth and decided to look for leaks another time and quickly climbed back down, stowing the ladder and closing the hatch firmly behind her.

She swallowed back the tears. "Prioritize." She said out loud.

A pale glow of light caught her attention, it seemed to be coming from the solarium. Amy followed the light into the glass room. It was filled with covered wicker furniture and dead plants. The pale light, she realised, was the early dawn as the sun began its ascent, she could see it clearly now that the misty rain had finally cleared. The sun's pale colours were being reflected in the lake, of which the solarium had a magnificent view. She looked around the sky for the remains of the moon, it could still be seen, but only just, its glow receding as the brightness of its astral companion became stronger as it gradually withdrew from view.

Removing one of the chair covers, folding it and placing it on the chair opposite, Amy coughed at the dust and sat down to watch the dawn. Its light rippled over the surface of the lake in a distinctly magical way, the wind made the water and colours shimmer. The sky was beginning to clear into a beautiful pale blue and she was truly in awe of the new morning's beauty.

The sky somehow seemed larger here than at home, almost as if it had swelled up or the land had shrunk back. Amy couldn't fathom why but there just seemed to be so much more of it. Perhaps it was the lack of buildings blocking the view, or the lack of grey clouds that seem always present in the English sky, but still, the sight of the open sky with such light was as breathtaking as it was intoxicating. She now understood what her mother had meant by a 'Canadian sky' and felt more connected to her at that moment than she had in a long time. To know that she was sitting looking at something her mother had so dearly loved, brought Amy a measure of joy she'd been missing of late and her mother's happiness and feelings for Canada naturally led her to think about her parents and how they had met.

Amy's mother, Selena, had loved visiting her husband's homeland. Eric, Selena's husband and Amy's father, had been in England studying when they fell in love. They had married and stayed in England but they had made many visits to Canada and to this cottage. Her father had refused to sell it because it was the 'family cottage' and, as soon as Selena had laid her eyes on it, she had fallen deeply in love with it, the lake and with Canada and its friendly people.

Amy had been born in England but had spent many happy summers with her brother and parents at the cottage during her childhood. Then her brother had sadly taken his own life and her father had a stroke and the cottage was closed up until he 'was well enough to travel again'. Sadly, he never was and, three months ago, a fire had ended both her parents' lives and it had fallen to Amy, their only surviving child, to deal with this cottage.

She closed her eyes, only now had she been able to build up the courage, and step away from her career, to come here and sort out the family's belongings. At least, with the fire, everything they had owned in England had been lost and, as sad as that was, it had saved her from having to go through every intimate detail of their lives, until now.

Amy resisted the urge to dwell on her parents any longer, at least for now, and she quietly watched the pale light grow stronger in the sky. Strangely, she was not feeling tired from her late night flight even though her internal clock was all messed up. Glancing at her watch, she remembered the flight attendant had told her it was best to alter her watch first thing during the flight, something to do with it being easier to adjust during the seven-hour flight. So it may be seven in the morning here, but to her it was mid-day. It would probably take a good night's sleep or two to readjust properly.

Stretching, Amy settled in her chair and watched the sun finally make its way into view and was greeted by a glorious sight. The land behind the cottage ran directly down to the lake and some of it had been cleared of trees, probably many years ago. At the edge of the lake there was a stony shoreline and a small landing heading out into the water for boats and she remembered it was great fun to dive from. The lake was huge and around it were beautiful hills and woodland. The trees were ablaze with colours, reds, oranges, browns and yellows; autumn in Canada had to be seen to be believed.

Amy was enchanted by the view and noticed there were also a few large houses dotted about in the woodland surrounding the lake. However, there were none like this cottage, they were all modern day mansions. Maybe she would get a good price for the old cottage and the forty acres surrounding it, she thought hopefully.

During the next hour, Amy pottered around with a cup of hot water in one hand, not having found any tea or coffee that was still, even remotely, in date. She fired up the old AGA oil fuelled stove in the kitchen that ran the heating for the cottage, removed dust sheets and found a linen cupboard filled with sheets, blankets and old-fashioned quilts. She took advantage of the lovely day to hang some bedding outside on the old washing line, so it could air out before she could make herself a bed for later that night.

When she eventually came to a standstill, Amy found some packets of dried soup that were, surprisingly, still in date. She tried not to ponder too long on that hideous thought and heated one for a late lunch, vowing to get to town soon to buy some proper food. While eating, Amy made a list of items she would need. The cottage was out of almost everything from cleaning products to tea.

I may not want to stay for long but I'm damned sure I'm going to make this place look good again, even if it'll only be the realtor who appreciates it, she thought.

After eating, Amy decided to stretch her legs and see if there was still a bicycle in the old barn, at least it would be quicker than walking to the nearby town of Morton Creek for supplies. Putting on her jacket and throwing the big, heavy bunch of keys in her pocket, she went out of the back door to investigate. The day was glorious with warm autumn sunshine, a deep blue sky and the beautiful leaves which seemed to glow on the trees from the sunlight. The old, mossy stone path led around the side of the house and joined with the gravel roadway. The unkempt road, full of overgrown weeds and potholes, ended abruptly in front of the large wooden barn.

In moments, she had the barn's rusty padlock in hand and was trying all the keys on the bunch for the right one. At last, she found it and with a little bit of waggling she managed to undo the old lock. She swung open the large, creaky old barn door and right there, in front of her, sat some sort of vehicle covered with yet another dust sheet. "No way." She said excitedly and rushed over to uncover it.

Sitting there majestically was her father's pride and joy. It was a 1950's blue Chevy, part car, part truck in immaculate condition. She smiled to herself remembering how her father had restored the car slowly and lovingly over the years, she was surprised she'd not remembered it earlier. More importantly, she now had a vehicle to get around town and to do chores with. Amy took a moment to appreciate all her father's hard work on the vehicle and then began to look around at the rest of the barn. Some of the planks on its walls had shrunk with age and the sunshine poured in through the gaps. The roof had a few small holes where she could see the sky through, but all in all, it was a functional barn. At some point, it had housed animals. There were stalls on each side, a hay loft above on the left. There was even an old lawn mower, the type you pushed with no engine to sit on. Everywhere, there were old rusty tools hanging from beams, some of them Amy recognised but many more she didn't.

By the time Amy had finished poking around the old barn, the light was beginning to fade and she decided to visit town the following day. Amy headed back to the house and finished removing the dust sheets in the lounge. She discovered that what she thought to be a table against the back wall was actually a beautiful old-fashioned mahogany desk with drawers, it looked like it had been made a hundred years ago. Surprisingly, she hadn't remembered it from her visits either, but then she knew that the eyes of a child saw very different things than the eyes of an adult. She tried the desk drawers and all but one was unlocked and full of various bits and bobs. However, none of the keys on the big bunch fit into the lock on the last drawer. Hopefully, she would find the key elsewhere, she thought.

The large cabinet against the wall turned out to be the old mahogany dresser when the cover was removed. The bottom was made up of three large draws and the top held three deep shelves, which were all covered with piles of books, old glass bottles, carved wooden toys, dried flowers and various other knick-knacks. Every shelf was filled to overflowing and she was surprised that nothing had fallen when she'd yanked the dust sheet off.   Amy   sighed, there was such a lot of sorting to do, more than she had imagined for what was basically a summer holiday home. You would think her parents lived there all year round by the amount of their possessions they stored here. At least, working for herself, as an author, she didn't have a set time to get back for, her friends knew she was out of the country until further notice and her agent was not expecting anything from her for a while, it was a good thing too, considering how much more sorting she would now have to do.

Amy knelt down and poked the fire, it roared into life once again and its warmth cheered her. She had always liked a real fire and it was one thing she had really wanted when she eventually bought herself a house. She chuckled to herself, here she was thinking about what she would like in a house, while sitting in a lovely old stone cottage, in the wilds of

Canada and not only did it belong to her but it also had many of the things she wanted in her dream house. Shaking her head at the crazy twist that life had thrown at her, she sat down in a nearby chair and was surprised by how squishy and comfortable it was, even if it was covered in some hideous 70's style orange and brown flowery material.

Leaning her head back and relaxing, she watched the flames lick the wood in the fireplace. It occurred to her that the flames were caressing and seducing the logs until they were no more. Her mind wandered as the warm fire relaxed her even more and she began to see images in the flames of people dancing and writhing around the logs. Amy began to fall into a deep sleep just as the images of the flame people began to scream and twist in agony as they were consumed by the insatiable fire.

The last thing she heard as she drifted away was the crackle of the fire and what could have been a woman's voice whispering gently in her ear, "Welcome home, Amy."

Chapter Three

Outside the building, the bright, beautiful day was marred by the police and emergency vehicles with their lights flashing and the colours reflecting in the windows like neon lights flashing in a downtown red light district.

The Ontario Provincial Police officers struggled to hold local newspaper reporters and TV crews back and the inquisitive crowd of public spectators was growing by the minute. It didn't help that the crime scene was at the side of a busy road, which brought it undue attention.

Inside the building, the sound of a camera clicking and whirring was all that could be heard as it echoed off the room's walls to the stunned silence of those at the scene.

Normally, the inside of a crime scene was a buzz of movement and noise, but this one was different.

So very different.

Not one of the five people now present at the scene had ever seen anything like this before, in all their many years of combined service.

The young OPP officer, who had received the call and been the first officer on the scene, stood apart from the rest and, outside of the room, in the motel's corridor. He had seen and smelt enough of these murders to last him a lifetime, maybe even several lifetimes. He was looking somewhat green and a little shamefaced as he had already vomited in the hallway when he first arrived. There was no way in hell he was going back into that room, not even if the Chief of Police asked him personally.

The corpulent Coroner, Dr. William Chester, hung around near the doorway waiting for the Forensic Identification Officer and his photographer to finish their work. He surveyed the hideous scene but all he could think about was the breakfast he had been so cruelly separated from when the call came in and he rushed to the scene. Now he wondered why he had left it and rushed over, it was such a waste of a good steak and eggs. He would just have to get a larger lunch that was all.

The last person to enter the room was Detective Inspector Andy Withers, he was a near retirement, and rather exhausted, cop who had seen too many things over the years. He hated being dragged out to the small towns in his area, especially so early in the morning. He hated even more the stench of blood and voided bowels, he'd expected to get used to it, during his years of service, but never had. Even he, as jaded as he was, had never seen anything quite like this horror and he was quite sure he'd never see anything like it again and he thanked God for that.

The room, which had revolted every single one of them, was a small motel room off the only road into the town of Morton Creek, it held twin double beds and all the usual furnishings, the room was a little run down but good enough for a cheap overnight stay. It was at present, however, almost completely covered with blood. The blood had come from the three occupants who were presently pinned to the walls. Each naked body had its own wall and each had its arms and legs stretched out wide and, more weirdly, the bodies were actually stuck half way up each wall, as if thrown there by a great force. Each victim had been tortured and every one of them had their entrails hanging out of their bodies, which cascaded down to the floor like a fleshy, blood-red waterfall. Almost everything in the room was red with dried or drying blood, the carpet squished underfoot gruesomely and bled onto the forensic shoe covers when walked upon. The only places that had escaped the carnage were the small bathroom, which shone bright white, a stark contrast against the rest of the room, and small patches of the wild flower wallpaper, especially around the main doorway. It was as if a blood bomb had exploded a few feet inside the room facing all its destructive power towards the twin double beds.

The smell in the room was so overwhelmingly horrendous that everyone was trying to work while retching and they all had to wear copious amounts of menthol rub under their noses, to avoid inhaling too much of the vomit inducing stench.

Detective Inspector Andy took one look at the bloody scene, put his gloved hand into his white forensic overall and reached for his phone on his uniform's utility belt and rang his junior partner's number. "Mitch, we've got a nasty one, can you come back from your vacation two days early? Yes, we can reschedule it, you can finish your deck later." Andy shook his head, closed his phone, shoved it back into his belt and zipped the white overall back up to the neck.

"When was the last time they were seen alive?" Andy said over his shoulder to the O.P.P. officer who stood in the hall.

"The motel clerk said he delivered them a note at 8:45pm last night and they were all alive then because he saw into the room and they were all there, sir. He said nothing seemed amiss at that time." The young man said.

"Right, go back to the clerk and get every detail you can off him about the note and who gave him it to pass on. Also, check if there are any working security cameras and, if there are, get the clerk to point out the person that handed him the note."

"Yes, sir." The officer moved quickly down the hallway, only too glad to be away from the horrific scene.

Looking around the chaos of the crime scene, Andy spotted a woman's handbag hung on the back of a chair near the small table against one of the walls. He carefully walked towards it to investigate, his feet squelched with every step and he tried really hard to ignore that he was walking on someone's internal body fluids. Trying not to shudder he picked the purse up, examined all the various contents typically found in a woman's bag and extracted an ID from within. "Amanda Hamilton, 38 from...who cares...somewhere out of town." He said out loud, sighed and placed the ID in an evidence bag and pocketed it.

On the small table, next to the chair, lay an amazingly spotless and perfectly white piece of paper that had been folded three times and a torn envelope, it had presumably come in, next to it. He peered at the paper and the only thing on it was a strange circular design, perhaps a tattoo design or a business logo, he thought.

Turning from this oddity, he watched his Forensic Identification Officer work the scene. "Lou, any idea what the fuck happened here?" He said.

Lou looked up from what he was doing and said, "Well, we've got a man, a woman and a teenage boy, probably a family. Maybe a robbery gone wrong, too early to tell, though." He stood, making his, now not so white overalls, rustle and crunch in the only way that the specially coated paper overalls can. "Never seen anything like this, they were tortured mercilessly. What a mess."

"How are they hung on the wall? I see no rope, straps or anything else." The Detective Inspector said as he took a step closer.

"Probably super glue, that shit will stick anything together." Lou said without any hint of humour.

"Seriously? The fucker super glued them to the wall and gutted them?"

"Maybe, won't know for sure until I've done some tests. Bry, can you make sure you get some close up shots of their adherence to the wall as I try to get them off it? Andy? Will? I'm going to need your help over here." He said as he stepped nearer to the woman.

The Forensic Photographer placed himself in position as the Coroner and the Detective Inspector came over to assist Lou. Carefully, the three of them took a limb each and tried to peel the woman off the wall. Without warning, she was suddenly free of it and the three men staggered back unsteadily with the dead weight of her.

Unfortunately, all of them got covered in her viscera. At exactly the same time, the other two bodies instantly dropped from the walls too, splashing blood and gore everywhere.

"Jesus!" The Coroner said as he got doused in the body fluids.

"Fuck!" Andy said as he stood there dripping with blood, not wanting to move a muscle.

Bryer was the only one not completely covered down his front as he was facing the wall taking the photographs, his back, however, looked like red rain had hit his white overalls and hit it hard.

Unfortunately, one of the bodies landed on a blood soaked bed and bounced off it onto the wet sticky carpet making even more of a splash, while the other body landed awkwardly over the small table and chair that held the handbag.

The body, crashing into the table, dislodged the pile of local attraction fliers, takeout menus and newspapers that lay on it. The single sheet of white paper, which was on top of that pile, fluttered downward in the rank air like a freshly plucked feather as it gently floated towards the wet, bloody floor and certain immersion in the wetness there.

Andy spotted the paper in mid-air and instinctively knew it was more important than any of the other items on that table and, as he was the nearest person to it, he rushed over and just managed to grab the piece of paper right out of the air, inches before it landed on the blood soaked carpet like all the other paperwork had just done.

In a flash, Andy saw the strange symbol again on the crisp white paper, as he did so he lost his balance, slipped and landed on his ass in a puddle of gore.

"Fuck." The Detective said through gritted teeth. "Some days I fucking hate my job."

Chapter Four

Amy had awoken with a fresh sense of purpose and had decided to go to Morton Creek, it was, as far as she could remember, the nearest town to the cottage and where she could buy all the supplies she was going to need. Amy was actually looking forward to driving her father's truck, it would be almost like connecting with him again, and she looked forward to seeing how much had changed in Morton Creek. She checked the tire pressure and the oil on the old Chevy and climbed in behind the wheel and turned the key. Surprisingly, it started almost straight away, she was truly impressed and had half thought it wouldn't after all these years.

At first, driving on the opposite side of the road from what she was used to in the UK, made her a little nervous but as she drove along the beautiful country roads, edged with a wonderful array of autumnal colours from the trees, she couldn't help but relax. She opened the window and breathed in the lovely fresh air of the warm autumn morning. She smiled to herself, driving in London was never this pleasant or relaxing, she truly enjoyed every minute of the twenty minute drive.

As she pulled to a stop outside the small general store, in downtown Morton Creek, she glanced down the road that led through the town. It was a typical small town with just one main street, a dozen shops and a few restaurants along it. It was, however, just as lovely as she remembered it from her childhood, each side of the road was lined with glorious autumnal trees and little flower and shrubbery beds and, although the flowers had come to the end of their beauty, the beds were still attractive to the eye and well maintained.

Climbing out of the truck, Amy smiled to herself as she breathed in the clean air and an unexpected feeling of peace entered her heart as she realised just how much she felt at home in this town from her past. It wasn't just the buildings of this town she loved, it was also the wooden area surrounding the town, the river at the east end of it and the clean, bright streets that were well cared for. The fresh air and blue skies made Amy feel at home, somewhat unlike the dirty streets, crowded roads and smog of London.

Over the years, not much had changed in Morton Creek she was surprised to see, the old fashioned street lamps still had banners on them advertising the next thing on the town's social calendar, this time it was the annual Pumpkin Ball, the highlight of this month's social calendar and the biggest event of the fall season.

The general store, she parked in front of, had been there as long as she could remember, it looked just the same to her now adult eyes. The store was a cross between a grocers and a hardware store. Boxes of apples and piles of pumpkins sat side by side on the pavement with planks of wood, brooms and old fashioned oil lamps. The store had been proudly owned and run by the MacArthur family since the town was founded in 1848, at least so said the plaque by the door. These days, it was run by Cyrus and Kathleen MacArthur, both of whom had been close friends of Amy's Mum and Dad. This was to be the first time she had seen them since her parents had died. Amy took a deep breath and bravely walked towards the open door of the store.

A bell jingled overhead as Amy stood on the welcome mat. Looking around her she was amazed that the inside of the store really hadn't changed either, it was still like walking into an Aladdin's cave. The two stores were bound together in one long crazy jumble, to the right there was all the hardware and its counter, now empty. Amy presumed Cyrus was off dealing with a customer in the bowels of the store.

To the left, another counter, but this one was surrounded by groceries bursting from every shelf, box and stand. There, Kathleen stood deep in conversation with a customer, she hadn't yet noticed Amy and that gave Amy a chance to look at the lady she had know as Aunt Kath, but whom she hadn't seen in many years.

Kathleen was a small round woman with a shock of grey curly hair that just had a life of its own. The perpetual smile on her face hadn't waned over the years, it had just deepened the happy look on her aged but beautiful face. Her eyes had a happy, almost mischievous glint, and those eyes now turned towards Amy, as the customer she had been serving, moved away from the counter.

"Good morning, are you looking for anything in particular?" Aunt Kath said.

"Morning, I'm looking for my Aunt Kath." Amy said as a joyous smile spread across her face.

Kathleen looked taken aback until she suddenly recognised Amy. "Amy! Oh my goodness, is

that you? What are you doing here? It's been years."
The little woman rushed around the counter and
bundled Amy into a warm hug that smelled
wonderfully of good, old fashioned lavender
perfume. Finally, breaking the hug, she held Amy at
arms length, "I was so sorry to hear about what
happened to Selena and Eric, it's a terrible, terrible
thing. You look just like your mom, you know." She
said and placed a gentle hand on Amy's cheek.

"So they say." The usual sadness, which came
whenever she thought of her parents, filled her heart
and clouded her vision with tears. Amy braced
herself for the painful sobs but this time they
didn't come and a single tear ran down her cheek.

Kathleen brushed away the tear, "Not to
worry, sweetheart, you were always part of our
family and that's not going to change any day soon,
indeed no." She smiled and patted Amy's shoulder.
"Wait 'til Cyrus sees you, the old fool will be
delirious."

"Old I can take, but who you callin' a fool?
You married me, remember." A man's gravelly voice
came from behind a stack of paint tins.

"Hush your silliness, man, come and see who's
on a visit." Kath said in the tone of one long
married.

"I'm a'comin', woman." A slim, balding man, in overalls, stepped out from behind the paint stand. His delightfully wrinkled face was tanned in the way of one who enjoys working outside. He peered at Amy and a huge smile lit up his face. "Amy Grey! Is that you all grown up?"

"Hello, Uncle Cy."

"Come here and give this old man some love, it's been too long, girl."

She went gladly into his bony but warm embrace and felt safe again.

The next three hours were filled with tea, homemade cookies and laughter as Amy sat with them in the store. It was just what Amy needed and it was a delight to catch up with them both. When Amy finally left, not only did she come away with groceries, a promise of a firewood delivery and a container of homemade soup but also an invitation to dinner the following night at their apartment above the store. For the first time since her arrival, Amy felt truly at home and loved, something she had been deeply missing of late.

After stowing her shopping in the truck, Amy decided to take a wander down Main Street. The sun was warm overhead as she walked along discovering new shops and remembering the old. She was delighted to find that 'Acker's Cafe' still existed. It was the place where her family went for brunch every Sunday during the summer. There is something so very reassuring in seeing beloved places from your childhood standing the test of time, despite the downward turn of the local economy, she thought. Such things can make your heart sing, and that's exactly what it did to Amy, a wave of nostalgia filled Amy's heart and she felt drawn into the place. Although the awnings had been changed over the windows, since her last visit many years ago, the cafe looked no different. The green door still showed the well-worn welcome sign and the windows were still full of shiny leafed plants.

Following her joy at seeing the old place, Amy decided to stop for lunch there before heading back to the cottage and all the emotionally tiring work that was awaiting her there. Determinedly, she stepped into another place from her childhood and, finding a booth by the window, she glanced around at the interior. The cafe was made to be as homey as possible, the walls were painted a warm terracotta colour with wooden shelving displaying old fashioned wares such as oil lamps, antique hand tools and quilts. There were a few stools at the wooden counter, some free standing chairs and tables, and over by the large brick fireplace, there were comfy chairs and coffee tables. Although the fire wasn't lit, the entire area gave the feeling of being cozy and warm. Amy imagined it was a perfect place to sit by the roaring fire, sipping hot chocolate on a cold, snowy day.

She noticed there were a few people in the cafe already and more continued to come in after Amy sat down, it seemed that 'Acker's Cafe' was still the place to go to for lunch. Amy looked at the menu on the table until a young, fair-haired waitress came and took Amy's order of a club sandwich with a green tea. Amy sat and looked at the other customers, she didn't recognise anyone, so she just sat and people watched while waiting for her meal. As a children's author, Amy loved to gather visual details about people, she would watch families and how they interacted with each other, and sometimes it gave her inspiration for her books. With this in mind, she sat watching a mum and three children, who all looked under ten years old, eat and talk with each other at a nearby table. She watched as two of the children began to squabble and smiled to herself as their mum quickly squashed the argument, it reminded her greatly of trips there with her family. Once again, she found herself wondering if having a family of her own was in her future, she sincerely hoped it was someday.

Her thoughts were disturbed by the waitress returning with her order.

"Does Ben Acker still run the cafe?" She asked the girl.

"No, sorry. He retired before I came here, I think about five years ago. His granddaughter, Annabeth, runs it now.' She said and placed the food on the table. "Enjoy your meal."

"Thanks." Amy said as the waitress turned away, her attention going back to her other customers.

"Annabeth, huh?" Amy said to herself and tried to remember her face. All she could remember of Annabeth was that she was the Acker's spoiled granddaughter who wanted nothing to do with the 'English girl' as Annabeth had called her. Amy's attention was diverted from her lunch and drawn out the window as two police cars pulled up outside the cafe, one of them had 'Coroner' written on the side. Four men got out of the cars, one carried a briefcase sized metal case, and he quickly spoke to the others then climbed into a truck and drove off. The two older, heavier set men headed for the cafe door, whilst the third, a handsome younger man who was carrying two similar metal cases, said his goodbyes and walked away heading down Main Street.

The two remaining men entered the cafe and walked across the room to hellos and nods from some of the customers. They both sat at the end of the counter, near Amy's booth.

A tall woman with perfect makeup and lots of brown hair, that was entirely too big even if this was the eighties, came over to take their order. "What can I do for you, Detective Andy?" She said and leant forward just a little so her cleavage was more prominent.

"Coffee. Black and strong, Annabeth." He said in a voice that couldn't be less interested in her if he tried. He leant his elbows on the counter and put his head in his hands.

So that was Annabeth, I didn't expect her to look like that somehow, Amy thought to herself as she tried to watch her without obviously staring.

Annabeth nodded as if used to the Detective's lack of interest, "And for you, Doc?"

"I'll have the lunch special with extra fries."

The detective's head shot up.

"Seriously? How the fuck can you eat after the morning we've had?" He said.

"You get used to it in my job." He then lowered his voice just a little, "After all, bodies are just meat in the end."

The detective looked repulsed and sighed, "When will you have some answers for me?"

"Maybe...two or three days. I'll start the autopsies after lunch, but honestly, I think cause of death is self-evident."

"Maybe, maybe not...there's just something odd about all this." Detective Andy frowned as he poured sugar in his newly arrived coffee.

Amy tried not to look like she was listening but it was hard not to stare, her imagination was taking over and she wanted to know what had happened, something rather nasty by the sounds of it. The two men went on to talk about fishing and everyday things, as if the last thing they wanted to talk about right now was their morning together. Of course, this only made Amy all the more intrigued.

The rest of her lunch in the cafe was quiet and uneventful, much to the disappointment of Amy's imagination.

Before Amy left town to return to the cottage, she made a quick stop at the realtor's office to book an appointment for the realtor to appraise the cottage in two days time. She also dropped into the local news and magazine store to order the daily newspaper to be delivered to the cottage.

On the road home, Amy felt like she was being watched or followed, she kept nervously glancing in her rear view mirror only to be greeted by an empty road. Still, she couldn't shake the strange feeling.

*

The following day she spent sorting and clearing out the attic, which was much easier than she had first thought as everything was already boxed up. All she had to do was go through each box or trunk and decide if the contents would be kept, given to charity or put in garbage bags. When she had finally managed to bring down all the boxes, bags and other paraphernalia of family life at the cottage, she was amazed at the size of the now empty attic. It was huge and because it spanned the entire length of the cottage, it would make a great studio for a painter or even an office for a small business or perhaps even a writer. She pondered this thought as she looked out of the small, dirty window towards the lake.

Seeing the dust, cobwebs and years of dirt around her, Amy had a great compulsion to clean and spent the rest of the afternoon doing just that in every room of the house. By the time it came to shower and dress for dinner at Aunt Kath's and Uncle Cy's, the cottage was much cleaner and Amy felt a lot more relaxed. Cleaning always had that effect on her, it was a great way to still the mind.

*

Arriving at the store, which was now closed, Amy took the outside staircase up to the second floor of the building where Kath and Cy's apartment was located. The store downstairs had originally been two stores and was converted into one big one by Cy's father, Harold, this made their apartment really rather large and they had never felt the need to rent the place out and buy a house elsewhere in town. They'd only had a small family, one son who had moved away at the age of eighteen to attend college and who had never come back, so their needs were small. They did, however, have a small piece of land behind the store where they had created a beautiful garden, which included Kath's kitchen garden that was full of vegetables and herbs.

Amy knocked on the green painted door and let herself in as she had always been told to. "Hello? Aunt Kath? Uncle Cy?" She called out as she removed her coat and hung it on the hooks by the door.

"We're in the kitchen, Amy." Came Aunt Kath's voice.

Amy took off her shoes and padded down the hallway in her purple socks.

The hallway opened into a wonderful large kitchen full of every appliance you could imagine, Aunt Kath was an avid cook and she liked the proper tools for the job. The copious amount of kitchen cabinets that lined the walls had white doors on them and the walls, what could be seen of them, were painted a bright sunny yellow. The whole effect made for one bright kitchen and, although it wasn't Amy's taste, it suited Aunt Kath's bright and happy nature.

"Hello Amy, dear. I do hope you are hungry, I've made my infamous chilli to warm us all up. I see the wind has turned and the cold will be coming in quickly now."

"Hello, smells good." Amy sat on one of the stools at the island in the centre of the kitchen, next to Uncle Cy who was flicking through a catalogue.

"Nice to have you back with us again, Amy. I was just saying so to Kath." He said and patted her on the hand.

"It's nice to be here actually, I wasn't sure it would be what with...well, you know."

Kath nodded and opened the fridge. "Do you want a beer with your dinner, I know Cy will have one."

"Yup." Cy said and took the beer can from his wife.

"Sure, why not." Amy said as she watched Kath open two cans and pour them into glasses, one for herself and one for Amy.

"Almost super time, Cy. Time to put work away for the night."

"Yup, just a minute. Finishing the order for the snow shovels and then I'll be done with it." He said as he scribbled down information on an order form. "I'll ring it through in the morning and we should have them by next week."

"We'll need them too, it's going to be a long hard winter this year." Kath said.

"How can you tell? It's so lovely and sunny every day here." Amy said as she took the offered glass of beer from Kath. "Thanks."

"When you've lived as long as we have, you get to know the signs. The wind changes direction and comes off the river with a cold mean streak, and especially when it happens in October and not November, then we know it's going to be a long cold one."

"And she feels it in her bones." Cy said mysteriously and wiggled his bushy eyebrows at Amy.

Amy laughed at him.

Kath swiped him with the tea towel. "Hush now." She said but chuckled too. "Who's ready to eat?"

Amy and Cy both said 'me' at the same time and laughed again.

"So I see, all right, Cy can you bring the chili pot through and Amy if you could bring the garlic bread?"

"Sure." Amy said and followed Cy and Kath out of the kitchen and into the dining room.

Their dining room was just off the kitchen and next to the lounge. The large mahogany table with eight chairs dominated the room, its dark sleek surface was an interesting contrast against the light coloured wallpaper with spring flowers on it. There was an old sideboard that matched the table, which held two beautiful silver candlesticks. Above the sideboard, was a painting of Cy's grandmother, an elegant lady who was obviously a part of a wealthy family by her clothes and jewellery.

Amy knew that Cy's family had once been great landowners and had lived in the largest house in the area and the store had been one of their many holdings, but over the years the family fortune had dwindled away and all that was now left was a few items from the big house including the items in this room, some jewellery and the store. Amy glanced at the painting of the woman and had the very same feeling about her as she had as a child, Mrs Ada MacArthur was a mean spirited, harsh woman who looked down on everyone. One look at the picture and Amy shuddered, she had never liked the look in her eyes. Trying to ignore the thought that the eyes were looking at her, perhaps even looking directly into her Soul, Amy forced herself to sit down at the table with Cy and Kath.

"So have you decided if you are still going to sell the cottage, Amy?" Kath said as she spooned out chilli for everyone.

"Yes. I think it's for the best. My life is in London." Amy said as she helped herself to the garlic bread. "Actually, the lady from Carpenter's Realty is coming out tomorrow to look at it."

"Ah...dear Emily, yes, she'll do a good job, get you what you want for it." Cy said as he enthusiastically began eating his chilli.

"I can't help but think it's sad." Kath said.

"Kathleen, we've talked about this. It's Amy's decision." Cy said as he looked sternly at her across the table.

"I know, I know. It's just... well, it's been in the family for so many years. It seems a shame to be giving up on it now."

"I'm not giving up on it, I'm giving it a chance to be lived in again, to have a family enjoy it." Amy said. She felt a little stung by the thought of giving up on her family's home.

"Perhaps, one day you will have a family of your own and then you could bring them out to the cottage yourself." Kath said hopefully trying to change Amy's mind.

"I hope I do, but I can't leave the cottage just sitting there slowly falling apart until that happens, can I?"

"Well, no, but you could come out for holidays and then we would get to see you more often too." Kath said.

"Hmm..." Amy said, not wanting to prolong the conversation. "Can I ask..." Amy ate a mouthful of delicious garlic bread, "have you ever felt anything at the cottage?"

"What do you mean?" Cy said.

"Well, I dunno...something, different, odd even."

"Now you're starting to sound like your Aunt." Cy laughed.

"I'm serious, sometimes it feels a bit creepy." Amy said and looked at her Aunt.

"Never when there are other people there, but once when I dropped something off for your mum, when they were out, it did feel like someone was watching me even standing behind me, but when I turned round there was nothing there of course." Kath said.

"You just spooked yourself, is all. To think anything else is nonsense." Cy said.

"Maybe." Kath said but looked at Amy with a look that said she wasn't convinced.

Amy knew how she felt, there was just something a little unnerving about the cottage sometimes.

Chapter Five

The following day, Amy was happy she'd spent some time the previous afternoon, before going out to dinner, cleaning and tidying. The cottage was now in the best shape for the realtor's appointment this morning and Amy knew she didn't have to rush around, she could enjoy a leisurely breakfast and relax, which she did.

After washing the few dishes from her breakfast, she glanced at the kitchen clock, Ms Carpenter, the Realtor, was due in thirty minutes and, as Amy was completely ready for her visit, she decided to take her second mug of tea and the newly delivered newspaper into the conservatory and enjoy a few moments to herself.

Again, the view was magnificent on yet another bright October day, the sunlight glinted off

the huge lake and the varied colours of the trees
shone like precious jewels around it. Amy sat and put
her feet up on the padded wicker stool, she decided
she was certainly going to miss that view when she
went home. Her flat, in London, didn't even have a
window box for her to grow anything in and it
looked down on the small concrete yard of her
neighbour's house, which was usually filled with
rubbish bins and bicycles. Amy longed for some
greenery or even a garden in her life, she had always
fancied being a bit of a gardener like her father. She
had also noticed that having greenery around her
always made her feel more relaxed and somehow
more whole, it lifted her heart with happiness and
she liked the feeling.

Taking a careful sip from her hot tea she
unfolded the newspaper and was surprised to see a
photo of Detective Inspector Andy Withers, whom
she had seen in the cafe yesterday, on the front page
next to the scary headline:

Family Killed in Motel Horror. Police Baffled.

"Oh my God." She said to herself as her
attention became glued to the page. The grizzly
details of the crime scene seemed to leap out at her
from the newsprint, making her shudder with

disgust. She was pretty sure the British newspapers didn't normally go into that much hideous detail, did they? Finally, she turned the page and read some of the other articles, but, reluctantly she put the paper aside as her mind kept going back to the murders and she did not want to be reminded of the horrors they had found in the motel room. Amy distracted herself by watching a white cloud slip slowly by in the perfectly serene blue sky. How can such disgusting things happen in such a beautiful world, she wondered to herself. Admittedly, it was not for the first time that such a thought had entered her mind, especially after seeing a disaster or horrible crime. There was so much beauty around us, but so few people even noticed it any more while they rushed around doing the things they thought were far more important. Perhaps, if everyone stopped to smell the roses once in a while, there wouldn't be quite so many horrible things happening in the world, she thought. She knew deep down that it was a vain hope but sometimes hope was all one had in life and she clung to it.

The dull sound of thudding woke her from her deep thoughts, she sat still trying to figure out what the noise was. There it was again. It sounded like someone knocking but oddly not, it was a very weird thudding sound. Realising it must have been the

Realtor lady arriving early, Amy hurried out of the conservatory, back through the kitchen and down the hallway to the front door. With a hard tug, the door gave way and creaked open as Amy peered out at a handsome man, who looked a little familiar, as he stood on her doorstep and in both of his hands he held silver coloured metal cases. He was quite tall, maybe six feet and well built.

"Can I help you?" Amy said, looking up at him and noticed his incredible blue eyes.

"Hi, I'm looking for Ms Amy Grey." He said.

"You've found her, how may I help?"

"Hi, sorry." The man said as he put down one of the metal cases and held out his hand. "I'm Bryer Burnett, but most folks around here just call me Bry. I'm the photographer for Carpenter Realty."

"Oh, right. Nice to meet you...Bryer. I think you're a little early, but you are most welcome to come in and make a start, if you would like." Amy said.

"Thank you, ma'am." He said and picked up his case again.

Amy moved aside to let him in and had to hide a smirk that had quickly appeared on her face, with a reply like that she'd expected him to be tipping his hat too, if he'd been wearing one. Although she was glad he wasn't as the sun shone on his lovely nut brown coloured hair making her want to play in it with her fingers, she'd always had a thing for men with longer hair and his, slightly wavy hair, just met the top of his shoulders. She tried, incredulously, to ignore her racing pulse, although she couldn't help but take in the rest of him and she gave him a furtive, and appreciative, once-over with her eyes.

He wore a green plaid shirt and jeans with what looked like cowboy boots sticking out from under them. Amy liked what she saw and her curiosity was not the only thing that was piqued by him, she found him very attractive indeed. Sometimes, you find people in your everyday life that you are inexplicably, and sexually, attracted to, even though you don't know them and that was exactly what she was feeling about Bryer Burnett. She tried really hard not to stare too much as he walked down her hallway.

It wasn't long before he had his photography equipment out and sorted, ready to shoot and he had proceeded to take pictures of each room when Ms Carpenter arrived.

Ms Emily Carpenter was a small, polite lady in her mid-sixties with a 1950's fashion sense and her attitude was extremely professional, if a little imperious. She introduced herself with a forceful handshake and immediately began taking measurements and making notes on every room, without making much conversation. Amy followed her around feeling quite unnecessary to the whole process. To make up for her inability to help, she offered both her visitors hot drinks but they declined and continued with their work, without needing anything from her.

Finally, the older woman said, "I think, Miss Grey, you will get a handsome price for this lovely cottage, very few of this age and location come up for sale and even if the buyer is not interested in the cottage, after all it is probably only a three season home, the land is incredibly sought after." With that comment Ms Carpenter turned away from Amy and walked out of the kitchen and into the conservatory.

Surprised, Amy followed her, "Oh, I hadn't considered that someone wouldn't want the cottage." She couldn't help but feel more than a little disappointed at the thought, who wouldn't want this lovely place? Were they mad?

"This area is well known for wealthy families buying the land and having a custom house built, as you can see from the view." She stretched out her arm to encompass the wonderful view of the lake and the huge mansions secreted around the edge of it and half hidden amongst the trees.

"I see." Amy said as indeed she did see, she looked at the massive houses that lined the lake and really rather disliked them for their lack of character, they were modern monstrosities to her eye.

"I think it would be a shame to tear this old place down." Bryer said from behind them.

Amy jumped, she hadn't heard him approach.

"Yes, well, that might be so, Bryer, but you are not the one purchasing it, now are you?" Ms Carpenter said in a curt and rather condescending voice.

"No, ma'am." He said, completely unfazed by her tone.

"I think that is all I need for the inside, Miss Grey." She said as she put her tape measure and note book back inside her handbag, fastened it and placed it over her left wrist. She then made her way to the back door. "Bryer? Have you photographed the land yet?"

"No ma'am, not yet, was just about to, though."

"Well, hurry up, will you? You know very well we have another property in Glendale to visit this afternoon and I want to be home in time for dinner." She said imperiously as she began to walk outside, not waiting for him. "You know how Henry dislikes it when I'm not home for dinner." She called over her shoulder as she continued outside and strode purposefully down the path to the lake and the wooden dock.

He silently saluted her with his forefinger touching his forehead as he walked past Amy with a mischievous look on his face. "By the way..." he said with a hushed conspiratorial tone, "'Henry' is her cat, not her husband." He grinned at Amy.

Amy chuckled at him and followed them both outside. She watched, from a distance, as they took measurements of the dock and photos of the land and the small overgrown gardens at the front and back of the property.

Eventually, they were finished and Ms Carpenter told Amy she would be in touch shortly as she bustled off to her car. She called back to Bryer, who was unlocking his truck and opening the door to stow his photographic equipment away, "I'll see you at the Henman's in Glendale, Bryer. Don't be late." She waved and drove off down the drive, without a second glance in Amy's direction.

"Well, that was interesting." Amy said as she watched Bryer put his two metal cases in his truck.

Admittedly, she was enjoying the view, he was rather nicely built and those jeans looked good on him after all.

"Yeah, Ms Emily can be a bit old fashioned and strict at times but she has a good heart." He said as he turned round.

"I didn't mean her, although I'm sure you are right. I was thinking about someone buying this place but not actually wanting the cottage. How sad." Amy said looking back at her family's vacation home, a place that had been a home to her family for several generations and over a couple of hundred years.

"I agree, there's not many of these old places left."

"Isn't there a law to stop old buildings being torn down here?" Amy said, wondering if it was like England in that respect.

"Sure, but you would have to get it listed as a heritage building first, to stop it. It's a lot of paperwork and many hoops to jump through, but worth it if you want to save the old place."

"Hmm..." Amy nodded.

"It was nice to meet you, Miss Grey." He smiled and held out his hand to shake hers.

Amy took his hand in hers and a warm tingle of excitement ran up her arm from his warm touch. A smile burst onto Amy's face and so did an unexpected blush, which she quickly tried to cover with her hand. "Please, call me Amy. Miss Grey makes me sound like an old maiden aunt or something."

His smile widened, "Only if you call me Bry." He said as he climbed up into his truck.

"Deal."

"Good." He started the engine, nodded goodbye to her and began to drive slowly down the gravel drive and make his way back towards the main road.

Amy watched him go but didn't see that he looked back in his mirror at her as she had already turned around to go back inside the cottage.

His truck screeched to a sudden halt just at the first bend.

Amy looked back towards the driveway but his truck was just out of view around the bend and she thought he must have stopped for a squirrel or something and she continued to walk back inside the cottage unconcerned.

Bryer had stamped on the brakes when he had looked in his rear view mirror at Amy.

He rubbed his eyes as if to clear away what he had just seen. He could have sworn he saw two women, instead of one, standing on the path outside the cottage. One was Amy for sure, but the other...the other looked odd and very out of place and, more importantly, he knew there was no one else in the cottage with Amy. He reversed just a couple of feet around the bend so he could see the cottage clearly again and saw there was no one at all standing outside. He took a deep breath and blew it out noisily.

He can't have seen another person, he was imagining it, he decided. I need more sleep, he murmured to himself and promised not to have caffeine before bed again, especially after recently working at a nasty, multiple murder scene. He ignored all his instincts which were presently screaming at him, telling him he had seen something important and it was not something that should be so easily brushed aside.

Shaking his head as if to dislodge the image like a nuisance cobweb, he cracked a joint in his neck and opened the window. Wanting a distraction, he turned on the radio and forced his brain to not think about what he thought he had seen, which he obviously couldn't have, and continued to drive out to Glendale and his next appointment.

Chapter Six

July, 1628, London, England.

The handsome gentleman, dressed in the finest clothes, remained seated on his wooden bench with an imperious and lofty air about him.

He watched the play from beginning to end and now waited while the crowd applauded the players as they came forward to the edge of the wooden stage and bowed, the footlights making their faces glow eerily.

He knew how to play people to get what he wanted, he'd had years of practice after all. He knew if he looked a little resistant to the enjoyment of this evening's entertainment then he would be offered something more for his favour. He slowly clapped, his eyes watching the crowded room like an eagle searching for its prey.

As usual, it didn't take long and he suppressed a smug smile that had crept onto his face, lest it be noticed, and replaced it with a perfected bored expression.

He watched Mathius Goodman climbing the wooden steps close to where he was seated. Sweat glistened on the man's round, ruddy face, his jowls and expansive belly wobbled with the effort of the climb, even though the seating area was but one flight up from the ground.

He swallowed his disdain for the corpulent owner of the theatre and nodded to him as he approached.

"Ah, how now, John?" Mathius wheezed, "A fine show, was it not?" He levered himself down on the edge of the wooden bench right next to the important and influential man and panted from the exertion.

The stench of Mathius' sweat and foul breath wafted towards John, he tried not to show his deep distaste for this common, little man and resisted the urge to hold his kerchief to his nose. "Thou hast chosen a singular word for it." John replied, with no hint of enjoyment.

Mathius looked at him worriedly, wheezed even more and wiped his sweating face with his kerchief. "Perchance and prithee, thou canst accompany myself to dinner on the morrow? I meet with an actor from The Globe theatre."

John raised an eyebrow in suspicion.

"Verily! He doth agree to read my play and put forth to show at The Globe. Wilt thou abide me and give good discourse on it? Thou wilt gladly attend super and late carousal at yonder theatre anon?"

John watched as the last of the unwashed public left the theatre, while the players spoke amongst themselves down by the stage. They were getting rowdy and patting each other on the back, pleased with their performance. He could hear plans being made to retire to a local tavern and bawdy house to celebrate.

John pulled his thoughts back to the conversation with Mathius. "Alas, I wilt be a'doctoring on the morrow, Mathius. An important man who wilt pay handsomely." At last, we have come to it, John thought to himself.

"I pray thee, such man of substance as thee doth add weight to my endeavour and happily I shall add weight to thy purse."

John held up his hand to pretend his resistance.

"Thou shalt not refuse my gift!" Mathius said looking stern and a little offended.

"As thou wilt, Mathius. Attend thee, I shalt." John said. With the deal struck, he watched Mathius descend the stair and rejoin his players looking overtly happy with himself and John allowed the smug satisfied smile creep upon his face again. "Tiresome, foul-stenched fool." John said quietly to himself as he stood and straightened his immaculate clothing.

John, still pleased by his manipulations, whistled tunelessly but happily to himself as he headed towards the door and left the theatre. The cool air of the summer night caressed his skin, refreshing him from the warmth and stink of the once crowded playhouse. On the breeze, though, he could smell the dirt of the streets of London and he took a kerchief from his pocket and quickly held it to his nose. Stepping carefully over the animal waste at his feet, and trying not to slip on it as he carefully stayed away from the drain down the centre of the street, which carried the human waste, amongst other things. He saw the half moon reflected in water upon the ground, the puddles were a remnant of a short but urgent and welcome summer storm earlier in the evening.

He was proud of his power and influence over Mathius, something he thought he'd lost after the trouble of the last few months. With the help of

George, his friend the 1st Duke of Buckingham, yet another man who could be easily manipulated, John had escaped the death penalty, although they called it a postponement. More importantly to him, his reputation had been tainted with the accusations of murder by magic, poisoning and rape. Of course, these charges were true, although he would never admit it to anyone, he knew too well how to survive, and life had taught him thoroughly. Such thoughts of his past left a sour taste in his mouth and he longed to reach home to swill the taste away with some fine brandy, but first he must get himself to the Dog & Duck to meet with the book collector, a man who worked for him and who scoured libraries and private collections for the rare works John required.

With his mind distracted, it took a while for him to hear the growing noise of a rabble behind him. Presuming it was just the last attendees of the play or perhaps the overflow from the nearby tavern, he thought nothing of it.

That is until he heard his name mentioned.

His heart skipped a beat and he had an urgent need to run. His instincts were screaming at him to get away and get away right now. However, being a man full of his own self-importance, and great depths of arrogance, he ignored his instincts and stood his ground, rounding on the group now forming nearby.

"'Tis 'im!" A voice called from the group.

"Aye, 'tis tha devil 'imself!" Another shouted.

The group moved closer as one, like seaweed moves on the tide, and as each person shouted abuse, the anger of the mob increased two fold.

"Away with ye, canst thou leave a Doctor to his thoughts?" John sighed, he'd had this trouble before, especially since walking away from the court and their charges.

"Thee's naught a Doctor, thee's tha devil and a murderer and rapist of that young'en Joan Seager, was 'er name. We knows thee, John Lambe." Said the man at the front, by his size and clothing a Blacksmith by trade.

The mob pushed ever closer as John stepped back a few paces and looked around him for assistance. The few people that were upon the street, and who were not with the mob, turned away from him. Abruptly, he found himself with his back against a stone wall, the mob formed a semi-circle around him and the large man began to walk to and fro in front of John, like a lion stalking its prey.

"Begone and alloweth me to go hither this night, I shalt bring no charges to bear. Wherefore doth thou hath the right to.... " John said and paused. His brain urgently looking for a way out of the tiresome situation, his only hope was to intimidate this insolent rabble. "Great influence within the household of the Duke of Buckingham and indeed with thy King I have. Step aside, I command you!"

"By my hammer and tongs, we shalt not!" Said the Blacksmith.

"Begone, I say." John said as he looked from one person to the next, trying to find a person he knew so he could intimidate or threaten them, when none could be found he looked for a gap, to escape through, in the wall of angry people.

"Devil!" A woman cried.

"Witch!" Another woman's voice called.

The mob cheered and surged forward menacingly.

"Thy court mayhap released ye, but God sees thee and wants justice for poor wee Joan." The Blacksmith roared.

That's when the first stone hit John on the chest and he doubled up in pain as the air rushed from his lungs.

For a moment nothing else happened, the people stood silently and watched him gasp for air. Then, like a ripple in a pond, the shouting began and grew until it became a deafening roar. The mob now began to shout, 'Kill 'im! Kill the Devil!" and rocks flew at him from every direction, pummelling John to the cobble stoned ground. One rock caught him in the eye, he screamed as pain shot through his head and he felt his eye socket crush inwards.

Still the rocks rained down upon him and he struggled to breathe through the excruciating pain from his broken body. He cowered like a street urchin in the filth and grime of a back street of London. His once elegant clothes were torn and covered with his blood as he curled up and tried to make himself as small as possible between the stone wall and the cobbled street. His final breath left his mouth when the large stone, thrown by the Blacksmith himself, smashed into his throat, collapsing his windpipe and crushing his spine.

John Lambe, astrologer to the peers of the realm, doctor, cunning man, extortionist, murderer and rapist died in a puddle of his own blood, gore and broken bones.

Chapter Seven

October, present day, Canada

As the evening closed in and the cold wind blew the brightly coloured leaves around the stone building, two young women sat in the small dorm room, surrounded by textbooks and posters. The room had a very basic kitchen, which was made up of a microwave, a toaster oven, a small fridge and a few shelves where the cheap food packets and tins, the staple of any student's menu, were a little too neatly stacked.

Both of the women sat eating their steaming noodles in a companionable silence, one young woman was sitting on the only chair in the room and the other sat on the bed. They had decided to take the opportunity of a food break from studying, due to the change in subject matter. Nikki, whose room it was, finished her noodles first, put her empty bowl on the bedside table and began to pull out another set of study books from her backpack.

"You know, Susannah is waiting for Billy to come over soon. Do you want to go to the library to study with me instead? You know how loud they get and we'll get more done that way." Olivia said as she too finished her noodles and looked apologetically at her friend.

"No, I'm tired and I don't want to carry all these books over there. Let's hope they go out or fall asleep tonight." Nikki said as she got comfortable on her bed again and began spreading out the books.

"Yeah, I think you're hoping but we will see." Olivia put her bowl in Nikki's. "I'm going to make a coffee before I start again, want one?"

"Yes, thanks."

Olivia practically lived in Nikki's room and not her own, next door, which she shared with Susannah. Olivia had become friends with Nikki on the first day at the university and she wished they were sharing a room together. Susannah was okay, but she was more interested in her boyfriend than actually doing any school work and, as Olivia was there on a scholarship, she simply didn't have that luxury. She had to keep up her grades or lose the scholarship and no boyfriend was worth that, she had decided.

Olivia boiled some water and added it to the instant coffee in the mugs, carefully crossing the room again, this time with the hot drinks, she put them on the small table by Nikki's bed next to the dirty bowls.

"Great, thanks." Nikki said.

"So what did you think of Dr Peterson's discussion today, was that awesome or what?" Olivia said enthusiastically.

The rest of their conversation was utterly drowned out by very loud music.

"Seriously?" Nikki said looking up at the wall behind her as it was the one that joined her room to Olivia's and Susannah's room.

The noise was definitely coming from the dorm room next door and it was deafening, the throbbing music was so loud that objects on the shelves were vibrating and now there was a tell-tale loud knocking coming through the wall, which told the girls exactly what Susannah and Billy were doing in Olivia's shared room.

Nikki and Olivia looked at each other.

Nikki sighed, this was becoming a regular thing most nights and she was truly getting sick of it. "For fuck's sake. Can't you tell your roomie to keep it down, Liv?" Nikki said and scowled at Olivia, "I'm trying to study here. You are trying to study too, it's time they stopped being so selfish."

"I'm sorry, Nikki, I did warn you and ask you to go to the library with me, you know how loud they can get."

"One of these days, she will get herself in trouble. Can't you go and tell her to shut the fuck up?" Nikki said as she untangled herself from her bed covers and books, got up and went over to her food shelves, where some of the cans had fallen due to the vibration. 'This is crazy." She said as she slammed them back into their rightful places.

"Yeah, I'll talk to her tomorrow."

"Sorry, Liv, it's not your fault if you have a pain in the ass for a roomy." Nikki regretted losing her temper with her friend.

All of a sudden there was complete silence.

"Oh, thank God!" Nikki said. "Perhaps I can learn something now, some of us care about the test tomorrow." Shaking her head, Nikki returned to her bed and her mountain of study books.

"Oh, that's so much better, I can think clearly now. I promise I'll mention it to Susannah in the morning." Olivia said as she made up the cot bed that only just fit between Nikki's bed and the window in the small dorm room, it was usually where she slept when Susannah had her boyfriend over. She sure as hell didn't want to sleep in her own bed with those two going at it all night long and anyway, Billy gave Olivia the creeps, he was just too smarmy and thought too highly of himself and his impressive ability, so he thought, to get any girl he wanted. Olivia thought he was a dick and had never been able to understand what Susannah saw in him.

Throwing herself on the narrow folding bed, she took off her trainers, threw them to the floor and pulled out a chocolate bar and a large book from her backpack. After offering Nikki some, she began biting off chunks of the chocolate and chewing it enthusiastically while she leant back against the wall, supported the textbook on her knees and began reading a chapter in her Psychology 101 book. She sat for a while like this and then moved to lay on her stomach so she could make some notes more easily, that was, of course, until the blood curdling scream rent the air in two and made her stop mid sentence and mid chew.

They both snapped their heads up at the same time and they stared at each other. It seemed like time around them had come to a stop for a moment and then, finally, so did the scream.

Olivia raised an eyebrow at her friend.

The universe seemed to hold its breath along with Olivia and Nikki in the odd silence that followed.

Neither woman moved a muscle.

Finally, the spell was broken and Olivia sat up. "Do ya think that was real or just someone messing about?" Olivia looked nervously at her friend.

Nikki shrugged her shoulders and shook her head, she had an unsure but worried look on her face. "No clue."

"Perhaps we should take a look out in the hall?" Olivia rose, walked across her friend's overly neat room and leant her ear against the door, trying to listen to what was happening on the other side of it.

"Can you hear anything?" Nikki said.

"No, it's all quiet." Taking a deep breath, Olivia slowly opened the door and peeked out. Other students were doing the same and she could see many heads nervously sticking out from their doorways.

Tom and Brandon, two of the university jocks, appeared in the corridor with baseball bats in their hands. They were dressed only in T-shirts, boxer shorts and they both had bare feet, they had obviously just run up the stairs from the male dorm below as they were also a little out of breath. They looked around nervously and walked further along the corridor.

"Liv, did you hear where it came from?" Tom said as he drew level with Nikki's door.

"What's happening?" Nikki said loudly from behind Olivia making her jump and squeal.

"Shit, Nikki, don't do that!" Liv said as she leant against the door frame breathing heavily.

"Sorry."

Olivia turned back to Tom, "I don't know where it came from but it sounded really close and very loud."

"Yeah, we heard it downstairs." Brandon said. "We thought it was our game at first but then Danny said his RPG character doesn't scream like a girl when shot." Brandon quietly laughed to himself in a nervous kind of way.

"Shut the fuck up." Tom said abruptly to Brandon. "Can you hear anything?" He asked Olivia.

She shook her head.

The young men began to creep forward listening hard but the tension had now been broken and other students were coming out into the hall and beginning to talk loudly, wondering what had happened. Some students were angry and complained about their noisy neighbours, others just looked around warily and then went back into their rooms as if they had decided it was just a stupid prank and nothing to do with them.

Tom knocked on each of the doors along the corridor, to check if the students were okay, a few doors remained closed, presumably the ones where the students were out. He worked his way back down the hallway towards Olivia and finally knocked on the door of Olivia's actual dorm room, next door, but no answer came. "Billy and Susannah were in tonight, right?"

"Yeah, we heard them...erm...earlier." Olivia said as she leaned out from the next doorway.

"Shit. Billy certainly knows how to score." Brandon said with an envious grin.

"Don't be a dick, Brandon." Olivia said.

With a deep breath, she plucked up some courage from the depths of her Soul and pushed past him into the corridor and stood in front of her dorm room door. Looking around her for backup and then looking directly at Tom, who nodded encouragingly, she turned the door handle.

It was locked.

She rushed back past everyone and almost flew back into Nikki's room to grab her keys from a pocket in her backpack and she then marched straight back to the locked door. Inserting the key and turning it slowly in the lock, she felt a horrible dread build up inside her and it crawled around under her skin making it prickle in an intense and uncomfortable way, her instincts were screaming that something was wrong, horribly and terribly wrong.

Before she had got the door open even an inch, the smell struck her like a blow to the chest, she staggered backwards under the weight of it as the stench of death assaulted her nostrils. The smell had now reached Tom and Brandon, who were standing behind her, they recoiled just as she had and began retching in the corridor.

"What the fuck is that smell?" Tom said as he put his hand over his nose and mouth. He stepped forward and stood beside Olivia.

"I don't think we should go in there." Brandon said meekly and stepped back a few steps from the door and the stink.

Pulling the neck of her t-shirt up over her nose, Olivia bravely opened the door and although the light was dim, due to the room only being lit by a single candle, she saw an image that would stay in her mind for the rest of her life.

The sound of retching and screaming came from behind her and forward through the open doorway to wash over her as Olivia gripped the door frame and tried to process what she was looking at.

Her friend, and roommate, Susannah was laid on the bed utterly naked with her boyfriend, Billy, next to her, and, as normal as that should be, it wasn't anything like normal. The bodies were on the bed, yes, except their body parts happened to be all mixed together. Their heads were on the pillows while their arms and legs were a jumbled bloody mess covering the entirety of the bed. Body parts and internal organs were strewn around the bed in no particular order, as if someone had collected them in a bucket and just thrown them at the bed, not caring where each of them landed. It was like a demented Picasso painting, if he had only painted in red and used dismembered limbs and organs as his models.

As the bloody image crawled and seeped into her mind, Olivia began to see weird dots before her eyes and a sudden dizziness gripped her making her stagger a little before she completely passed out. Unfortunately, she collapsed face first into the warm blood soaked carpet of her dorm room.

*

When Olivia awoke, and only for a brief moment, she thought, just maybe, she was laid in an ambulance. She blinked and tried to focus on exactly where she was and what had happened, but then everything changed and all she could see, and smell, was her roommate's body parts strewn all over the bed. She trembled as a deep shudder rippled around her body melting her bones and making her feel sickly weak, she rubbed her eyes as if to rub away the horrific images.

Finally, removing her hands from her face, she looked around her again, this time she saw the inside of the ambulance properly and allowed herself a few deep breaths to try to make her racing heart relax a little, before it burst out of her chest like some alien in a movie.

She stared around her, shock having dulled her senses. She could see out of the back of the ambulance and she simply stared at the many cars, emergency vehicles with flashing lights and people moving about, many of them coming out of the university's residential hall.

Two men, who she didn't recognise, approached the ambulance looking directly at her. She gazed at them uncomprehendingly.

"Miss Olivia Hamilton? May I ask you some questions?" The middle aged man asked as he stood at the end of the stretcher by the ambulance door. The other, younger man stood next to him with a notebook in hand, looking at her.

"I...err...yeah." Olivia looked at them while a Paramedic checked her pulse and then wrapped a blanket around her.

"I am Detective Inspector Andy Withers and this is Detective Staff Sergeant Mitch Roberts, we are with the Criminal Investigation Branch of the O.P.P. Are you well enough to talk to us?"

Olivia nodded.

"Thank you. Can you tell me everything that happened tonight? In as much detail as possible please."

"Sure." Olivia explained everything she did and saw that night in a very monotone voice, she recalled every small detail as if watching a movie and she saw it all again, in her mind and in a strangely detached way.

"Thank you, Miss Hamilton. I think that's all we need for now. I believe they're going to take you to the hospital for observation shortly."

The Paramedic nodded.

"Okay." She said without really focusing.

"Is there anyone we can call for you?" Mitch said, pen poised above his notepad.

"No. Thanks." She said with no emotion either in her voice nor on her face.

Poor kid, thought Andy, when the shock wears off she will probably need therapy and lots of it. With a sigh he and his partner moved away from the ambulance and headed back towards the residential hall building. All the students from the floor had been evacuated and had already been questioned by the local police, but no obvious suspects had been found at this time.

Andy sent Mitch off to find the camp security and see if there were any security cameras that could help clarify what had happened. From all accounts the perp, or perps, were in and out very quickly with no known witnesses. Andy entered the stone clad building that housed the male and female dorms and took the stairs to the second floor. "Well, Lou, what do we have this time?" He said as he reached the corridor near the crime scene. Standing by Lou's side, he began to put on the forensic clothing in the dorm hallway.

"You are not going to like it, Andy." Lou said as he waited for Andy to get properly dressed and then began to walk a little further down the corridor to the door of the crime scene. "Bry has almost finished with the photos then you can go on in."

"Right." Andy tried not to breathe too deeply as he could already smell what was behind the door.

"Fuck me." He said through gritted teeth as the room door swung open and the gruesome scene was revealed in all its horrific glory.

"It's all yours." Bryer said as he collected together his equipment and carefully stepped back through the doorway. "Thankfully, I'll be outside if you need me." He said, grateful his job was done and he could escape. He stood on the plastic sheet in the hallway and removed his overalls, shoe protectors and hair cover, placing them all in a large evidence bag for forensic examination of any particulates.

"Thanks, Bry." Andy said to him and patted him on the back as he brushed past. "Lucky you were out this way, huh?"

"Yeah, I was in Glendale doing a house shoot." He said as he left, putting as much distance between himself and the crime scene as possible.

"So, what did you find, Lou?" Andy said.

"You mean apart from the butcher shop display on the bed?" He said, raising his eyebrows.

"Yeah, apart from that." Andy tried hard not to stare at it, his mind kept trying to connect the parts like some psycho version of 'Dem Bones'.

"Well, there's this." Lou said while handing an evidence bag over to Andy.

In the bag was a white sheet of paper folded in three places with an envelope, it had the exact same strange circular symbol on it as the one they had found at the last murder scene in the Motel.

"Well, isn't that interesting?" Andy said as he peered at the image, his curiosity seriously piqued. "Not had a chance to get anywhere with the last one yet, but at least we know now that there's a connection between the two crime scenes. Sometimes, perps can be so helpful, even if they are sick fuckers."

"Yeah, the sooner you solve these crimes and get that crazy unsub off the streets, the better." Lou said, disdain obvious on his face. "Too many have died horribly already."

"No pressure then?!" Andy said and swore again, loudly.

Chapter Eight

The loud shrilling of the phone woke Amy abruptly, and, for a few moments she didn't know where she was nor why she had been woken up in the middle of the night. She picked up her cell phone and blinked several times so she could focus on the number. It was Felicity, her agent, calling from the UK. Amy groaned and then began to worry, she quickly tapped the screen over the word 'answer'.

"Felicity? Is everything alright?" She said as she sat upright and turned on the bedside light.

"Amy, darling!" Felicity purred into the phone, "Of course it is, why in heaven's name would it not be?"

Amy could almost hear Felicity's perfectly plucked and Kohl lined eyebrow rise. Felicity had one of those English accents that always made you want to take elocution lessons just to be worthy of talking to her and, rather annoyingly, she always pronounced darling as an extended word that sounded like dahhling.

"You do realise it's four in the morning here, don't you, Felicity?" Amy said as she pulled the covers up around her more, the temperature in her bedroom had dropped quite a lot overnight.

"It is? Well darling, what are you doing up so late? Your lovely creative brain needs its sleep you know." Felicity said seriously.

Amy shook her head. Although she liked Felicity considerably, Amy knew she lived in a different world than the rest of the human population. She was about to explain that this phone call had awoken her and then she changed her mind. It would just be too much effort for four in the morning. "What can I do for you, Felicity?" She said in a resigned, tired voice.

"Just checking in, darling. Making sure my prize winning author is alive and well, as one does."

"Yes, I'm fine...just sorting things out here." Amy said as she snuggled down more under the covers to stay warm.

"Excellent, just excellent. Any clue how long it will be before you return to civilization, darling?"

"Not really, but, like I said, I'll phone you when I leave...Felicity, you did know this when I left, so why are you asking again? What are you up to?"

"Such a clever girl to know Felicity is up to no good." Her deep throaty laugh tumbled over the connection. "Well, darling, I met a rather dashing chap at Adriana's last night and thought how marvellous it would be to get you two together but he is leaving for the Americas in three weeks."

"Felicity, I've told you, several times before, I don't need you to fix me up with one of your friends no matter how dashing they are."

"Technically, darling, he is not one of mine, actually he is one of Adriana's friends."

Amy could hear the pout in Felicity's voice, she did so love to play the matchmaker.

"Be that as it may, please stop. I don't need a man and if I happen to find one I like...well, it'll be me that finds him, okay?"

"Alright, darling. I won't apologise as I know you truly love the attention, but do hurry up and come home, I'm missing our lunches."

"I will be back before you know it, now I must get some sleep."

"Of course, of course. Ciao Bella!" Felicity said and hung up, leaving Amy no room to say goodbye.

Amy stared at the phone and shook her head, placing it back on the nightstand, she snuggled back down under the blankets and went back to a sleep filled with strange voices whispering in her ears.

*

As the sun began to shine through her curtains, Amy started to wake up, she was just at that lovely relaxed place between being asleep and being awake.

"Amy? Amy? Canst thee hear me?" The voice said.

Amy's sleepy mind was instantly wide awake and her eyes shot open, she was sure she heard someone say her name. She lay in her bed and listened hard, perhaps there was someone at the door and she waited for a knock but none came, or perhaps she was dreaming it, she told herself. No, the truth was she had felt the air from the spoken words tickle her ear as they were being said. Amy's eyes darted around the room searching for someone, but she could see no one. Her breath had sped up and her heart was beating like it was trying to get out of her chest.

"Amy?"

The sound came as a whisper in her left ear. Amy's heart froze and her breath became shallow, she slowly turned her head towards the sound, terrified at the thought of finding someone there, but just as terrified if there wasn't anyone.

There was nothing next to her except the pillow on the left side of the bed. Feeling like a small child, Amy moved across the bed and slowly peered over the edge to look around on the floor and under the bed, all the while holding her breath in case something jumped out at her. There was nothing there except the woven rug on a wooden floor that really needed sweeping.

"Get a grip." Amy said out loud to fortify herself and forced her body to climb out of bed and head for a warm refreshing shower.

By the time she had eaten breakfast, she had just about blocked out the feeling of someone's breath on her ear but she couldn't shake the feeling that someone or something was with her in the house watching her, she had that creepy skin feeling one gets in the middle of the night when heading to the bathroom with hardly any lights on. That distinct feeling that any moment some ghostly, skeletal hand will reach out and touch you on the shoulder just before it murders you. That same feeling that makes a grown person rush back to the safety of their bed and leap under the covers.

Trying to shake the feeling off, Amy decided today would be the day to sort the old dresser in the living room. Armed with boxes and black garbage bags, Amy stood in front of the overflowing piece of furniture and decided to put on the radio for company. She found a station of classical music, re-lit the fire and set to work.

Sitting on the floor, she opened the bottom and largest drawer, it was full of children's games. They were so well loved and over used by Amy and her brother, Richard, that the boxes were falling apart. Amy carefully checked if all the pieces were there and the complete ones she placed in the box for the goodwill store, the ones with parts missing she put in the garbage bag. Flashes of her childhood came back to her as she sat and worked her way through the pile. Eventually, she came across her father's old game box, it had a lovely set of chess and backgammon, with all the pieces in it, and she decided she wanted to keep it and placed it in yet another 'keep' box. The morning flew by and by the time the old, wooden cased clock, on the mantel over the fire, chimed eleven, Amy only had the top shelf left. Pleased with her progress she decided she needed to make a cup of tea before tackling the final shelf. Climbing over the various and now full boxes and bags, she headed for the kitchen and the kettle.

With a hot mug of tea in hand, she was soon back in the lounge and looking at the top shelf, it was just as full as the others but she would need a stool to reach it.

"Hello?" The voice said behind her.

Amy jumped and dropped her mug on the floor where it smashed to pieces and sent hot tea everywhere. Spinning round, her breath caught in her throat.

"Whoa, sorry. I didn't mean to make you jump, I knocked on the back door several times but you didn't answer, but I knew you were in because I could hear your radio." Bryer said as he stood next to the sofa, only three feet away from her.

"Shit. Sorry. Erm what...what do you want?" Amy felt nervous, and disoriented from being so jumpy.

"Here let me help you get that." Bryer bent down and started picking up the pieces of the broken mug. "Cyrus MacArthur asked me to deliver your firewood, he's having trouble with Bessie again."

He said and smiled, a strikingly handsome smile that relieved Amy's edginess just a little bit.

"Bessie?"Amy said.

"That's what he calls his old truck, says he's been married to that truck as long as he's been married to his wife." Bryer said as he held out the pieces of the cup, "Where do you want these?"

"Oh, in that black bag there." Amy said, pointing to the open bag and laughed, "Yeah, sounds like something Uncle Cy would say."

"I didn't realise he's your uncle." He said as he dropped the pieces of the mug into the plastic bag.

"Not by blood but he and Kath have been family friends from before I was born and so I've always known them as aunt and uncle." Amy said and smiled fondly at the good memories she'd had with them over the years.

Her smile faded as her mind came back to the present and she realised an awkward silence had grown between them.

"So, fire wood, huh?" Amy said, mentally slapping herself for the lack of conversation skills.

"Yup, where do you want it?"

"I'll show you, follow me." Amy said as she led the way through the cottage and round the outside towards the lean-to covered woodpile. All the way round she wondered if he was checking out her back profile, she knew she would be if she was following him. They both came to a stop in front of the almost depleted pile.

"Just here would be great." She said.

"Okay, I'll bring my truck closer." He said and walked away towards the front of the cottage.

She couldn't help watching him as he went to fetch his truck and bring it further down the drive to unload. Yup, he looked great from behind just as she knew he would. Knowing it would take some time for him to unload and not wanting to stand here watching him and drooling like a teenage girl, Amy decided to grab her dad's old garden gloves and give him a hand.

Although surprised by her appearance at his side, Bryer said nothing as he watched Amy pick up load after load and place them on the wood pile. He did, however, think to himself how much he liked her curves along with her willingness to just get on with a job and he watched her quietly work away.

Amy stopped as they were half way through the wood pile and re-tied her hair back in a ponytail, she looked out over the lake, of which they had a wonderful view from the back of the cottage.

"It's quite lovely here, isn't it?" She said to herself more than anything.

"Yes, it is." Bryer said as he came to stand next to her. "How long do you intend on staying?"

"Oh, I dunno...until I've sorted everything and sold the place, I guess." She said as she let her eyes wander over the view taking in the beautiful autumnal colours of the trees and the blue sky that was reflected in the perfectly calm, quiet lake again. "This would make a lovely spot to work from though." Her words surprised her but it was true, it really would be a great place to write.

"What work do you do?" Bryer said.

"I'm a writer, I usually write children's fiction." Amy said and turned to face him. Unnervingly, he stood close and was looking directly at her with the most intense blue eyes. Amy felt a sudden surge of attraction to this handsome man and she could feel her cheeks getting warm as she began to blush.

"A writer, huh? That must be an interesting job." He said and tilted his head on one side. "Have you been published?"

"I...err...yes, I have an award winning series that I've just finished a book tour for. That's one of the reasons why I've not come out here before now to sort the cottage." She had been on tour, but she had also been putting this trip off for a while now.

"Ah, yeah Cyrus told me about the loss of your parents, I'm sorry." He said and looked away to hide his own pain that had appeared on his face.

"Thanks." Amy was unsure what to say next, she didn't want to pry into his life but she also didn't want to talk about her parents. She fiddled with her father's old work gloves.

"Yes," he said, "this would be a great place to write." He turned and smiled at her again, all traces of sadness were now wiped from his face. Without any further words he returned to stacking the wood.

By the time they had finished, the wood pile was satisfyingly high and it was lunchtime.

"Would you like something to eat or drink?" Amy offered.

"Thanks but no, I've promised to make another delivery for Cyrus." He said and gestured at the remaining wood in his truck.

"Ah, okay." Amy said and tried really hard not to sound too disappointed.

"Although, I could take a rain-check." He said with a cheeky grin.

"Rain-check it is then." Amy said, her heart raced just a little more than usual. "Thanks for the wood."

"Anytime." He said and climbed back into his truck. Waving his hand out of the window, he drove off down her gravel drive and made a conscious effort not to look back this time. He was not sure what he would see and decided he didn't want to know.

"Hmm...he might be fun." She said as she watched his truck vanish round the corner.

Amy turned back to the glorious view, took off her father's gloves, placed them on top of the wood pile and decided to take a walk down the path to the lake. As she walked along she admired the view more and more and began to realise just how big the lake really was. It was so quiet and serene, there was no one on the lake, no boats, canoes or even swimmers. Amy guessed the water would be pretty cold as near to the end of October as it was. She stood on the wooden dock and peered down into the water, it was really very clear and she could see it was quite shallow beneath the dock, it had always seemed so deep when she was little.

Amy's stomach growled and she took the hint that it was time for food and turned to walk back up the path. The cottage was set slightly higher than where she was and it looked lovely with the trees full of autumn colours behind it and the lovely blue sky above. It was like one of those beautiful images you get on a box of chocolates or a tin of cookies. She smiled to herself, the old place really did have character and charm.

On her way back to the cottage, she paused at the old kitchen garden. Once it had grown tomatoes, chilli peppers and garlic now it was all overgrown with plants that had gone to seed and many different types of weeds. She remembered what her mum used to say about weeds, 'Weeds are just plants in the wrong place.' She could hear her mother's voice in her mind as she said it and she remembered her Mum fondly, and for the first time, she didn't feel the sad pain in her heart and the need to cry. She let the happy memories flood over her and thoroughly revelled in it.

"I think it's time for lunch." Amy said to the black squirrel that rushed past her and shot up a tree. She headed back inside the cottage to sort some food and tackle that final shelf.

Amy made herself a toasted cheese sandwich and ate it by the fire surrounded by the boxes and bags of her morning's work. How sad and odd it was to think that life comes down to boxes for charity and bags for the garbage, she thought a little morbidly as she ate.

Having finished her meal she finally decided she had to get off her butt and get back to it and she grabbed the small kitchen stool. She picked up the many bunches of dried flowers that covered the front of the shelf, dropping them to the floor below, she only just managed to hit the garbage bag and dust fluttered into the air making Amy sneeze a couple of times. Behind, where the flowers had sat, was a roll of paper, Amy grabbed it and stepped down off her stool to see what it was. Sneezing again at more disturbed dust she unravelled the paper, it was an old roll of hideous 1970's wallpaper that had been rolled inside out and written on. Amy realised what she was looking at, it was a handwritten family tree and at the bottom was her and her brother Richard's names with their dates of birth and his date of death. Amy swallowed hard not wanting to think about Ricky. She unrolled the paper more and she saw the names of her parents and both sets of grandparents, then the line went directly back on her father's side many, many generations. She decided she would study it further tonight, after dinner, and placed it safely on the sofa.

Climbing back up the stool, Amy reached out for the last things on the shelf, there was a box of old photos, a few ornaments, some lovely old glass bottles with a large stoneware bottle, they all looked a bit battered and dirty as if they'd been dug up. Finally, the shelf was clear apart from the thick layer of dust that had settled around everything leaving ghostly impressions of what used to be there. Arms full, Amy carefully climbed down off the stool and placed the items on the now cluttered coffee table.

The box of photos she placed on the sofa alongside the family tree to look at later and she examined the bottles. She could tell the glass ones were old because when she looked through them the other side of the room was distorted from the old glass. The bottles were all different shapes and sizes, there were seven in total and they were all empty and, although pretty, Amy wasn't sure what to do with them. She wavered between the goodwill box and the garbage, eventually putting them in the good will. "Well, if they don't want them, then they can throw them out, can't they?" She said to herself.

The ornaments were of no particular value to Amy as they were not her taste and she placed them in the charity box.

All that was left was the large stoneware bottle on the coffee table, it looked like a flagon, and Amy tried to lift it, as if to drink from it, and was amazed at how heavy it was. "Ya needed strong wrists in the old days, huh?" It had no cork and was completely empty but she rather liked it and put it back on the coffee table.

Amy, pleased with her progress so far, dusted off the old dresser and then sat down on the sofa next to the box of old photos and began to look through them. There were many photos of her parents and of her and her brother as children, they were mostly of them outside playing, some were of birthdays. Finally, she came across an image of the four of them with Aunt Kath, presumably Uncle Cy had taken the picture. Everyone looked so young and Amy decided she must have been about ten years old in the picture, which meant her brother would then have been twelve.

Tears welled in her eyes, all of her family had gone and although Aunt Kath and Uncle Cy were close, they weren't blood family. Brushing the tears away, she decided to do something less painful and pushed the box of photos off her lap and onto the sofa cushion. Amy heard a rattle come from the box so she picked it up again and gently shook it, but carefully, so as to not make the pictures fly out. Again she heard the rattle, Amy removed some of the images and found a small metal key at the bottom of the box.

"Well, hello." She said to the key, "I wonder where you belong?" Her eyes slid to the locked drawer in the lovely old desk by the window. "I wonder...."

She rose and stood next to the desk, a flutter of excitement gripped her as she inserted the key into the keyhole and turned it, a satisfying click made her heart beat faster and with an intake of breath she slowly slid the drawer out.

"Oh, is that all?" She said, feeling somewhat disappointed.

The drawer was filled to capacity with various notebooks and sheets of paper with hand written notes on. Amy peered at the writing, it looked like it was her father's and the same hand that had written out the family tree on the roll of old wallpaper. As she flicked through some of the rough notes, reading a few, she soon realised they were all family history notes, dates and names.

"Why lock this stuff away?" She said aloud, "How odd." She continued to look through the drawer and found an old bible dating from 1827 and a small stoneware bottle, similar to the one she found on the shelf but this one had a stopper in it. Amy lifted it and shook it to see if there was anything inside. It sounded like something might have rattled, in fact she was pretty sure it had and she shook it again a little harder, yes, definitely something in there, she thought.

Amy pulled at the stopper but nothing happened, she tried again but it was well stuck with age, she peered closely and it looked like it was sealed with wax. "How interesting." She said as she sat back down, on the sofa and looked at the lovely old bottle in her hand, wondering what could possibly be inside.

Something quick and dark moved on the other side of the room and it caught the corner of her eye, she spun her head round to see what it was, however, there was nothing there but the empty room. However, the creepy feeling of someone standing near her had returned and she shuddered.

"Look whoever you are, stop creeping up on me. Show yourself or leave me alone, okay?" Amy tried to say bravely, as one does when alone and nervous.

Of course, the last thing Amy expected to happen was for something to actually materialise directly in front of her.

Chapter Nine

The Voice believed it was absolutely in charge, as it had been since its arrival.

The Host's body and mind had submitted remarkably easily and now did the incontrovertible bidding of the Voice. The Host's mind had been allowed to remain at the surface to interact with the Voice, and the world at large, to deceive all but the Voice and deceive it, it did. The Host only appeared normal to those that might look and no one ever did.

"Why dost thou bawdy noise nay abate? Canst thou nay kill thy accursed box?" The Voice demanded.

"It's the TV, I've told you before, and we need to watch it for the news. It will make you pleased again, you will see." The Host replied and although they sat at the desk with many books opened before them, the Host's eyes kept flitting across the room to look at the TV screen.

"Look hither at thy parchment, damn thee!" The Voice said.

"Hush now, we need to see this." The Host's hand reached out and grabbed the control, pressing the volume button so the sound rose enough to hear the newscaster.

"More murder and mayhem tonight as we are getting in reports of two students murdered at the Henry Dale University Campus just a few days after the gruesome murder of the family at a local motel. James Munroe, our roving newshound, is on the scene. What can you tell us, James?" The glamorous blond said into the camera.

Her colleague, a handsome man with a movie star smile, immediately appeared on the screen. "Well, Mary, I can confirm two students are dead tonight in another gruesome scene, it's like something from a horror film here at Henry Dale University." He said and smiled inappropriately. "Apparently, the bodies of a young woman and her boyfriend were found in her dorm room at 7:20 this evening. The bodies have been removed by the Coroner and although I tried to interview the detective in charge of the investigation, he wouldn't speak to me. We do know, however, that the names have not been released by the police until the families have been notified, but I can guarantee you, no parent will sleep well tonight." He said with another 'aren't I wonderful and famous' smile on his face, despite the fact that the actual news he was telling the audience was about a horrendous tragedy.

"Terrible, terrible news. Do the police have any suspects yet?" Mary said. She tried to look concerned but it wasn't very convincing.

"Not as far as I know, but then they aren't talking to the press. One thing I did find out though, the student who found the bodies of her roommate and her roommate's boyfriend has been taken to the Henry Dale Memorial Hospital and is being treated for shock."

"The roommate survived? Well, that is good news on such a terrible night." She said with another Hollywood smile flashed at the camera, full of teeth and disinterest in anything but herself.

"Yes, apparently, and lucky for her, she was in the next room studying with a friend, I have her name here...erm." James flicked through his notebook, "Olivia Hamilton, yes, that's her name." More teeth flashed at the screen.

"Well, Olivia we wish you a speedy recovery and our sincerest condolences go out to the two families tonight who have lost loved ones. Thank you, James Munroe from Henry Dale University Campus, the scene of more horrific murders." Mary paused for just a moment. "We'll have the weather for you with Carly, after this break." Mary smiled sweetly into the camera just as the remote control smashed into the TV screen.

"Nay, it canst nay be truth." The Voice raged.

"I don't understand how we missed her, how did we get the wrong girl?" The Host said aloud, the tone of disbelief obvious in their voice.

"Thine incompetence defeats thee."

"Our incompetence, we are doing this together, remember?" The Host said.

"How darest thou speak to me thus? I am that which gives thee thy power, thou wilt do well to remember."

"And I am the one who released you and gave you this life." The Host said, "You should remember also that I can easily remove you and send you back to the nether you came from." A firmness had crept into the Host's voice.

"Come now. We must nay bicker and move forward with our conspiracies." The Voice soothed and spoke gently to its Host, like a parent trying to calm an angry child, but the intent was lost on the Host, it just heard the words as an example of the Host's control over the Voice.

"That's more like it. So, now I guess we need to visit the hospital and finish what we started." The Host said as it's hand drummed noisily on the desk in irritation.

"Doest thou requirest me to draw a'nother Sigil?" The Voice asked.

"No, this time we shall visit in the normal manner and do what needs to be done." The Host said.

A sick sense of calm came over the Host and the Host took that as the Voice's agreement of the plan.

The Voice said nothing else, pleased that more blood would be shed shortly and it would soon be free from the mind and body that presently held it.

Chapter Ten

The air by the old dresser and directly in front of Amy, shimmered almost like in a heat wave. Only the temperature of the room had dropped slightly instead of increasing, which would normally cause such an effect.

Amy watched, her eyes glued to the spot as if by an outside force, the area seemed to shimmer like an illusion of an oasis in the desert sun.

The sunlight that streamed in from her window shone on the spot and appeared to bend oddly around the shape that was slowly forming there as if the very air were changing into something more solid.

Amy's eyes grew wide and she gasped with fright. Her hands automatically gripped the sofa cushions, each side of her, in pure fear. She wanted to scream, to run, to do anything but be stuck in that spot, in front of whatever it was, but she was unable to move a single muscle.

The shape began to swirl and darken and it started to become more distinct around the edges as the seconds ticked slowly by. The outline widened and the solid form came more into focus.

Amy blinked several times, her mind was telling her over and over again that it was just a dream, inside her head she shouted back at her mind, telling it to wake up. WAKE UP! But deep down she knew she was actually awake, she could feel the goosebumps on her arms prickle as the image of a woman slowly and steadily appeared before her.

"Good a'fter noon, Amy." The apparition said in a calm, gentle voice.

Amy stared in horror, frozen to her seat. It was the voice, the one she'd heard all along, and the one that had whispered so close to her ear that she could feel the breath brush past it. Amy wanted to scream with fear but the fear wouldn't let her move any muscles in her throat and, worst of all, she was pinned to her seat by that same fear.

"Nay be a'feared. I pray thee." The woman reached out a hand, with her palm up, in what seemed like a friendly gesture.

Afraid of being touched by it, whatever this thing was, Amy's flight reflex finally kicked in as she scrambled up the back of the sofa and climbed over it and she backed into the hallway of the cottage. Bravely, she turned her back on the apparition and made a run for the front door, not knowing where she was going only knowing that she had to get out of the cottage right then. After two attempts to turn the door handle with her sweaty hands, she finally got the door open and she shot out of the cottage and onto the garden path. She ran down the path and onto the gravel drive, she slipped and went down hard on the gravel, painfully grazing her hands and knees as she did so. Amy quickly got back onto her feet and continued to run up the drive, she didn't look back, not wanting to know if it was behind and following her, nor did she stop until she met the junction onto the main road at the end of her drive. There she paused to try to catch her breath and quickly turned around to make sure the thing, it, whatever that was, hadn't actually followed her.

Amy was panting and she bent double trying to catch her breath and think a little more rationally. She looked around again and saw she was alone so she took a moment to look at her hands, she had grazed her right one quite badly and she picked the small pieces of gravel out of it, the graze burned but had stopped bleeding. She also felt her knees through her jeans, both were sore but the skin didn't seem broken or her jeans would have been torn. She would, however, be getting a few bruises.

A crow cawed somewhere in the trees above her and made Amy jump. "Shit." She said and tried to calm her breathing again.

A bright red car whizzed by and caught Amy's eye as it did so, strangely it comforted her to know that there were people using the road and she could find help as she escaped from...a ghost? Was this all real? It couldn't be could it? She thought. "It was just a dream, or sleep walking...perhaps too much stress...yes, stress, that's it. Nothing to worry about, just a hallucination from stress." She said to the trees, trying to convince herself. She turned around to look at the calming, rustling leaves as the warm breeze brushed against them when it came off the lake. The sound and sight, along with the breeze, was soothing and Amy began to feel more like herself again.

"Please, I wouldst nay hurt thee." The woman said.

Amy spun round to find the woman stood behind her and in the middle of the drive, blocking her exit to the main road. Amy staggered backwards.

"Go away, you're not real. I'm tired and overcome by being here with all my memories. You are not real, leave me alone." Amy turned and determinedly marched back towards the house and away from the strange woman, she wanted to put as much distance between them as possible. All she wanted, with her entire being, was to be away from this hallucination or whatever it was, these thoughts made her walk even faster. She wouldn't run, no, she was not going to run again from something that wasn't real, she decided.

"Some believe I am real and some nay do, none canst see such but thyself, Amy." The woman said as if she had read Amy's mind when she suddenly appeared next to Amy and walked along with her at a rushed pace that matched Amy's.

"Shit, don't do that!" Amy jumped at the sudden closeness of the hallucinated woman. "Only, I can see you, huh? I guess I'm going crazy then." Amy pointed to her forehead, near her temple and rotated her finger to signify she had lost her mind.

"Thou canst see because I wish it so." The woman said simply.

They had reached the garden path that led to the front door of the cottage. "I see, well, that solves everything then. Perhaps, I should get a check up, maybe it's a brain tumour...they make you hallucinate, I think. Yeah, I'm pretty sure they do." Amy said a little too calmly. Not able to understand nor take in what was happening to her, Amy's self preservation instinct took over and rationalized everything until it made some sort of sense and, at that moment, a brain tumour made an awful lot of sense.

"Thou art in shock, a tisane 'twould do thee well."

"Tea? You want me to drink tea?" Amy said as her eyebrows rose, "What sort of hallucination wants people to drink tea? God, I am nuts." Amy sighed as she walked up the path more slowly and in a resigned manner, she walked back through the open front door, the very one she hadn't closed in her rush to escape just a short while ago.

"A Teil tisane for thee." The woman said and didn't follow Amy in the house.

Amy closed the front door firmly behind her and locked it, sincerely hoping and wishing that the hallucination couldn't pick locks and open doors. She looked around her, everything seemed normal inside, there was nothing out of place at all, no sign that she had just run out of the cottage like a crazed mad woman. Amy laughed at herself nervously, shook her head in disbelief and dragged herself towards the kitchen to make a hot drink. Perhaps the hallucination was right, a cup of tea is good for shock, she was pretty sure she had remembered hearing that somewhere before.

"Bloody hell." Amy stood at the doorway to the kitchen and gaped at the sight before her eyes.

The woman stood at the range, boiling water, she then put lime green leaves into a mug and waited for the water to heat. "Be seated and at peace, there be much to discuss."

"So now you want to talk too, fine. What do I care, they will lock me up sooner or later anyway, might as well have a conversation with you first, it could actually be interesting. Perhaps I will discover a new insight into the human psyche. How much worse can it get?" Amy knew she was rambling and sighed. Feeling resigned, Amy sat at her kitchen table and watched the woman. The woman's long brown hair hung loosely down her back and her clothes were strange, she wore a long dark brown skirt with a white blouse that was tied instead of buttoned up the front, she had some sort of weird fitted jacket over the blouse and an apron over the front of the skirt. It seemed Amy's imagination had no bounds, apparently she could think up a whole wardrobe for her hallucination. She was so proud.

However, Amy could make no sense of why her hallucination would look like an extra from some 17th century drama or re-enactment group, but went with it anyway. What the hell? What did she have to lose? Her mind? Hmm...it was probably too late to worry about that, she thought.

The woman poured the hot water slowly and carefully over the leaves.

"Yup, I've definitely lost the plot." Amy put her head in her hands because she just didn't want to see anymore.

The woman placed the mug of steaming tea in front of Amy.

Amy lifted her head and looked at it, she slowly reached out with her index finger and put it into the liquid as if it was some bizarre, other worldly substance sitting before her. "Ow, it's real!" She said and stuffed the burnt finger in her mouth, sucking it to relieve the sharp but short lasting pain.

"Thou art an oddity, truly. Tisane is hot, thy should knowest this." The woman looked puzzled and sat down at the kitchen table opposite Amy.

"I know tea is hot but...I...how can a hallucination make me tea?" Amy frowned, stared at the mug and then at the strange woman sitting across from her.

"I cometh nay from thy mind, Amy. I am Spirit."

"Now I know I'm crazy, there are no such things as Spirits." Amy said directly to the woman, "Next you'll be telling me there are demons too."

"Many things exist in ye world, thee art nay knowledgeable about all." The woman said.

"Really? C'mon. If you are a Spirit, bloody prove it." Amy said as she grabbed the mug determinedly and sniffed the tea suspiciously.

The woman vanished and instantly reappeared standing by Amy's side.

"Shit!" Amy said and, as she jumped, she dropped the mug on the table and the tea spilt all over it like an unstoppable tidal wave. It was the second time she had wasted a good mug of tea in as many days. Amy sat there staring at the woman trying to ignore the spilt tea as the woman calmly walked back over to the chair, she had so suddenly vacated, and sat back down again.

"Okay, okay...I have either utterly lost my mind or you...are..."

"Spirit." The woman finished the sentence for her.

The tea reached the edge of the table and dripped off it making small splashing noises as it hit the stone floor of the kitchen. It was the only sound that could be heard as the two women looked at each other for several moments.

It was Amy who moved first and gave in to her OCD impulse. She sprang up out of her seat, grabbed a cloth and proceeded to wipe the table and floor. Once it was cleaned up to her satisfaction, she placed the now empty mug in the sink. "What was in that anyway?"

"Teil tree leaves, I believe thee call it now... a Lindon Tree?" The woman said.

"Don't ask me, not that knowledgeable about trees." Amy said as she sat down again. "So who are you? What do you want with me? And why are you haunting me?"

"Art ye naught? Well, I shalt hath to teach thee knowledge of trees and plants, many art curers and magical." She said and paused. "Ye canst call me Erda, Erda Miller, if thy likes. Alive I was but a Cunning Woman and, through nay fault of mine, I am now Spirit, forever affixed betwixt and between living and dead." Erda said.

"Oh." Amy wasn't sure how to respond to this new information.

She frowned.

"A Cunning Woman? What's that? Is that like a con artist?"

"Thee hath nay heard of a Cunning Woman? A Wise Woman? A Spae Wife?"

"Wise Woman? Ah, so you are a Witch?" Amy said, not feeling at all comforted by this bit of news.

"Nay a Witch, a Cunning Woman a'though here, in thy time, 'tis much a'same." Erda said.

"But where do you come from, why are you here? How come you can do things like 'make tea' if you are a Spirit? What do you want with me?" Amy could not help but tumble out question after question, her mind wanted to know everything right then and there.

"Thee needs to take time to pause and perchance I wilt tell thee." Erda smiled as if talking to a small child.

Amy looked at the smiling face of Erda, the Spirit, and noticed the smile lit up her attractive face and made her seem more friendly than Amy had noticed before. "Okay." Amy said and leant back in her chair, thinking 'This should be good.' She still wasn't completely convinced that this was at all real, she was still betting on the brain tumour, it seemed the most suitable choice for this particular problem.

"'Twas birthed in the Year of Our Lord, 1600. Much happened upon me whilst alive, my parents died of plague when I was but of thrice years. My dame's dame took me by her side and taught me much. I helped her heal wounds, cast charms and make protection upon chattels of those who couldst pay and some who nay couldst."

"I know what it is like to lose your parents, I recently have too." Amy said, suddenly feeling in a very sombre mood.

"Aye, 'twas nay something I remember but a'miss all a'same."

Amy wiped away a lone tear that had tumbled silently down her cheek.

"I canst tell thee my long tale but 'twould be better if I show thee, mayhaps." Erda looked at Amy as if sizing her up for something important. "If thou art willing?"

"What? Did you actually say 'show' me? How is that even possible?" Amy's eyebrows rose up towards her hairline.

"Thy must trust me."

"Trust you, I don't think I can do that just yet." Amy looked at Erda nervously.

"Nay a'fear thee, thou wilt be safe. Upon my word." Erda stood and evaporated.

Amy looked around her not understanding where Erda had gone, but before Amy could get out of her chair to look around the cottage, Erda reappeared in the kitchen, by the stove, and she had a handful of leaves from what looked to be several different species of plants.

"Doest thou hath beeswax and tway iron pots?"

"I...um...I have candles." Amy went to the under-sink cupboard and rummaged behind all the cleaning supplies until she pulled out a handful of old candles, which had been kept there for years, in case of power cuts. They had originally been white but they were now a little discoloured with a yellow tinge and several were warped and bent.

"'Twill do." Erda took four of the candles.

Amy rooted through another cupboard, full of old pots and pans and found two old aluminium pans, one large one and a smaller one, the latter had the handle broken off.

"These okay?" Amy held them up for Erda to see.

"Aye."

Amy watched as Erda placed water in the large pan and boiled it on the stove, she then placed the small pan in the hot water and the four candles within that pan, while they melted, and she chopped up the leaves and crushed them with the flat blade of the knife until they were wet with their own juices. She poured the melted wax immediately into a cereal bowl and added the crushed, chopped leaves and then quickly mixed them thoroughly together, creating a waxy ointment that had already started to solidify.

"If you are from the 1600's, how come you know how to use a stove?" Amy said, pleased that her brain was working again and thinking logically.

"'Twas birthed in 1600, beyond my death, in the Year of Our Lord 1628, I found I couldst a'wander unfettered and I learned much by it, learned some of thy ways and strange words. I hath seen much in my four hundred years of a' wandering."

"Learnt, you mean learnt not learned. Wait...you've been wandering around for four hundred years?" Amy said, horrified by the thought. She couldn't wrap her mind around that much time, where had she been? What had she seen during all those years?

Erda nodded, "Aye, four hundred years. Now let us repair to thy room." She led the way to Amy's bedroom and it was obvious she had been wandering around the rooms of Amy's cottage and knew the place well.

Amy followed her, wondering what was going to happen next and what she had been dragged into. Was it a wise and safe thing to do, to follow instructions and do what one's own hallucination told you to do? Surely, that's how crazy people blew innocent people up and got locked up, she thought to herself.

"Lay thee down." Erda stood at the edge of Amy's bed.

Amy lay on top of her bed and thought to herself, hopefully, I will wake up any moment and this will all be a dream. Yup, that's it...a dream. Of course, it is. She laid there waiting, wishing and praying it would happen and happen quickly, but it didn't.

Erda came closer and sat down on the bed beside Amy. "'Tis warm but wilt nay burn thee." She put her index finger in the greasy ointment and smeared it across Amy's brow.

Amy felt the warmth of it upon her face and found it comforting like a hot chocolate on a cold winter day. The warmth of her body seemed to make the ointment smell stronger and she could now smell the plants and their pungent aroma, the mixture smelt odd but it was a pleasant smell of gardens and cut grass, of sweet herbs and green growing things. Her mind began to wander and she dreamily wondered what Erda had put on her forehead. "What is it? It smells lovely. I'm feeling all warm and relaxed too." She said feeling all her worries melt away.

"'Tis a partitive unguent, 'twill separate thy Spirit from thy body and thou wilt travel with me."

"Wait...what? You...are...stealing...my Spirit?" Amy said as she tried to sit up but she felt her body go numb and she could not move. Her mind struggled to find some clear, rational thoughts but it couldn't find a single one and it completely shut down.

Then there was only deep, unyielding darkness.

Chapter Eleven

The cold October wind blew the beautifully coloured autumn leaves around the pair of feet that stood on the hospital pathway, their owner looked up at the large, modern building and the blue sky beyond. The Host's feet walked up the pedestrian path from the car park and the Host paused to smell fresh, crisp air, their eyes moved along the building until they saw their destination point and their face lit up with glee.

The hospital doors automatically opened with a swoosh as the Host and the Voice entered the Henry Dale Memorial Hospital. They made their way past the sitting area and the reception desk, where a nurse sat typing on the computer and they headed over to the vending machine in the far corner of the emergency room. Placing their sports bag on the floor by their feet, they watched the desk from the corner of their eyes while they pretended to be interested in the various chocolate bars and bags of chips inside the vending machine.

"Why dost thou loiter?" The Voice said.

"Just waiting for...ah, there we are." The Host said quietly so as not to be overheard, not that there was much chance of that in the deserted emergency room so early in the morning.

The nurse at the station, looked around her and assessed she wasn't needed for a few moments, then quickly made her way into the washroom opposite, leaving the desk unmanned, which, technically she was not allowed to do but sometimes the call of nature was just too strong to ignore.

This was what the Host had been counting on.

Without pausing for an instant, the Host quickly manoeuvred themselves around the desk and typed the name 'Olivia Hamilton' into the computer, finding the floor and room number. The Host quickly returned the screen to its original page and was standing in front of the elevator, next to the desk, just in time as the nurse returned to her station looking somewhat more relaxed.

"What 'twas thy box thou touched?" The Voice asked.

"It is a device that gave us the location of the girl."

"A useful device thy hath knowledge of."

'You have no idea." The Host said as it watched the button calling the lift light up and the doors open directly in front of them. "I've booked a real check-up for myself on the fifth floor in just over 30 minutes, so we have a valid reason to be here, just in case."

"Thou art wise, pray tell what is a 'checkup?' The Voice asked.

'Don't worry about it now." The Host said and pressed the button for the required floor.

As they made their way along the corridor of the third floor, the few patients and nurses that passed by barely noticed their presence. The Host watched the room numbers until they came upon the one they needed. Looking through the side window, they could see the young woman was asleep in one of the two beds in the room.

With purpose but also stealth, they opened the door, walked in and closed it quietly behind them. Luckily, the other bed in the room was empty but had obviously been slept in and they knew they didn't have much time. As quietly as possible, they drew the curtain around Olivia's bed and then peered closely at her. The Host checked the chart to ensure they had the right girl this time after the last debacle and saw that the girl was on tranquilisers, the Host was pleased, and it meant she wouldn't wake up straight away and call for help.

"Allow me a'use of thy limbs, I crave the feel of it again." The Voice said.

"As you wish, but hurry we have little time." The Host said and yielded their body over to the Voice.

The hands, now controlled by the Voice, pulled on the medical gloves they had brought with them and reached out to stroke the fair features of the young woman, she stirred in her sleep but didn't wake. Without a second thought, one hand covered Olivia's mouth while the other crushed her windpipe. Olivia instantly woke despite her medication and struggled against the attack. Surprise and shock showed on her terrified face as she recognised her attacker and disbelief clouded her eyes. Olivia kicked against the covers which held her in place, for a short time, as she felt unconsciousness creep over her. She tried hard to scream but the combination of the hand over her mouth and the lack of air made no noise escape her lips. Finally, she fell into the deep, inky black well of unconsciousness.

"Is it done?" The Host asked.

"Nay, she is but without senses."

The Voice made the Host's hands stroke the hair away from the young woman's face so tenderly that the Host was surprised. "Are you going to finish the job or shall I?" The Host said a little impatiently.

"Thou hast no need, I shalt complete my will. 'Tis just she doth remind me of a woman, I knowest a'fore."

"Oh?" The Host said, looking at Olivia.

"Aye, 'tis naught but a fancy." The Voice said and withdrew a blade from the Host's pocket. Feeling the sharpness of the edge of the blade with the Host's thumb, the Voice then made the Host's hands plunge the knife deep into the girl's neck, withdrawing the knife and allowing the arterial spray to cover the curtain, the Voice then thrust the knife into the girl's heart making it cease beating immediately. The knife was then quickly forced into the body cavity just below the ribs, the Voice used their combined strength to force both of their hands into the body, breaking ribs as it went. Feeling around in the wet stickiness that was the young woman's chest cavity, the hands found what they were looking for and finally began cutting free both the left and right lungs. When the gruesome task was completed, the hands placed the lungs inside a large, plastic resealable bag which was full of ice. Then the bloodied hands covered the body of Olivia with her own blood splattered covers.

Pulling off and placing the now dripping medical gloves in a Ziploc bag and sealing it, the Voice returned the use of the body back to the Host and the Host placed both bags into the sports bag they had brought with them.

"Did you enjoy that?" The Host asked.

"Mightily, thank thee." The Voice said, it sounded revitalized from the experience.

Gathering the bag and placing it over their shoulder, the Voice and Host left the third floor of the hospital without anyone knowing they had been there at all and headed off to their appointment on the fifth floor without a care in the world.

Chapter Twelve

May, 1622, London, England.

Amy's eyes flew open in an effort to stop the room from spinning and to cease the need to vomit. She was laid on a single, straw filled mattress on a hard bed, in a room she didn't recognise, and there in front of her was Erda standing by the window looking out while brushing her long hair.

"Where are we?" Amy said.

Erda ignored her and continued to brush her hair.

"Oh, so now you don't speak to me. You could have done that earlier, instead of whispering in my ear and frightening the hell out of me." Amy said and sat up, the dizziness feeling having left her.

"She canst nay speak to thee 'cus she canst nay hear thee."

Amy's head spun round to the opposite corner of the room and there stood Erda, leant against the wooden planked wall of the room.

"How? What?" Amy looked between the two Erda's utterly confused.

"She is me but a me a'fore all good withered and was taken from me." Erda said from the corner, as she watched herself with a sad look on her face.

"Oh, um...okay." Amy said, unsure of what that meant as she watched the other Erda. "How are we here watching her, I mean you."

"The partitive unguent worked, thy are Spirit with me." Erda came and sat by Amy on the bed.

"But not quite like you...because I could see and hear you before...when I...when I was in my body, why can't she? My body is okay, isn't it? I can get back to it, I'm not stuck like this am I?" Amy could hear the beginning of panic in her voice as she moved to the edge of the bed.

"Thy body is well, it rests whilst thy Spirit walks." Erda said, "Thou canst return when thee wants, 'tis simply to think of thy return and so shalt it be, but I want thee to see how I became such." Erda gestured at her Spirit self and gave a sad smile to Amy.

Amy felt sorry for her, was Erda trapped as a Spirit forever to wander and haunt people? She wondered. "If I can leave and go to my body, what about you? Can you return to yours, do you have...a body...still?"

"I am always Spirit now, my body is naught but ash, but you will understand soon." Erda said as she followed her other self out of the small room.

Amy quickly followed both Erdas, good job they are wearing different clothes or this could get even more confusing, she thought.

They walked into another room which was also small, it held a large fireplace and a wooden table with benches on either side.

Erda and Amy watched as the corporeal Erda collected her shawl and baskets off wooden pegs by the door and headed out of the cottage, up a short earthen path and into the meadows nearby. She walked along a stream collecting wild plants and herbs, placing them in her basket, until she came to the edge of the woods, there she climbed over the rocky outcrop and continued into the trees.

The version of Erda that was alive, walked around the woods collecting different types of flowers and leaves and she hummed to herself happily. After a while, she reached a grove of trees with a small meadow at its centre. The meadow was filled with wild grasses and flowers. She stopped collecting nature's offerings and lay down in the sun drenched grove. As if by magic, a man appeared at the edge of the clearing, he watched Erda laying in the sun for a few minutes without moving a muscle.

Slowly the man crept forward, careful not to make a noise and disturb Erda. As he approached he removed his jacket and unlaced his shirt. He was a tall, handsome man with strong features and dark brown eyes. When he got closer to the relaxing woman he began to smile, a knowing sly smile of one who knows he is getting what he wants.

A crack of a twig, under his foot, made both of the watching Spirits jump.

The version of Erda, which lay upon the ground, twitched at the noise but didn't move at all, she already knew he was there.

"Thy footfalls are heavy, thou wilt need more care if thou wish to startle me." She said but remained relaxed on the grass, fully reclined with her eyes closed.

"Ah, my love, thou art as beautiful as thy art wise." The man said as he lay down next to her on the warm grass.

Erda's spirit looked away, "I canst abide this, let us move on." She said.

"Wait, who is he?" Amy asked as she watched the man begin to seduce Erda by kissing her throat, undoing her gown and placing his hand on her bare breast.

"He's...'twas the love a'my life, John. A knave whom I believed to be my heart's soul." Erda began to move away and reached out for Amy's hand. "Come there is much to see."

Amy took hold of Erda's offered and somewhat cold hand, "You didn't have to show me that, you are torturing yourself aren't you?"

Erda ignored Amy's comment and walked back into the tree line.

The trees before Amy's eyes shimmered and melted away to reveal another image, the inside of a small, dark cottage. It was lit by tallow lights and the smell of the pig fat burning made Amy's nose wrinkle in disgust. In front of Amy, on a blood soaked bed, sat Erda propped up against the wall, holding a newly born child. The mucus and blood smears were still on the infant's head and Erda was obviously all alone in the dirty hovel.

The Spirit of Erda walked over to the bed and gently laid her fingers on the child's head.

"You had a child?" Amy said, looking at Erda in a new light.

"Aye, a bastard child of John's."

"Why are you alone, where is he?" Amy said as she moved closer to the bed and noticed that the Erda in the bed was looking around her as if she could hear them. "Can she...you...hear us?"

"Nay, though I fancied I felt something at the time." Erda looked sadly down at the mother and child. "John and I were estranged, he wanted me to teach him a darker path but I saith nay for he hath a temper and 'twas nay suited."

"A darker path?"

"Aye, 'tis using skills of root and herb, with thy will to harm, to make receipts against folk, to hex them. I would nay teach him, thus he hunted me and the unborn. I knew, once born, the babe 'twould be used against me so I hid and birthed it in the shadows."

"Oh, that's terrible." Amy really didn't know what to say.

"Once healed and strong again, I travelled long and far to a cousin's house. They raised her as their own. Rachel, a good woman, and Ethan, her husband, a wealthy wool merchant, took her within. They had nay surviving babes of their own." Erda said not moving her gaze from the head of her newborn daughter.

"What was her name? Your daughter, I mean."

"Abigail." Erda said simply.

"Did you ever see her again?" Amy didn't like to ask but her curiosity got the better of her.

"Nay, until she was full grown."

"Why didn't you go to see her earlier?"

"John found me after I hid Abigail. He locked me in his house, in the very room we had tupped to bring her life. He endeavoured to force me to teach him hexes and curses."

Everything shimmered and once again the scene changed, this time the two Spirits stood outside a large partial brick, Elizabethan style house presumably in the country due to the peace and quiet and the lovely fresh air. The full moon glinted off the leaded glass windows seeming to make the house glow with an eerie light.

"Wow, that's beautiful." Amy said. She had always rather liked the Elizabethan architecture. "Where are we?"

"'Tis John's house in London. I once thought as thee, but now 'tis just a prison." Erda said as she walked towards a door in the brick wall that ran the length of the garden.

Following behind, Amy asked, "How long did he keep you here?"

"Two years whilst he begged, cajoled and bribed a'ways out of me. Until he came upon the news I hath produced a child, I knowest nay how, he swore to find our child and threaten her life against me. I gave him little things over time after, to stave him off, but his hunger grew. More he knew, more he desired. His desperation for finding our child became an obsession. He hath me beaten every other dawn as he steadily became mad with desire for darkness he craved. Lastly, he knowest that I would nay give him his need so he plotted my death hoping 'twould give up the location of Abigail if I knowest I was to die."

"Dear God, I'm sorry."

"'Tis nay thy fault, Amy." Erda said as she leant on the brick wall by the side of the wooden door.

"I know, but still, I'm sorry for what you went through protecting your child."

"Naught canst be a'changed now, nay one knowest where she was and I knowest she was safe..."

A piercing scream punctured the air and froze Erda mid sentence.

"What the hell was that?" Amy looked around in alarm.

"Go through the door yonder and see for thyself." Erda said and walked away, "I wilt be yonder...after."

Amy looked at Erda with a puzzled frown as more screams rent the very air in two. So loud were they that Amy could hear the voice of the person who was screaming break with the effort. Amy took a deep breath and steeled herself, she had no idea what was to come but knew by that sound it wasn't going to be pleasant. Putting one foot in front of the other, Amy approached the door with caution, stepping through the opening she saw the most hideous sight she had ever seen in her life.

In the centre of the vegetable and herb garden was a pyre, a large pile of wood around a pole that was set alight and a woman was tied to the pole. Amy could just see through the curtain of smoke that the flames had just reached the bottom of her skirts. Amy's heart sank in horror as she recognised the woman, it was Erda. She felt vomit rise in her throat but she couldn't be sick as she was without her body, so the sensation was purely in her mind.

An unknown hulk of a man was stoking the fire, spreading it around the pyre...around Erda. There was another man there who she barely recognised as John, he stood arrogantly before Erda, the woman he'd once professed to love, with a look on his face of murderous glee. He truly looked evil and Amy instinctively and deeply hated the man.

A waft of smoke from the pyre blew towards Amy and she smelt the unmistakable smell of burning flesh. She could see John was speaking and Erda was shouting something back but Amy couldn't quite hear what, so she moved closer. She had an unwilling, yet an overwhelming, need to hear Erda's last words but it was John she heard speak first.

"Before thy fate takes thee, knowest verily thy secret is loose. Dwell thy last stretch of time and lack thy joy. Thy daughter is found." The maniacal joy in John's voice could not be mistaken.

"Nay!" Erda shouted until the smoke dried her throat and a scream of agony burst forth again from her. With the last of her strength she cried, "Thy life shalt be crushed from thee, thou shalt not rest. Thy body and soul shalt rot in thy own mess akin to the cabbages upon a wet field. I hex thee, John Lambe, I hex thee!"

Before John could make the sign to ward against Erda's words, she gave out her last agonising breath and sealed the curse as her flesh blacked and the fire roared over her.

Amy looked away, unable to watch the last of Erda burn away.

"Holy fuck!" Were the only words she could muster. Staggering away, Amy made her way back through the doorway and into the open gardens around the house. The moon shone brightly, lighting her way but with a cold light, almost as if it was mourning the death of the young mother.

Amy went and stood next to Erda, she reached out and held her cold hand as they looked out over the ornamental pond together, neither of them seeing it.

After several minutes had passed, Amy said, "Why did you show me this?"

"I needed someone to knowest the truth, to knowest why I died and canst nay be a mother to my child...but also to see what became of me next." Erda said, turning to Amy. "You must go back and witness. I have never been able to do so."

"What am I to see? You are...gone now."

"He wilt perform a small ritual, thee must tell me exactly what he dost, I beseech thee."

"Why? Why can't you come with me?"

"I was nay there, with my mind, so I canst nay see it, I canst remember...dying...and then being Spirit after his death but nay at this time. But thy cometh and thou wilt see it. I nay understand it all but this I knowest."

"Alright, I'll try." Amy looked a little hopeful and began retracing her steps back to the door in the wall and the private garden. The smell of burning flesh was still in the air but the fire had just about been put out, the large man was talking to John near the remains of the fire. Amy forced herself not to think of the other remains that lay there too.

She watched as an old, male servant came out of the house with a small chest and a lit lamp, placing them on the ground at John's feet. John sent the large man and the old servant back to the house before kneeling down and opening the chest. Amy stepped closer to see what he was doing, John's head snapped up and he looked directly at her. Amy froze to the spot, her mind screaming, 'He can see me, oh my God, he can see me!'

Finally, his gaze moved away from her but he continued to look around him as if feeling someone nearby. After a few moments his attention returned to the chest in front of him. "Thoust will nay keep thy hex, loathsome bitch." He said viciously as he removed a sharp looking knife and a bottle from within. Without hesitating and acting with urgent speed he slit his hand open with the knife.

Amy gasped as she saw the knife drop to the ground and drops of blood dripped from his left hand.

Again John looked around him as if expecting someone to be there with him. "I knowest thou wilt haunt me until thy hex is dissolved with success. Knowest thee I wilt bind thee instead and prevent thy hex purchase." John shouted the last words to the air.

"He thinks I'm Erda haunting him already." Amy murmured to herself.

John let a few drops of his blood fall into the bottle, then he placed several other items in it too, some small, too small for Amy to see what they were, but she did see him add an iron nail. Mumbling words over the bottle he moved forward and scooped up ash from the remains of Erda and the fire, placing them in the bottle also. He continued to mumble words as he placed the stopper in it, melted the end of a candle, he withdrew from the box, in the lamp and smeared it around the stopper and bottle, effectively sealing it. He held the bottle out in front of him and smiled. Amy decided that his smile was the most evil thing she had ever seen and, if she was in her body, she would have had shudders down her spine just for that smile. She watched him place the bottle back in the chest and carry it back to the house without even a second look at the spot where he'd just killed the mother of his child.

Amy breathed deeply, as she thought she recognised that bottle, it looked like the one she had found in her father's desk. It was Erda's bottle, her home and her curse which had been placed upon her by her murderer, ex-lover and father to her child. Saddened, she kept playing the scene over and over in her head until she reached Erda out in the garden.

"Didst thou see?" Erda said and wrung her cold, cold hands. "Pray thee, tell me thou didst."

"Well, I'm not sure what you wanted me to see but here's what I saw." Amy recalled what she had seen John do, although she couldn't tell Erda the words he'd used as they were mumbled and sounded foreign to her ears.

"Ah, now I doth see. I hath nay knowest John hath bound me with his blood." Erda looked pleased.

"How does that help?"

"To be bound by blood is a'most powerful way to bind, canst only be broken upon death. 'Twas lost between dying and being Spirit, now I knowest why. He hath bound me and, when my hex killed him, I was set free to a'wander as Spirit."

"Your hex killed him?' Amy blinked, finally realising that hexes and curses must be real, not some fiction from a fairy tale.

"'Tis certes." Erda said matter-of-factly.

"Oh. Wait, that bottle...is that the one I found at home in the desk?" Amy said as she remembered the idea that had dawned on her earlier. "It looked the same."

"Aye, 'tis a very one."

"So are you attached to it in some way?"

"My ashes are within, so 'tis part of me and I part of it."

"Right." Amy said not really understanding.

"Come, 'tis time to return, thee hast done well for thy first partitive flight." Erda took Amy's hand.

The garden blurred and became Amy's bedroom at the cottage again. Amy tried to move but her body seemed incredibly heavy and she felt very tired.

Erda lay her hand on Amy's arm, "Rest now, flying can make thee tired until thee is used to it. Sleep and I shalt watch over thee."

Amy, closed her eyes and felt the edge of sleep, she marvelled at how comforted she felt knowing Erda was there watching over her and how she instinctively didn't find it at all creepy. Vaguely, Amy wondered if Erda could haunt her dreams as well. Amazingly, after all she had seen, Amy felt relaxed and rather safe knowing Erda was nearby. She soon drifted off into a peaceful sleep, this time there were no voices disturbing her slumber nor, surprisingly, images of burning bodies to give her nightmares.

Chapter Thirteen

October, present day, Canada

Detective Inspector Andy Withers sat in his chair, with his feet up on his desk, chewing the end of his pen and wondering when the autopsy findings would come in on the motel and university murder cases. Both of them were weird and extremely violent and they disturbed him just a little bit more than his murder cases usually did. And that pissed him off immensely, there was only a certain level of sicko he could handle and this person or persons' level was just way above that. His desk phone rang and made him jump, but it was not the call he hoped for. Swearing profusely, he hung up on Glendale's police dispatch and stalked out of the office, he made his way down the stairs and out of the rear of the building to his car. Before starting the engine, he rummaged in his pocket for his phone, pressed the number three on the speed dial and left a voicemail on his partner Mitch's phone. Punching the car into drive, he pulled out of the parking lot and headed across town in a foul mood.

Andy arrived at the Henry Dale Memorial Hospital in a matter of minutes as for once and most unusually, all the traffic lights from the east to west side of town were in his favour, this helped to lighten his mood slightly but not by much. Exiting the lift on the third floor, he stalked through the chaos that burst forth from the usually quiet corridors of the hospital. There were so many uniformed police officers, hospital security staff, nurses, doctors and patients, it was impossible for him to spot Mitch and Lou in the crowd. Over the heads of the noisy people, he finally saw Bryer at the other end of the hall, who waved him in his direction and towards the end of the corridor.

Andy pushed his way through the panicked people, pausing to tell a uniformed officer to clear away as many unnecessary hospital staff as possible, on the way.

"Looking casual today, aren't you Bryer?" Andy said as he noticed the photographer was in sweats and carrying a gym bag.

"Yeah, just got here. I was upstairs." Bryer said and looked away, not allowing for any further discussion on his reason for being there.

Andy filed the reaction in his brain, there was something secretive about the guy, he decided. Andy caught Mitch's eye as he walked out of the elevator into the chaos just as Andy had, he called him over with a tilt of the head. Andy watched as his young partner managed to make his way quickly across the room. As usual, Mitch was dressed in a uniform but his unruly curly hair, which always looked like it needed a good brushing, looked particularly wild today. Andy thought it made him look a bit like a hippy, however, he was good at his job and a whiz on the computer and so Andy liked him. In fact, despite their age difference, Andy and Mitch got on so well, they could have been brothers in another life.

"Mitch, can you canvas the various members of staff and see if we can get more info out of them than the O.P.P. have managed to so far? I'll be at the scene."

"Will do, boss." He said, pulled out a notepad from his trouser pocket and headed directly for the group of staff, who were huddled at the nurse's station talking excitedly.

"Mr Burnett? Here's the equipment you wanted from your truck." A fresh faced uniformed officer said as he passed over two metal suitcases and the truck keys.

"Thanks, Haynes. Appreciate it." Bryer said, took the cases and began to head down a side corridor. "The scene's this way, Andy." He called behind him as he walked off, his sneakers squeaking on the polished floor with each step.

Andy followed behind as Bryer led the way down to a more quiet corridor that had already been sectioned off by the police and the two policemen guarding the entrance to the hallway nodded them through. Eventually, Andy and Bryer arrived outside a room that had its door wide open and by it stood Lou putting on his forensic overalls.

"You two got here quick, not even been in there yet myself." Lou said as he covered his hair with a plastic hat.

"Yeah." Andy said as he meaningfully looked at Bryer, who ignored Lou's comment and began to put on his own overalls.

Within a couple of minutes they were all dressed identically and walking into the small, two bed hospital room. Lou was the first to reach the bed in question, which had its curtains pulled almost all the way around it, he peered around the open space at the edge of the curtain. "Crap, that's nasty." He said, checked if he could pull the curtain back more without compromising the evidence, which he could, so he drew it back a foot and everyone was able to look at the grisly scene.

The bed covers were no longer the pale blue that they were supposed to be, they had soaked up much of the blood on the body, although the arterial spray had squirted up the curtains on one side, then had run down and left dark puddles on the otherwise pristine floor.

"Jesus. You think that's nasty after what we've seen recently?" Andy said, relieved that it wasn't as bad as he had been preparing himself for. These gruesome murders were beginning to fill his mind with disgusting images and he didn't like that, not one fucking bit.

"Yeah, it doesn't help that I freaking hate hospitals though." Lou said as he carefully peeled back the sodden cover to reveal the woman's open chest cavity.

"Shit. Poor girl." Bryer said as he paused to look at her before he began using plotting markers to form grids and then photograph the scene.

"Who found her?" Andy asked.

"The uniform who was first on the scene said it was a nurse doing her hourly rounds." Lou said.

"That must have sucked big time for the nurse, not a surprise you want to find. Did she have any visitors today?" Andy inclined his head towards the girl.

"Not as far as I know but the nurse was rather out of it when I arrived, probably still is, come to that. The officer probably didn't get much more from her." Lou said and opened one of his metal cases to begin work.

"More murdered bodies, what's this world coming to?" Said the throaty voice of the Coroner as he peered around the curtain. His large sized forensic overalls making him look like an anaemic Santa.

"Hey, Will." Andy said in a resigned voice.

"Dr. Chester." Lou nodded to his colleague.

"Dr. Chan." Will said to Lou as if there was some sort of professional rivalry between them.

Bryer silently continued to take photographs, his camera constantly whirring in the background.

"Well, she's dead." Will said with an amused look on his face. He quickly looked serious again as he realised no one enjoyed his inappropriate and smart ass remark.

"Thanks, Doc. I can see that. How about some more useful information?" Andy said.

"Not until I do an autopsy, you know I don't like to guess, Andy." Will said pushing his wire rimmed glasses up his nose and peering closely at the corpse. "I can tell you her lungs have been removed though."

"Her lungs? What the fuck? What sort of crazy do we have now?" Andy said, frowning at the sick news, would the weirdness on these murders ever end? He wondered.

"Not a clue, but that's your territory not mine. Lou, let me know when you're done so we can take her out of here." Will said as he stepped back a little to give Lou and Bryer room to work unhindered.

"Sure thing, Will." Lou said, all rivalry seemingly set aside as he got down to the nasty business that comes with crime scene forensics.

Dr Chester stepped back from the scene and walked over to the other side of the room to the empty bed and sat on it. "Andy, I have those autopsy results you've been waiting for downstairs, I was about to ring you. I think you'll find them really very interesting, especially after this." He said, gesticulating his hand towards the girl's body.

"I'll come and collect them from you after." Andy said as he picked up the chart from the end of the bed with his gloved hands. "Fuck me, I bet that's not a coincidence."

"What?" The Coroner said with a startled look on his face.

"This poor young woman is Olivia Hamilton, the roommate of the murdered girl at the university." Andy said shaking his head, "What the fuck is going on?"

Nobody replied because not a single one of them had any idea.

"Any sign of that weird symbol here?" Andy said.

"Not seen it." Said Lou, 'You Bry?"

"Nope, not this time."

"Ever find out what it was?" Lou asked as he taped plastic bags over the girl's hands as a precaution in case there was any DNA evidence, from her attacker, either on her hands or under her nails.

"Not yet, got an appointment with some guy at the university later, hopefully he'll know. Found him online, some sort of historian or something, the website said that this Dr. Renshaw's speciality is symbols." Andy said but he didn't sound too hopeful as he also stepped back a little and watched the forensic team work.

Later, once Bry and Lou had finished, the Coroner and his staff removed the body and took it to the morgue downstairs. Detective Inspector Andy followed them down because he wanted to get a look at those autopsy results from the previous five murders.

As he waited, he watched while Olivia's body was put in a mortuary fridge cabinet and he couldn't help thinking how sad it was for her to have such a short life. What was she 18, maybe 19 years old? It was a fucking shame, he decided.

Will Chester's voice brought Andy out of his sad revere.

"Come into the office, Andy." Will said from his office doorway, "And take a seat."

Sitting in Will's stark white office, Andy wondered how the Chief Coroner ever got anything done or indeed found anything on his desk as it was piled so high with files and books, it looked like one sneeze and the entire thing would collapse burying the Coroner alive. Andy looked around the messy room. Apart from a tall bookshelf overflowing with books and magazines, the only things that broke the sea of white walls was a faded poster of a tropical beach on one wall and a couple of discoloured old certificates on the wall behind Will's chair. It certainly wasn't the most cosy of offices that Andy had seen, he knew it was the morgue but still this place needed a bit of life in it to cheer the place up, perhaps a plant or two, Andy thought as his mind wandered.

Will leaned over his desk and waded into the huge piles of files, he quite quickly found the two buff coloured folders and passed them over to Andy. "Here, have a read."

Andy took the files and began to look through the blood curdling images and, as usual, tried his hardest to read the medical jargon that always seemed like a foreign language to him.

"Here, you will need this too."

Andy looked up to find Will handing him a glass of amber liquid. "Scotch, at this time of the day?"

"With these crimes, it's Scotch at any time of the day." Will said, sat down heavily in his old, worn leather chair and picked up his own glass of liquid delight.

"Yeah, I know what you mean." Andy said and took such a deep draught of the liquid that it burned his throat and reminded him he was still alive, unlike these poor fuckers, he thought to himself.

"What am I looking at exactly?" Andy eventually said, having given up on deciphering the medical terms.

"Essentially, all five bodies were tortured and then mercilessly cut up while the victims were alive." Will said, taking a slug of his drink.

"Nice." Andy said in a disgusted, humourless tone.

"Here's the kicker, several of them were missing an internal organ or two."

"What? Fuck." Andy let out a long sigh. Yup, he had a special type of crazy on his hands with these cases, he thought.

"Yeah, but here's the odd thing...it's not like it's a signature...you know where the unsub takes the same thing like a finger or tongue or something...no, this guy takes a different piece each time. With the family in the motel room he took a spleen and the two kidneys from the woman, and the liver from the boy, but nothing was missing from the older male. With the students, he took the lungs from the female but the male had nothing missing."

"This shit gets weirder." Andy said while his brain tried to understand the mentality of the murderer or murderers. He shook his head and gave up, he would never understand him or them...whoever.

"Yeah, I know. And now the roommate of the girl also loses her lungs?" Will brushed his hand over his eyes in an attempt to counteract his weariness, he'd been working flat out on these cases. "Why would anyone need lungs, let alone two sets of them?"

"Perhaps we're looking at a black market organ supplier?" Andy said, hoping it wasn't the case because those were near impossible to find and the perps would be well gone by now. Those types knew how to cover their tracks too well.

"No, I can't see it. The problem is that although some skill was used to remove the organs, it was not the skill of a surgeon and you would need that if the organ was to be viable afterwards."

"Hmm..." Andy frowned and took another mouthful of the strong liquid.

"My best guess is that it's some sicko, more weird than the usual sicko, who is collecting various body parts as trophies but this is a new one on me. I've never seen anything quite like this in all my years working in the Coroner's office." Will said and knocked back the last of his Scotch.

"Yeah, me neither, we have got one sick fuck on our hands, don't we? This could well be a landmark case or it could come back and kick us in the ass, if we don't catch the fucker. It could go either way. Anyway, let me know what you find with Miss Hamilton's body." Andy said, finished his drink in one big gulp and left the Coroner's office nodding his thanks as he did so.

*

By two-thirty that afternoon, Andy sat alone in yet another office but this one was the complete opposite to the Coroner's. This office was dark wooden panelled with several huge book cases full to the brim with old looking books. The room was so neat that Andy wondered if dust even dared to land in here. The desk only had a pen, a laptop and one tray, with a few documents in it. In fact, it was so clean and tidy it didn't actually look used by anyone let alone a professor at a university. As he waited for the professor to arrive, he could hear the university students milling about in the hall outside, presumably going from one class to another.

The door opened allowing the noise of the hall to flood into the room and in walked an extremely good looking woman of about thirty-five years.

"Detective Inspector Withers, I presume?" The woman's honeyed voice said as she offered him her hand.

"I...erm...yes." It'd been a while since a beautiful woman had flustered Andy, especially when he was expecting to meet a man, but he stood and shook her hand trying hard not to look her up and down in an unprofessional but very appreciative way.

"I'm Dr. Renshaw, pleased to meet you, do sit down." She said and sat behind the immaculate desk.

"Thanks and thank you for meeting with me on such short notice." He said, feeling a little more comfortable after his initial confusion.

"My pleasure, Detective Inspector." She smiled, flashing perfectly neat and white teeth.

"Please, call me Andy." He said impulsively and he could feel his body temperature raise in response to that smile. I'm too fucking old for this, he thought to himself and tried to arrange his thoughts in a more professional manner.

"Andy. Then, you must call me Charlotte." She said with another sexy smile.

Forcing himself to concentrate on the reason why he was there, Andy said, "Did you have an opportunity to take a look at the drawings I emailed you?"

"Why, yes I did." She said as she opened a desk drawer and withdrew a blue folder, opening it she removed copies of the strange circular drawings and lay them out on her desk. "Intriguing they are, too."

"Oh, why so?"

"It's a little out of my specific field, which, as you know, is the symbology of Christian religions, but they look like Sigils to me. To be more precise, they look like Magical Sigils. Something one would expect to find in the accounts of Witch trials, I think." Charlotte said.

"Witch trials?" Andy's eyebrows rose in surprise and a smile appeared on his face, "You're kidding, right?"

"No, I'm not. I've passed them to a friend of mine who knows more about this area than I. I hope you don't mind?" She said as she placed the images back into the file.

"No, that's fine. Anything that will help figure them out is good by me." He said feeling more than a little confused and frustrated by these murders and their stupid symbols. His pocket came alive as his phone vibrated with a call, he withdrew it and looked at the caller's name.

"Excuse me a moment, I must take this call." He said to Charlotte, stood up and went out of her office and into the stone clad hall of the university. "What's up, Lou?"

"Thought you'd want to know, we've finished the crime scene reports for the motel and university and one thing certainly sticks out." Lou said.

"Oh? And what might that be?" Andy said, wondering what the hell was coming now.

"Both scenes gave no forensic evidence whatsoever, no fingerprints, no hair nor fibre, nothing."

"Fuck." Andy said and kicked the empty wooden bench by the wall, he quickly looked around him and was pleased to see all the students had gone and no one saw his outburst. "What else?"

"The papers with the symbol on, again had no finger prints on them...not even smudges. The envelopes were self-sealing so no DNA either and the only finger prints on them were the clerk's at the motel and the victim's. Basically, each crime scene only had evidence of the victims and not the perpetrator or perpetrators, and, this is odd, both doors were locked from the inside and showed no evidence of tampering either to unlock or force the doors."

"What? So you're telling me these people were tortured and murdered by the invisible man inside locked rooms?"

"No, I'm telling you there is no evidence of anyone else being in there with them." Lou said, sounding a little perturbed by his own unusual findings.

"Are you sure, you've run your tests twice and double checked everything?"

"Yup, three times, actually, to be sure. There is no evidence of the murderer or murderers at either scene."

"Right, thanks for letting me know, Lou." Andy said and hung up. "Fuck, fuck, fuckety, fuck!" He said through gritted teeth as he rammed his phone back in his pocket.

"Is there a problem?"

Andy spun round to find Charlotte standing behind him. "Ah...no. Just a frustrating day. Sorry." He said feeling more than a little embarrassed for his outburst and, more specifically, for her seeing and hearing it.

"Not a problem. I have heard that type of language before, you know. I do work with students

every day." She said as she locked her office door.
"I'll let you know if I hear anything back from my
friend. Did you need anything further?" She looked
at him with an alluring half smile on her face.

"No...err...thanks." Andy said as he watched
her walk away.

He tried not to stare at her toned ass and
lovely long legs and wondered if she had meant
police work or something other, when she asked him
if he needed anything else. He certainly hoped he
would hear from her soon and for more than one
reason. He watched her walk towards the end of the
hall and turn the corner, he could have sworn she was
putting on that sexy walk just for him. Well, he
definitely hoped so anyway and suddenly his day
didn't seem quite so bad after all.

Chapter Fourteen

Amy awoke feeling refreshed and relaxed, something she had not really been feeling of late. She stretched out her body under the covers wondering what the day held for her. She began to think about Erda and opened her eyes to scan the room. She had kept to her word and was sitting on the old chair, in the corner of the bedroom, watching over Amy while she slept. Amy stretched again and yawned loudly, she finally pushed the old fashioned quilt back and sat on the side of the bed, her feet resting on the woven rug.

"Art thou refreshed?" Erda said.

"Yes, thanks. Did I dream it or did we really just go into your past and see you...see you die?" Amy said as she rubbed a hand over her face and tried hard to gather her thoughts about what she had witnessed.

"Aye, thoust saw my truth." Erda nodded.

"I'm sorry, Erda...what you went through...it was horrific."

"'Twas and 'tis done. 'Tis naught to be done of it now."

"I guess that's true." Amy nodded, rose, put on her dressing gown and went to make herself a cup of tea.

Minutes later, she was sitting at the table, in the kitchen, sipping her warm brew. Amy looked over at Erda and wondered what she had seen in all those years of wandering through the lives of the living, lives that she could never truly be part of. Several thoughts came to her at once, "What happened to John? And your daughter, Abigail?"

"Thee evil doer thou knowest as John, he succumbed to my hex nay three years hence my death. Abigail who he hath indeed found, was taken in by John's sister, Catherine and her husband Nathaniel, 'twas given station befitting her father's place despite being his bastard and heir to naught. Later, I found she married well and I hath been watching my family through hundreds of years hence." Erda looked out of the kitchen window seemingly lost in thought and time.

"That is good news, about Abigail I mean. How did you and your bottle come to be here then?" Amy asked, but before Erda could answer Amy's phone rang.

"Darling, is that you? Amy, darling?" The upper class voice said loudly in the ear piece.

"Felicity! How lovely to hear from you again, how's London?"

"Freezing darling, all it does is rain here in October! Time for Felicity to go somewhere warm until Spring, perhaps the Maldives or Hawaii...."

"What a lovely idea, Felicity. Now what can I do for you?" Amy quickly changed the subject as she knew Felicity would be inviting her along to help find Amy a suitably rich husband. Amy had fallen in that trap twice before and she did not intend to fall in it again, no matter what.

"Oh, yes. Right, of course, darling. I'm calling with good news, your last book just reached the New York Times Children's Best Seller list, you went straight in at number nine. Congrats, darling!"

"Oh, wow! That is excellent news." Amy said and perked up with joy.

"That means a lovely plump royalty payment and bonus will be lodged in your account soon, I know it's vulgar to talk of such things, but, honestly darling, now you can afford to get out of the horrid little apartment you have here..."

The disdain in her voice seeped out of the phone and crawled into Amy's ear.

"...and buy something more suitable for a best-selling children's novelist." Felicity's voice rose with excitement as if she had just heard that Hermes had a sale on.

"I rather like my little flat in London." Amy said feeling a bit homesick for her home, things and especially for Bilsby, her cat, which she had safely lodged at a friend's while she was out of the country. She missed cuddling with him.

'Don't be ridiculous, darling, no one can love living in a closet." Felicity said imperiously. "Oh, yes, I almost forgot, you will need to get new head-shots done too, as soon as possible, as we'll be getting a lot more attention now and your last ones are well, frankly a tad...well, unsuitable for you now, darling, obviously."

Glad of the change of subject, as Felicity's superiority complex had begun to grate on Amy, she said, "Okay, I'll get on to it and send the invoice to your secretary as usual."

"Right-oh! Okay, darling, I must dash as I'm meeting the Wetherington-Smythes for dinner and one mustn't keep one's friends waiting. Toodle-pip, darling!"

The call ended before Amy had even gotten the chance to say goodbye.

Amy put the phone back down on the table and let out a deep sigh, sometimes talking to Felicity was hard work but she refused to let it get her down, after all, it was extremely good news that she had rung up for and so Amy let her irritation go. She sat back down at the kitchen table with her cup of tea and wondered where she could get new head-shots done around here. It was time to explore more, she decided.

After a quick breakfast of bagel, cream cheese and more tea, Amy showered, dressed and headed into Morton Creek to have a proper look round the old town and perhaps find out if there was a decent photographer in any of the nearby towns, although she wasn't sure who she was going to ask about it. She parked on Main Street and, after noticing Cy and Kath were both busy serving customers, she waved a quick hello at them through their shop window. She decided she would walk down one side of the road exploring the shops and stop for lunch, then walk back up the other side doing the same and hopefully just in time for dinner. She felt the need to spoil herself today after the excellent news from Felicity. She might even do a bit of shopping while she was at it.

It was yet another beautiful day in October as Amy walked down the street, there was a warm breeze which made the multi-coloured leaves on the maple trees rustle and the ones on the ground swirl around her feet. The colours and sounds of the quiet town in a beautiful autumn soothed Amy's Soul, which is exactly what she needed after the horror of what she'd seen on her recent Spirit journey into Erda's past.

Amy visited many of the small stores, she looked through cafe windows and even visited the small public library that was housed in a beautiful 19th Century building right in the centre of town. Eventually, she came upon an outdoor sports equipment store and she thought that perhaps they would know of a good photographer in the area. After all, what hunter or fisherman doesn't want proof of the big catch?

The bell over the door rattled as she entered and surveyed the place. The store had a long counter at the back with various sized guns behind it and a stout, middle aged man in a checked shirt leaning on the counter, talking on the phone. Amy looked around her as she walked to the back of the store, everywhere she looked she could see fishing rods, camping equipment, hunting outfits on racks and camouflage nets. The store had a strange smell, sort of dusty and metallic. She paused a few steps away from the counter and waited patiently for the man to finish his conversation, which he did within moments.

"Can I help you today?" He said pleasantly and his face lit up with a kindly smile, his missing teeth did nothing to deter the warmth of it.

Amy moved closer to the counter. "I hope so. I'm looking for a photographer, do you know of any in the area?"

"A photographer, eh? Well, there's Burnett's Photography on Alexander Street just past the White Oak bar. It's just down on the left there." He said pointing to his left, "But that's the only one I know of round here."

"Oh, that's great, I'll try there. Thank you so much for your help." Amy smiled, turned and began heading towards the door.

The man called from behind her, "Anytime. If you need any hunting or fishing gear, you know where to come, right?" He said hopefully.

"Sure do, thanks again." Amy said and waved goodbye as she left his store, delighted to find that the people in the town were so friendly and helpful.

Following the store owner's instructions, Amy headed down the road until she came to the White Oak bar. It was an old building but the sign looked newly painted and it portrayed a large white oak tree which stood in a green field. She could hear music coming from within but she didn't enter. Continuing past the bar, and promising herself she would visit it soon, she turned the corner onto Alexander Street. It was a small side street with a launderette, a delightful little book store and, at the far end, a black and white sign showed her that she had found 'Burnett's Photography'. She walked down to the end of the street to take a closer look.

The shop window frames and door were painted black and the two display windows, one on each side of the door, were tastefully decorated with portraits and landscape images. Stepping into the shop was like stepping into another world, the bottom half of the walls were covered in dark wood panelling whilst the top had vertical striped wallpaper of cream and very pale green. On the walls were various photographs, some looking like they were from the 19th century and some were more modern, they all complemented each other well as they were all black and white or sepia, except for the massive picture of a landscape behind the old-fashioned desk.

The large colour picture was of mountains and a lake, it was so big it felt like it drew you into the image and Amy found it difficult to tear her eyes away from it. When she eventually did, she spotted what looked like a small doorbell on the old desk, between a laptop and a cash register. She pressed the bell just once and heard it ring, the sound came back at her from down the dark corridor next to the large painting, from what, she presumed, was an office at the back of the store.

"I'll be with you in a moment." Came the disembodied voice from within the dark caverns of the store.

Amy smiled to herself as she imagined all sorts of hidden worlds back there and turned to more closely admire the large landscape.

"Feels like it's pulling you in doesn't it, ma'am?"

"Yes..." Amy turned and was surprised by the person standing in front of her, "You!?"

"Me." Bryer said with a smile, "Did you expect someone else?"

"Well, I hadn't thought about it actually, now that I do it makes sense, of course." Amy said and became flustered as the heat rose in her cheeks, she had almost forgotten how handsome he was.

"What can I do for you today, Amy?"

He remembered her name too and, as exciting as that was, sadly it only made her brain falter more, "I...erm...well, yes. You see, I need some new head-shots, is that something you do?"

"Absolutely." He turned and sat at the desk, 'When were you thinking?"

"Whenever you're free, although the sooner the better."

After consulting his laptop, Bryer said, "I have a space at two-thirty tomorrow, would that be okay?"

"Sure, that's great."

He asked her for her contact details and quickly typed them into his laptop's calendar and said, "So for head-shots, I suggest you bring one or two changes of clothing with you and we'll shoot a whole load, then you can go through the proofs and choose the ones you want, okay?" He scribbled the time on a card and held it out to her.

"Yes, that's just fine. Thank you." Amy said and took the appointment card from his outstretched hand. She then realised she didn't know what else to say, her brain scrambled madly for a subject. "Have you been to the White Oak, is it any good?" Words at last, she thought to herself with relief.

Bryer looked surprised but then smiled, "Sure, lots of times. That place has been here longer than me."

"Of course you have, how silly of me. I've never been in so I was wondering if I should go there for lunch today." Amy felt like she was rambling incoherently.

"It's old and a bit worn but the food is good." Bryer stood and came around the desk. "If you give me an hour, I'll be finished with the project I'm in the middle of and ready for some food, I'd be happy to show you around and cash in that rain-check." He said with a friendly smile.

Amy's innards melted. "Oh, erm...yes, that would be great."

"Meet me back here in an hour then." He said with another massive smile that truly made his face light up.

"Right, will do. I was just thinking of exploring the book shop next door anyway." Amy said.

Without another word she left the shop, trying really hard not to look back, or, for that matter, trip over the doorstep and make a fool of herself. Although she managed to stay on her feet, looking back at him was something she failed at, and, when she closed the shop door, she couldn't resist a quick peek through the glass, to her embarrassment he was watching her the whole time. Flustered again, she quickly looked away and tried to calmly walk along the pavement and into the book store. It was not an easy thing to do because her heart was hammering like crazy and her head was full of excitement like a teenager in love.

Amy peered into the window of the book store and was surprised to find a copy of her latest children's book, 'Maud and the Tea of Dume', sat on a shelf under 'New Releases'. A spark of pure joy ran wildly about her brain, she always had a deep sense of satisfaction and joy whenever she saw one of her books in print and even more so when it was in a book store window, even though she had been writing professionally for ten years and probably should have gotten used to it by now. Pushing the door open, she heard the tinkle of the bell above it and a lady with the most beautiful red hair came out from the store room.

"Welcome to The Blinded Eye book store." She smiled pleasantly and continued to walk to the small counter by the door placing a pile of books on the counter next to her.

"Hello." Amy said, aware that her English accent might stand out in a small book store in a small town and she waited for the inevitable comment.

"Is that an English accent I hear?"

"Yes, it is." Amy said and smiled.

"Oh, I love the English accent." She said and held her hand out to Amy. "I'm Maggie Moon and I own this book store."

Amy shook her hand. "Amy Grey, nice to meet you." Amy glanced round the store. "Nice place you have here." The store was quite large but still seemed cosy somehow. It was filled with shelf after shelf of books like any other book store but it also had cosy little reading nooks with soft looking chairs, little tables and small lamps. There was even a lovely little cafe at the back of the store which had just four tables and a counter selling beverages and cakes and snacks. Amy fell in love with the store immediately, it was exactly how she would have a bookstore if she ever owned one.

"Thanks, I'm so pleased you like it." Maggie looked at Amy for a moment. "I'm sorry and I understand if you think I'm crazy but you look familiar, have we met before?"

"No, but you may have seen my face on one of your books in the window." Amy said mischievously. She was amazed to realise she instinctively liked Maggie already, some people you just know you will be close friends with right from the start.

"Really?" She looked puzzled for a moment. "Wait, you're Amy Grey? The Amy Grey, the children's book author?"

"Yup." Amy grinned, being recognised still made her feel like an excited twelve year old.

"That's awesome. I love your books, I don't care if they are for children, they rock." Maggie said with enthusiasm obvious in her voice.

"Thanks, I appreciate that." Amy laughed.

"You should do a signing here? Hey, are you busy for lunch? We could go to Lacey's restaurant, her pumpkin soup is to die for, and we can set something up over lunch." Maggie said.

"I'd love to but I can't today. Can I call you later and sort something?"

"Sure, here take a business card. If you're busy during the day, we could go for dinner and maybe have some of the local wine, we have an excellent winery here." Maggie smiled a truly friendly smile, it was the type of smile that said we are going to have so much fun and you know it.

"Love to, I'll give you a ring."

"Excellent." Maggie said as she grabbed the pile of books and began walking over to a shelf, "Let me know if you need anything."

"Will do, thanks." Amy said and smiled. For the next hour, she perused the many books in the comfort and safety of the lovely bookstore. She ended up sitting down with a cup of green tea and looking over the couple of books she had been tempted to buy. Her time in the store passed pleasantly and before long she was saying goodbye to Maggie and heading back to the photography shop.

She was so very pleased she had found a nice local book store as well as somewhere to have her photos taken, to top it all she believed she just made a new friend and was now about to go and, hopefully, have a nice lunch with a sexy man. The day was going very well, she decided.

*

The inside of the White Oak bar was like any other small town bar, a long dark wooden bar counter with several stools dominated the place, there were a few tables and booths around the walls, a small pool table at the back and they even had an old jukebox in the corner, which was playing November Rain by Guns 'n' Roses when Amy and Bryer arrived. Sitting in a booth, opposite each other, they made small talk and looked at the menu. A skinny man with long, tied-back hair, who Bryer called Jack, came to take their order. He brought them each a bottle of beer and offered Amy a glass but she declined.

Amy sat watching the few people who were in the bar, at lunchtime, on a weekday. There were only four other people, an old man with long grey hair who sat at the bar talking to the bartender, a business man who was talking on the phone while sipping a coke, having just finished his food by the look of his empty plate in front of him, and a young couple who were playing pool and laughing.

"Are you sending them home to someone special?" Bryer said.

"Sorry, what?"

"The head-shots, are they for someone back home?"

"Oh, no. They're for my agent, apparently they want new photos as I just hit the New York Times Children's Best Seller list." Amy smiled from ear to ear. She couldn't help but boast, she was so very pleased with herself.

"Really? Well, congratulations! Lunch is my treat then in celebration."

"Oh, I couldn't do that."

"Of course you could and it's done, so enjoy it." Bryer said just as Jack walked over to their table and delivered their meals.

"Wow!" Amy said as she looked down at the huge amount of food on the plate before her.

She had ordered the Bison Burger and fries, thinking it would be a normal sized meal, instead the burger would take two hands to hold, it was fighting for room on the plate with the huge pile of fries, and, next to that was the salad decoration which was actually the size of a side salad, even the larger than normal plate was overflowing with all the deliciousness.

Bryer watched her eyeing the full plate. "This is Canada, remember, go big or go home." He said and laughed. "I did tell you the food was good here, wait until you taste it. Oh wait, you're not one of those women who is afraid of eating a decent meal, are you?" He said with a cheeky look in his eye.

"Hell, no." Amy said as she grabbed the burger with two hands and took a huge bite. She grinned at him with her cheeks bulging and ketchup smeared on her chin.

Bryer burst into laughter as he sat back in the booth fascinated by her. Picking up his beer bottle he held the bottom of it out towards her in salute and said, "Welcome to Canada, eh!"

After that they fell into an easy conversation about their lives, favourite movies and all the usual things a couple on a first date talk about. In fact, their conversation lasted well past their food and their second beers.

Chapter Fifteen

Most of the building was dark and the car park was almost empty, nearly everyone had gone home for the night, although there were two or three office lights still on. It was already six-thirty and Detective Inspector Andy Withers was still sitting at his desk staring at the report from Lou, it confirmed what he had told him on the phone yesterday, there was simply no forensic evidence what-so-ever in any of these recent murder cases. He put the file down and picked up another, this one told him that the cameras at the motel hadn't worked for years and the clerk couldn't remember seeing anyone bring the note for the murdered family, in fact, he had said that it had just suddenly appeared on the motel's desk with a room number written on the envelope.

He threw the report down and picked up yet

another, which was from his partner Mitch detailing that the Henry Dale University Campus Security saw nothing out of the ordinary on the night of the murders. "For fuck's sake, there has to be something, somewhere." Angrily he threw down the last file onto the pile on his desk and rubbed his temples.

Yet again, there was no evidence to help him solve these cases, the only link was that they were all the most horrendous and bloody crime scenes he had ever seen and that sure as shit wouldn't help catch anyone. He rubbed his brow and tried not to think about the headache that was threatening to turn into a migraine and make his day even worse. The desk phone suddenly rang, the noise jabbed bolts of pain through his head making him wince and angrily he grabbed at it, not because he cared who was calling but because he just wanted to stop all the damn noise. "What?"

"Andy?" The other voice hesitated, "There's an Emily Carpenter on line one for you."

Andy softened his voice a little, it wasn't Mitch's fault he was having a bad day or even week, "Who?"

"Emily Carpenter, she said you are expecting her call."

"I am?" Andy frowned, picked up his cell phone and looked at an entirely empty calendar app on it, knowing it was the only place where he listed his appointments, it didn't really help him much and it struck him just how sad it was to have nothing listed in it at all.

"Boss?" Mitch said, wondering if Andy had heard him.

"Yeah, yeah." He said with a puzzled look on his face, "Put her through." Then he sighed deeply wishing he was at home with a beer or something stronger. "Hello, Detective Inspector Withers, how can I help you?"

"Ah, good evening Detective Inspector, I am so glad I caught you. This is Emily Carpenter calling." The woman said in an authoritative voice and paused.

"Yes?" Andy said absentmindedly, while searching through his desk drawers for pain killers.

"I was asked to call you but if I am disturbing you or you are about to leave for home, I can always call back tomorrow." She said.

"No, no. Who asked you to call me?"

"Dr. Charlotte Renshaw, she said you needed some advice."

Andy's attention perked up and he closed the drawer he was looking in, "Oh, Yes, Dr. Renshaw."

He said with a happy look on his face as he sat back in his chair, he liked being reminded about her and those long legs.

"I'm telephoning about the Sigils she sent me, I can confirm they are what's known as 'Magical Sigils', in fact, they are quite rare. There is only one other known extant source of the image. Where was this image found? Charlotte didn't give me any details, she just asked me to confirm her suspicions and then to call you with my thoughts on this remarkable find, as she is presently away lecturing."

"They are part of an active investigation and I'm afraid I can't discuss the location where they were found."

"Ah, right, I understand, Detective Inspector." Emily cleared her throat as if she was about to address a class of students. "Well, as far as we know, they were used in spells for the Transportation of the Soul. At least, that was one of their uses."

"Excuse me?" Andy blinked in astonishment.

"They are a symbol of Witchcraft and used in spells for the Transportation of the Soul." She said without a hint of laughter and in an utterly serious voice.

"Yeah, right." Andy half laughed into the phone.

"I am quite serious, Detective Inspector, I can assure you this is no laughing matter, many people have lost their lives through persecution because of this type of thing." Emily said, her voice sounding more hardened and on the edge of anger.

"I don't mean to offend you, Ms Carpenter, it's just not something you expect to hear about the evidence from a crime scene. Can you explain what you mean by 'Transportation of the Soul'."

"Today, it would be known by another name, Astral Projection, I believe. Basically, the Soul leaves the body and can wander across this plane of existence or others." She said matter of factly, her voice having softened again, now that he was being more receptive to the idea.

Andy decided to let the crazy notion of planes of existence slide for now, "So whoever used this symbol..."

"Sigil." Emily interrupted.

"Sigil, thought they had left their body and it was their Soul that was floating around?"

"Essentially, yes."

"And there are people out there who actually believe this?" Andy couldn't help his voice from sounding incredulous.

"Of course."

"Are they in cults?"

"No, not at all. It is now a time honoured practice of the New Age movement. Although the Sigil is not used anymore, as far as I am aware that is."

"How is it that you are aware about such things anyway, Ms Carpenter?" Andy said and wondered about the sanity of the woman.

Emily laughed, "Don't worry, Detective Inspector, I am far too old to be jumping out of my body and letting my Soul run around, as it were. No, indeed. Many years ago, I studied History at university and focused my doctoral thesis on the folklore of 17th century England and North America, concluding my work with the Salem Witch Trials."

"Oh, right." Andy wasn't quite sure how to reply to this news and he rubbed his eyes as the pressure in his head increased. "This New Age Movement you mentioned, where would I find its members?" Andy said, thinking just how much it sounded like a cult anyway.

"They aren't members of anything, Detective Inspector, like I said before it's not a cult but a belief system. These types of people can easily be found in esoteric book shops. In fact, I do believe there is one in Morton Creek, um...'The Blinded Eye', if I recall correctly. Do you know the town, Detective Inspector?

"Yes, I'm familiar with it." He said as he wrote the name of the bookstore down on his notepad and circled it.

"Ah good. Well, when you are able to speak about where you found the Sigil, I'd be very interested to know the details, from an historical point of view, you understand."

"Of course. Thank you for your insights, Ms Carpenter. You've been most helpful to our inquiries."

"Pleased to help, Detective Inspector. Do contact me if you need anything further. Although, I am away for this entire weekend, visiting my family, but I will be back on Monday morning and I have already left my number with your colleague."

"Right, I will do. Bye." Andy hung up and pondered on what he had just learnt.

Andy found the medicine bottle he was looking for and popped a couple of the pills in his mouth and drank them down with the cold, stale coffee which had been sitting on his desk for the last hour. He shuddered with revulsion at the coffee as the pills slipped down. Tapping the end of his pen on his notebook, he sat and pondered the cult angle of this case for possibly the twentieth time, wondering if these murders were actually ritual killings. He was now pleased he, at last, had a place to start looking for the perp or perps. As he continued to sit and mull over all the facts in his head, an idea formed in his mind and filled him with intrigue. If he was right it would certainly change the case to a huge degree. He picked up the receiver of his desk phone and quickly punched in an international number, and, after a couple of rings, the call was answered. "Hey, Mac, how you doing?" He said into the phone.

The gruff, sleepy voice on the other end of the line replied, "Andy, that you? Do you have any clue what bloody time it is here?"

"Yeah, sorry bud. I realised as soon as you answered but then it was too late. Listen, do you remember when I was over the pond a couple of years ago, during that excellent fishing trip with you and the boys from Scotland Yard?"

"'Course." Mac cleared his throat and sounded a little more awake as he propped himself up with pillows against the headboard and attempted to rub the sleep from his eyes.

"I remember that you were talking about a case you'd thought was some sort of cult case, with murdered victims who'd had parts of their body removed. Anything ever come of it?" Andy said.

"Ah, the Olerenshaw Case. Nope, the case completely dried up, we had no evidence and no leads, it's a cold case now. Why are you ringing me so late at night to talk about it?"

"Because I think I have something similar going on here, maybe my cases are by part of the same cult or something. Any chance you can send me a copy of the files, Mac?"

"Seeing as it's you doing the asking, I don't see why not. I'll get one of the lads to email you it in the morning. So, when are you coming back for more salmon fishing on these fair isles? I know of some great trout spots now too."

"Thanks, Mac. I don't know when I can return but I'll be retiring in a couple of years and I might just come out there permanently, if it all works out." Andy grinned, talking about his long term dream always made him happy, despite his pounding headache.

"Sounds like a great plan, Andy, we could spend our weekends finding out who's the best angler." Mac laughed, it had been a competitive joke between them for many years.

"I know who I'd put my money on." Andy said and grinned.

"Yeah, right. Anyway, you know where to find me if you need anything else about the case, but just try to remember next time that we are five hours ahead of you here."

"Yeah, sorry again about that, Mac, apologise to Claire for me will you?" Andy felt really guilty now as he knew they'd recently had a baby.

"No worries, she's up with Michael at the moment anyway. Talk to you soon, mate."

"Yeah, bye Mac." Andy replaced the receiver, looked at his notes and decided to call it a night, he grabbed his coat and headed out the door.

*

By seven-thirty the next morning, Andy was back at his desk staring at the image of the Sigil and found himself wondering if it did have magic powers after all. Shaking himself mentally, he grabbed his mug and headed to the coffee maker in the canteen. It might not make the best coffee in the world but it was always full and hot. While pouring himself a cup of black nectar, he decided he would head into Morton Creek today and see if he could find himself some 'New Agers' or whatever they called themselves.

Returning to his desk with his hot drink in hand, he discovered he'd received an email from DI Paul 'Mac' MacAdam of Scotland Yard. Andy quickly clicked on the attached file and began reading the documents of the Olerenshaw case.

"I knew it." He said, to no one except himself.

As he continued to read through the various documents, he realised it was the same perpetrator or groups of perpetrators because the details of the cases were almost identical, even down to the drawings of the Sigil found at some of the crime scenes.

Again he chewed the end of his pen while thinking, the cult must have moved over here when their crimes were discovered in the UK, he thought to himself, or perhaps this is just another branch of the same cult.

Andy realised there were hand written comments on the edge of one of the scanned documents, he zoomed in on it so he could try to read it more clearly and he recognised Mac's handwriting, the note simply said: 'Victims were related' with no further explanation. Andy tapped his chin with his pen, his mind lost in thought.

Finally, he phoned the extension number of the small office next door. "Mitch?" He said.

"Yeah, boss?" The distracted voice said.

"Can you do some of your computer whiz kid stuff and look into something for me?"

"Sure, what do you need?" His partner said, sounding a lot more interested than before.

Chapter Sixteen

Amy came out of the lovely hot shower feeling all warm and toasty, she wrapped herself in the big fluffy towel and combed her hair through. Making her way to her bedroom, she turned off all the lights as she went. Changing into her PJ's, Amy lay snuggled up in her warm bed covers happily reading, she paused and placed the open book upside down on her lap as she sat and thought about Erda and her sad, lonely life. It was a shame she'd not had the chance to be with her child and she had died so young, at the hands of a madman, although twenty-two years in her time was not so young, Amy supposed. Things were so different in the 1600's and so much dirtier and smellier then too, indeed much more so than Amy had ever imagined.

She wondered where Erda had gone this time, she wasn't in the cottage, so Amy could only guess she had gone to wherever it was she went to when not here, Amy decided she would like to understand where exactly that was. It must be nice though, to travel anywhere in the world, and even in time, by just a thought. Oh, the things one could see, Amy thought. She closed her book and placed it on the small side table by the bed, deciding her mind was too busy to read and perhaps an early night would be good for her.

Amy reached out to turn off the bedside lamp and glanced at the bowl of waxy herbal mixture that was still sitting on the small table, it was the partitive unguent as Erda had called it, which she'd used to travel back in time. She looked at it for some time, wondering many things. "What if..." Amy said quietly to herself and reached out for the bowl.

Holding the bowl in both hands, she looked at the milky coloured contents which were speckled with small green pieces of plants, she poked it with a finger and it was solid, it left only a slight smear on her fingertip. She gazed at the contents for a long time trying to make up her mind, the inner conflicts of her thoughts making her edgy and nervous. Should she do this? More importantly, could she do this alone?

"Sod it." She said determinedly and, with some difficulty scraped and prised a small amount of the wax out with her fingernails. She managed to get enough for a small ball, which she held tightly in her hand to warm it through and make it soft again. It took a little while to make it pliable but once she'd done it there was no stopping her. Amy laid down fully in her bed, took a deep breath and smeared the powerful unguent on her forehead just as Erda had done. She began to feel the relaxing properties of the unguent and she tried to focus her mind on the time and place she wanted to go, she began to feel the numb sensation and then she felt herself drift off into the now welcome darkness.

Amy opened her eyes and found herself standing in the middle of a mall, the bright lights of it startled her, she blinked and looked around, somewhat confused. "Where the hell did I land?" She said and began to walk around, having no clue where she was nor why she was there. Of course, she couldn't ask anyone as she is a Spirit and could be neither seen nor heard by anyone she passed by. Eventually, she came to a 'You Are Here' board and she saw, from the name on the top of the board, that she was in the Meadow Grove Shopping Mall. "Of course." She said as she realised where she was. This was the spot where her parent's old house used to be.

When she had thought of going to her parents, this was the house address that had popped into her mind, not the new address where they had moved to only a couple of years before their death.

Amy closed her eyes and concentrated on their house at their new address. She felt a strange tremble in the air around her and then it was so quiet she knew she must have moved locations. Amy opened her eyes and smiled, she was outside the right house at, hopefully, the right time. She had arrived at night and quickly realised she was standing in the middle of the road and she began to walk across the dark, wet tarmac towards her parent's bungalow.

Although it was night and she couldn't see any storm clouds, she knew there had recently been a shower. The air smelt as if a quick summer rain storm had just passed by, leaving its watery gift for the plants and trees as if to honour them. She could smell the tarmac but also the earth, that damp glorious smell of wet soil, leaves and of life growing.

She began to walk up her parent's garden path, as memories of her childhood flooded her mind. She remembered there being a huge willow tree in the front garden of their old house when she was a child, she used to play inside its long arms and pretend she was in her own world. Sadly, there was no tree at this new house, just grass, shrubs and flower beds. The gardens both at the front and back were usually a blaze of colour, full of different flowers that bloomed at different times of year. Her father had been a very keen gardener, and, even with his reduced physical capacity, and with the help of her mother, he had kept the gardens just as beautiful as they were before. By the blooming of the flowers, it was obvious to Amy that she had arrived sometime in mid summer, possibly June by the look of it, just as she had wanted.

The bungalow itself was fairly small, after all there were only the two of them at home now and her mother had always said it was just large enough for them. The hall and bedroom windows faced outward toward the street on one side of the door and the living room window on the other side. Her father had hired contractors to build, this was before his stroke, the garage onto the right side of the bungalow and a new kitchen at the back.

Amy could smell the delicious scent of the roses by the front door as she got near to it. It was a smell she had always associated with visiting her parents. They also had a lot of roses at their old place, and it made her heart soar knowing she would see them again very soon. Although she was sad she couldn't talk to them, at least she could see them, even if they couldn't see her. Her pulse raced with excitement as she stepped up to front the door and she was so glad she had decided to do this.

For a brief moment there was utter silence but then a deafening sound burst forth and a wave of heat hit Amy. It all seemed to happen in slow motion as the door blew off its hinges and passed through Amy, the windows shattered and the glass flew outward as a huge explosion rippled through the house like a ripple on a pond and literally blew the house apart. What was left of the building was burning with such intensity that Amy could feel the air sucked into it from around her.

She staggered backwards as she watched, knowing there had been absolutely no chance to save her parents who were inside, the devastation was so total that they would have died instantly. In fact, that was exactly what she'd been told by the police when they'd informed her of the fire on that horrible day. Tears streamed down Amy's face as she sobbed and watched as her parents' neighbours rushed out into the street to see what had happened and she could hear the far off sound of the fire truck sirens coming closer.

Amy had not intended to be here for this, she was just supposed to see her parents when they were happy and living their lives, she wanted to remember them that way and not like this. Amy was angry at herself for not aiming her Spirit properly through time, perhaps this took more practice than she had first thought and maybe she should have come with Erda after all. Hoping to do better this time, she took a deep breath and concentrated on being where she was but in a time before the deadly explosion and fire.

Once again, she felt the air tremble around her and, when she opened her eyes, it was a wonderfully sunny summer's day and her parent's house stood before her, utterly undamaged and indescribably beautiful to her eyes. A flood of happiness washed over her because, at last, she was exactly where she'd wanted to be all along. Again she walked up the garden path, past the glorious smelling roses and stepped up to the front door. This time she heard a sound coming from the back of the house and thought her parents would probably be in the garden on such a lovely day. I bet Dad is pottering around the garden tweaking out dead heads of plants while Mum sits on the patio reading, she thought and could see it all in her mind's eye.

Amy walked around the house and along the side area that separated her parent's house from their neighbours. At the end, there was a huge trellis arch, which was covered with climbing clematis, its blooms covered every inch of the trellis with big white flowers. She walked under the trellis and into their lovely and well tended garden and saw the small patio with a table and four chairs, around the patio sat several pots full of flowers. Although no one was outside at present, she had been right about what her parents were doing that afternoon. Her father's gardening gloves were on the patio table next to his pruning shears, there were two glasses of cloudy liquid, possibly homemade lemonade or ginger beer and a women's romance novel with a pair of ladies sunglasses sitting on it.

Amy smiled to herself knowingly and walked across the patio and into the bungalow through the open patio doors. The newly built, modern kitchen was empty but smelt of chicken roasting in the oven, on the counter were salad leaves, tomatoes and cucumber which were all washed and ready to be cut up, they sat alongside a chopping board and a very sharp looking knife. She realised they must have come in from the garden to make an early evening meal, which they were probably going to eat outside as they usually did during summer. The thought brought back pleasant summer memories of visiting her parents and sharing a home cooked meal with them on that very patio during the summer. The sound of the phone ringing disturbed Amy's thoughts and she walked through into the living room to where the phone sat on the table by the sofa.

Amy only got one step into the living room before she stopped and surveyed the room that had been the place for many celebrations of birthdays, Christmases and her parent's wedding anniversary parties over the last few years. It was a room usually full with happy memories but now it was filled with unimaginable horror.

Both of Amy's parents were sitting on the sofa, although their posture looked somewhat awkward from the angle she was at. Amy cautiously walked further into the room and saw why they looked like that. Both of her parents had their throats cut and they had bled out over the autumnal, multicoloured pattern of the sofa making it seem just one dark hideous colour. Their heads hung loosely and oddly to one side and their eyes were open. Amy felt like they were both looking at her but their eyes were horribly opaque and unseeing.

Amy screamed as the image forced itself into her brain and buried its claws into her mind, making her unable to look away.

She noticed her father's body was far more mutilated than her mother's, not only was his throat slit but his torso had been cut open from neck to groan and the skin flaps lay open. With the quick look Amy got, before she finally forced her eyes to turn away, and, although she wasn't absolutely sure, it looked like some of his internal organs were missing due to the large gaping empty hole.

Amy collapsed on the floor, her legs unable to hold her weight any longer. She rocked back and forth with silent tears streaming down her face. The only words that left her mouth were: 'They were murdered, they were murdered', she said them over and over again.

She sat for a long time not looking at them and waiting for someone to come and find her parents, but no one did. The phone didn't ring again and no one came to the door. How could people not know, not have heard? She wondered.

The three of them sat there alone in their silence.

Amy knew she couldn't be with them any longer and climbed up off the floor. She wanted to go out of the house and stand by any of the beautiful smelling roses that surrounded it, she wanted one last smell of something pleasant before she walked away and returned to her time, never to come back again. She left the lounge, walked back through the kitchen and when she got out onto the patio, a huge heatwave forced its way through her as the house exploded again, sending debris and flames in all directions. The sound was deafening and the heat so intense that if Amy had been in her body she would have been burnt alive on the spot. Screaming with the sudden fright, she scrambled over the broken glass, wood and brick and made her way to the front of the house again.

Sitting down on the concrete path by the edge of the front garden, Amy watched the world burn. She now realised why she hadn't known her parents had been murdered, it was now obvious that the fire had destroyed all the evidence. She swore to herself that once she was back in her body, she would contact the police, make them aware and force them to find her parents' killer.

As she sat and watched the remains of the bungalow burn for the second time in an incredibly short space of time, she could only see the horrific images of her murdered parents in her mind. The tears began to run down her face until she couldn't hold them back any longer and deep, painful sobs wracked her body.

Eventually, the fire trucks arrived with the police and ambulances but nothing could be done, her parents were gone and she knew she could change nothing in this time, no matter what she tried to do, after all, no one could see or hear her.

Amy felt a cool hand on her shoulder and she looked up to see Erda standing above her. Erda knelt and gathered her in a cool embrace.

"Thy should nay hath come."

Amy cried into her shoulder. "I wanted to see them once more...I wanted to save them."

"Aye, I told thee we canst change naught."

Amy pulled back to look in Erda's eyes, "They were murdered. My parents were murdered and the fire hid that fact. Who would do that? Who would kill two innocent old people? They were lovely and everyone loved them." Agony clouded Amy's vision again with tears and she fell back into Erda's arms.

"Come, let us go home." Erda said while still holding Amy.

Amy awoke in her bed with Erda sat next to her, she rolled over and away from her, not able to talk about what happened and, eventually, she cried herself to sleep.

Erda watched her as she slept fitfully, whimpering in her dreams. She stroked her hot forehead until Amy rested a little more peacefully. She thoughtfully glanced across at the partitive unguent on Amy's bedside table and vanished.

*

Erda reappeared, some time earlier, in the living room and could hear Amy in the shower. Keeping an ear listening to the sound of the shower, Erda went into Amy's bedroom and walked around the bed towards the small bedside table. She picked up the bowl of the unguent and disappeared again. This time she reappeared in the attic and placed the bowl on the ledge of the window that faced out toward the lake. Erda looked down at the bowl of waxy unguent and smiled sadly to herself, "Aye, we canst only change small things, sometimes they lead to a'larger one." She said and once again she disappeared.

*

Amy came out of the lovely hot shower feeling all warm and toasty, she wrapped herself in the big fluffy towel and combed her hair through. Making her way to her bedroom, she turned off all the lights as she went. Changing into her PJ's, Amy lay snuggled up in her warm bed covers happily reading, she paused and placed the open book upside down on her lap as she sat and thought about Erda and her sad, lonely life. It was a shame she'd not had the chance to be with her child and she had died so young, at the hands of a mad man, although twenty-two years in her time was not so young, Amy supposed. Things were so different in the 1600's and so much dirtier and smellier then too, indeed much more so than Amy had ever imagined.

She wondered where Erda had gone this time, she wasn't in the cottage, so Amy could only guess she had gone to wherever it was she went to when not here, Amy decided she would like to understand where exactly that was. It must be nice though, to travel anywhere in the world, and even in time, by just a thought. Oh, the things one could see, Amy thought. She closed her book and placed it on the small side table by the bed, deciding her mind was too busy to read and perhaps an early night would be good for her. She reached over to turn off the bedside lamp and fell straight into a sleep filled with happy, safe dreams.

She would never know that she had done it differently last time.

Thanks to Erda's quick thinking, and travelling back in time to remove the unguent from Amy's bedside table, Amy never experienced the heart breaking, agonising pain of the horrific truth about her parent's death from a Spirit travel that no longer happened.

Erda appeared at Amy's bedroom doorway and looked at the sleeping woman. "'Tis best thee goes forth with good memories of thy parents, nay ones

'twill harm thee each time thy mind turns to them."
She whispered and vanished.

Chapter Seventeen

Amy glanced at her watch, for the tenth time in less than two minutes. She was early and she was nervous. She tried to gather her thoughts but she felt like an excited teenager on a first date, she shook her head, what was wrong with her? This is crazy, she thought. She was only early for the appointment and was now debating whether to sit in her truck to wait for a while, but, unfortunately in plain view, or to just go into the store early and be done with it. Sense won the day and, taking a deep breath, she grabbed her bag and climbed out of her truck.

She entered the photographic store at 2:18pm precisely, she knew because she, yet again, checked her watch. Luckily, Bryer wasn't in the front of the store and it gave her a moment to gather herself. "Come on, pull yaself together." She chided herself and then thought, it's not like you've never done this before, even if he's handsome and you like him. She unzipped her coat and took it off. "Get a grip." She mumbled to herself. She stood waiting quietly, wondering if he had forgotten about their appointment for her new head-shots.

A door opened along the corridor, that lead off the foyer of the store, and Bryer's head popped out around the door frame, "I'll be with you in five minutes just finishing a print run. You can go up the stairs, at the end of the corridor, and make yourself at home. There should still be some coffee in the pot, help yourself."

Before she could reply, his head vanished and she heard the door close.

Doing as she was told, she followed the dark corridor down to the end where, indeed, there was a flight of stairs leading upwards to a closed door at the top and another flight heading downward into darkness. Amy followed his instructions, and figuring it would be his studio, she confidently went up the stairs and opened the wooden door. She stopped mid-step through the doorway as the light flooded her vision, blinding her momentarily. Her eyes quickly adjusted and she realised she was not in a studio at all, but in what appeared to be Bryer's own apartment. Interested in his taste, and thinking she must have made a mistake with the directions, she quickly took the opportunity to look around her. It is always interesting, and very telling, to see where a man lived and how he actually lived.

The apartment had obviously had quite a lot of work done to it because most of the internal walls had been removed, which had flooded the space with the natural light from the six huge, old fashioned styled sash windows that faced out onto the street. The walls were painted a mellow brick red colour and covered with various photos in all shapes and sizes. There was a bed by the far left hand wall and an old wooden wardrobe next to it. To the far right, there were two huge, brown, soft looking leather sofas, which created an illusion of a separation from the bedroom into the living room. To her immediate left there was a half opened door, she could see a white and blue tiled bathroom that lay beyond and to her immediate right was a large brick arch leading into a rustic looking kitchen with all the modern conveniences. Although the apartment was open plan, the warm tones of the browns, red and toffee colours used to decorate it made it seem particularly warm, intimate and somewhat cosy. She was happy to say that she was pleasantly surprised by it all, and pleased that Bryer had good taste.

Amy walked towards the sofas and a thought occurred to her, had he said go upstairs or downstairs, she couldn't remember now. After all, there was no studio up here, so why would he tell her to go to his apartment? She didn't know whether to stay or go and the indecision rooted her to the spot. On the one hand, it was fascinating for her to see where he lived and how his place was decorated, but, on the other hand, she felt like she was intruding on his private life without permission. She was now definitely unsure of what directions he'd given her because she knew she had been flustered and overly excited when she had first arrived. "Bugger." She said to herself because she was now feeling like an idiot.

"Did you help yourself to coffee?" The voice suddenly came from behind her, making her jump.

"Shit!" She said as she swung round feeling guilty like the proverbial child caught with their hand in the cookie jar.

"Sorry, didn't mean to surprise you." Bryer said as he walked into his kitchen and got two mugs out of a cupboard, "Coffee?"

"Erm…no, thanks. Do you have any tea? Coffee gives me palpitations so I can't drink the stuff." She said as she walked towards him and leant on the lovely brick archway. "Love your place by the way, but I wasn't sure you said upstairs once I got here as I was expecting to be standing in your studio."

"Sorry, no tea, I never drink it."

"I'll just take some water then, please."

"Okay," He replaced the second mug with a glass and poured in some filtered water from the fridge. "When I'm doing portraits, or in your case headshots, I usually sit and have a coffee with the client up here to relax them and get more of an idea of what they want before heading down to the basement."

"The basement?"

Bryer handed her the glass of water and went over to sit on one of the sofas.

"Thanks." Amy said. She followed him and sat on the edge of the other sofa opposite.

"Yes, the studio is in the basement, it's the best place for me to control the lighting."

"Ah, I see, well that makes sense. Talking of light, I love how this apartment is set out, it has lots of lovely light and, if I'm not mistaken, those windows face east so I bet you get a glorious view of the sunrise through them."

"Yeah, it's one of my favourite views." He said and smiled at her. "So, any offers on your cottage yet?" Bryer leaned back and crossed one jean covered leg over the other, resting his ankle on his knee.

"No, not yet. Early days yet though I suppose."

"I'm sure there will be a lot of interest, it's in a great spot. There's really good light for photographing the lake from there."

"You should come and take some photos then."

"Thanks, I will take you up on that offer." He took a drink from his mug. "Now these headshots, they're for your agent, right?"

"Yes, I can pay you or you can bill them directly, it's up to you."

"I can bill them, don't worry about that. Do you want a formal or informal pose?"

"Informal, my readers like to see me as me and not in some boring publicity shot, if you know what I mean."

"I do and we can do that, no problem."

*

An hour and a half later, and after two shirt changes in the little changing room just off the main room of the basement, the photos were done at last.

Although she had enjoyed working with Bryer, he was easy going and very professional, the thought of him looking at her for nearly two hours was as unnerving as it was arousing and it had been very hard for her to concentrate on what she was doing and not daydream about other more gratifying pursuits.

"Okay, I think we're done here. Do you want to come back upstairs for a coff...I mean, a glass of water?" Bryer said as he switched on the overhead main light and began turning off his directional studio lighting.

"Sure, why not? Smiling all that time under those lights makes you thirsty." She said. "I'll just gather my stuff and meet you up there, if that's okay?"

"Sure."

Amy got off the stool they had used for the shoot, and went into the dressing room to gather the extra shirts she'd brought for changes of pose. She also put away her brush and make-up, which she had brought to do touch-ups during the changes, she had come fully prepared, after all, she'd done all this before in the UK.

Bryer had already gone ahead as she climbed the stairs from the basement when she heard a phone ring. It continued to ring but no one answered it, when she got to the top of the stairs and onto the corridor landing, she realised the phone was ringing in one of the rooms off the corridor and not upstairs where Bryer was. Suddenly, there was a crash upstairs and several swear words floated down to Amy's ears. "You okay up there?"Amy called up the ascending staircase.

"Yeah, just dropped your glass."

"Your phone is ringing down here."

"Can you grab it and bring it up, I've gotta find a band-aid." He said, sounding a little harassed.

"Sure." Amy followed the sound of the phone and she thought it was coming from the store front but when she passed a closed door in the corridor, she realised it was coming from there. She paused to make sure by listening at the door and then opened it. The room was completely dark so she felt on the wall for the light switch and flicked it on and she was utterly struck dumb with horror by what she saw. She stood on the threshold unable to move or scream and she definitely wanted to do both.

The room was small, with a single blacked out window and it held a desk with a computer on it and a printer. The phone, which was ringing endlessly, sat on the desk but none of these things were what had rooted Amy to the spot. Her eyes roamed the room taking in all the bloody images of murder and carnage, which were posted upon the walls. Her stomach rolled and she knew she was going to vomit at any moment, her hand rushed to her face and she covered her mouth, tried to breathe through her nose and gritted her teeth. Without grabbing the still ringing phone, she backed away from the doorway and bumped into something warm and solid. A sudden scream burst from her throat.

"It's okay, it's okay." Bryer said as he held her against him.

Amy panted against his chest. "What the hell..."

Bryer leaned forward and kicked the door shut with his foot and didn't let go of her. "I'm sorry you saw that."

Amy pushed away from him suddenly frightened. "What the hell is going on?" She backed away towards the front of the store and tried to envision her path to escape to the outside world.

"It's okay, you're not in any danger, I promise. It's my work."

"What?" That stopped her cold.

"I'm a part-time photographer for the Forensic Identification Unit of the Canadian Police. That's my private office where I deal with all the police work."

"Oh." Amy still felt nervous but also a little foolish.

"I'm not an axe murderer, honest." Bryer said and then realised that's exactly what an axe murderer would say. He didn't move an inch, not wanting to make her more nervous of him. "I'm sorry you saw that, I thought I'd left my phone on the front desk. I would never have asked you to get it if I knew it was in the office. Are you okay?" He frowned and worriedly looked at her, silently praying she would understand and believe him.

"I...think so. It was just such an unexpected shock." Amy's breathing had begun to slow as she began to relax a little. "So you work for the police too?"

"Yeah, I do crime photos; also, as you know, I do realty work, of which there is only usually a couple of a month and my studio work, of course."

"Makes sense, I guess." She shuddered at the images still stuck in her mind. "Why do you have the...those images up on the walls like that though?"

"I have to check that I have every possible shot of the scene or of any evidence and I do that by recreating and plotting the scene out on my wallboards with the relevant images. Gruesome, I know, but it works."

"Oh. I see."

"Look, I'll go buy some tea while you wait for me upstairs, okay?" Bryer said and began heading to the front door.

"I...I think perhaps I should be going." Amy said, not feeling a hundred percent after what she had seen.

"You have just had a nasty shock and I hear Brits like tea when that happens." He said with an amused glint in his eye.

"Well, yes...we do." She nodded.

"Right, good, I'll be back in five minutes. You go upstairs and relax, okay?"

"Well...if you insist."

"I do." He said as he closed the store door behind him and quickly vanished around the corner of the building.

Amy weighed the pros and cons of staying and her instincts told her he was telling the truth and she was safe. She mentally shook herself and tried not to see the ugly images floating around in her mind as she slowly turned around and climbed back up the staircase to Bryer's apartment. The bright autumnal sunlight streaming in the windows cheered her up somewhat as she sat on the squishy sofa again and breathed in and out deeply.

Bryer appeared in the doorway only moments later clutching a box of tea. "Had no clue what you like so I just got the basic Orange Pekoe. Bessy, at the store, said that was a good choice."

"Yes, that's just fine. Thank you."

'It's the least I can do after what I just put you through." He said as he switched on his kettle and got two mugs out, he opened the box of tea and threw a tea bag into one mug and then poured the already perked coffee into the other mug. "Milk, sugar?"

"No thanks. Just black, but take the bag out please." Amy watched him make her drink. She realised she was watching how he moved and she liked what she saw, she began to imagine what he would look like without his clothes on. A little shocked that her mind would so quickly go from gruesome images to fantasizing about Bryer that she looked away. Was it her mind's way of distracting her? Well, it was bloody working, she thought.

"You okay?" He was suddenly standing next to her holding out a mug of steaming black tea.

Amy blushed and said, "Yeah, I just wished I'd let the phone ring now."

"So do I." Bryer said and sat on the other sofa with his coffee in hand, still looking concerned. He could really have kicked himself for his stupidity, what was he thinking?

The ensuing silence was awkward, neither of them knew what to say, both of them mortified by the events of the last twenty minutes.

"Erm...so, when will the photos be ready for viewing?" Amy said.

"I'll transfer them to the computer tonight and filter out any unusable ones, so perhaps you could come by on Monday and take a look?" He said hopefully.

"Sure, just let me know what time." Amy said and sipped her tea.

Bryer, desperate to find a way to repair the damage said, "You know, tomorrow night is the Pumpkin Ball at the town hall, it's a big tradition around here. I wondered if you would like to come with me, as my guest?"

"Oh, erm...Okay. Yes, actually that would be rather nice." Amy said surprised by the invitation and thoroughly flattered by it at the same time, her qualms about him had now mostly disappeared and she felt much more relaxed.

"It's actually a costume ball, do you think you can come up with a Halloween costume that quickly?"

"I'm sure I can, I bet there's a costume shop in one of the nearby towns who would be happy to help."

"There's a good one in Glendale, I've been to it before. I'll text you the address."

"Oh, great, thanks. Do you have a costume already?" She said between sips of her tea.

"No, but I have one in mind." He smugly smiled at her. "It will be a surprise though."

"Well, as long as it's not an axe murderer we'll be fine." Amy said and timidly smiled at him and looked happily surprised when he burst out laughing.

Once again they heard his phone ring, Bryer jumped up and rushed downstairs, presumably to the office to answer it.

He was quickly back upstairs with the phone to his ear. "Sure thing and it's for Detective Inspector Withers? Yup, I can do that, I'll email you them shortly. Okay, yes. Will do. Bye."

Amy looked up at him as he ended the call and placed the phone on the wooden coffee table between them. "Sorry, work call and I have to deal with it."

"It's okay, don't worry I understand." Amy had recognised the policeman's name from her lunch at Acker's Cafe. Deep down Amy was thoroughly relieved, it seemed that everything Bryer had told her was absolutely true. "I'll see you tomorrow for the ball, what time shall I be ready for?"

"I'll pick you up at seven." He said and smiled brightly.

Amy stared at that smile, it was the type of smile women might climb over hot coals to get a closer look at, well she would anyway. Her stomach fluttered with excitement and she felt the heat of her blood in her face rise as she began to blush again, just like a hopeless teenager. Disconcerted by her body's physical reaction to this man, she grabbed her bag, and, after saying a quick 'goodbye', she headed for the stairs and home, leaving her mug sitting on the coffee table and only half drunk.

Chapter Eighteen

Saturday, 27th October, Canada.

Amy rushed inside, dropped her bags on the floor and closed the door firmly behind her. The cold had soaked through her insubstantial British jacket and made her shiver. She quickly took off her coat, scarf and shoes and with her teeth chattering from the cold, she rubbed her arms and rushed into the living room of the cottage to light a fire. Once satisfied it would burn away of its own accord, she headed to the kitchen to switch on the heating powered by the AGA.

If she had thought about it before she went out, she would have put it on and then the cottage would be warm and toasty by now. She could have kicked herself, she made a mental note to leave it on the timer setting in future, That way she could happily forget about it and the cottage would always be warm. Sighing, she switched the kettle on for a hot cup of tea to hopefully warm her through. October had suddenly turned very cold, it was still so odd to Amy that the days could be so beautiful with their clear, pale blue skies and bright sunshine, but also so bitingly cold. In England, the sky was rarely blue especially when the day was cold, in fact, it was usually cloudy and grey on such days.

"Didst thou get what thy wanted from thy merchant?" Erda said as she appeared sitting on a chair at the kitchen table.

"Yup, the lady at the fancy dress store in Glendale was lovely and very helpful indeed. She said I was lucky to find anything decent seeing as I was going in for a costume so late and on the actual day most of the Hallowe'en events were held." Amy decided against a cup of tea and made herself a hot chocolate instead and spooned the powdered chocolate into her mug. Placing the steaming and delicious smelling mug of chocolate on the table, she went back to the hallway and picked up her bags to bring them into the kitchen to empty. She first put the grocery shopping away in the fridge and on the pantry shelves and then got her costume out to show Erda. "Well, what do you think?"

"'Tis becoming, thy wilt look fine."

"Thank you, Erda. I'm really looking forward to tonight, it's been many years since I've been to a Hallowe'en party, never mind a ball."

"Perchance, I canst come with thee for I nay hath thy pleasure either." Erda looked hopeful.

"Of course! But since when do you ask me if you can be in a certain place?"

"Nay, thy mistook my words. My intent is to accompany thee as a true guest, one with a body."

"How would you do that? You won't be possessing someone will you? Because I don't like the thought of that."

"Nay, naught of such. I canst let others see me as if I am like thee."

"You mean you can appear to be real? Solid?"

"Aye, 'tis a'trick but one I canst do."

"Really? Wow, go on then, show me." Amy said.

"'Tis how I touch things." Erda said and shimmered slightly and became more distinct and more into focus, she seemed sharper around the edges somehow.

"Oh, you look...kinda different." Amy reached out her hand to touch Erda's arm and indeed she felt the cotton of her old fashioned clothing and then the rough wool of her overdress, finally she touched the flesh on Erda's arm, it was still cool but not cold. "You really do feel real, if a little cool blooded."

"I'm still Spirit a'course, but thy thinketh I pass?"

"Oh yes, I 'thinketh' you could." Amy smiled and stared at Erda amazed, "I never knew Spirits could be solid if they chose."

"Aye, but it took many a'year to be such. A'many Spirits nay canst cus they are too young and nay full of practice."

"Won't it be dangerous for you, what if you fade out or something?"

"Nay, I wilt remain as such until I decide t'otherwise. More a'portant, people see what they want to see." Erda said, looking confident.

"Well, you learn something new every day, don't you? I mean about Spirits being able to actually be temporarily corporeal, not that people can be duped, of course." Amy said as she hung her costume on the back of the kitchen door, it had a few creases on it and she hoped they would drop out before her date tonight. "What costume will you be wearing?" She said as she returned to the table.

Erda raised an eyebrow.

Amy looked at her and looked at the 17th century clothing she wore. "I see your point." She said and laughed. "Hmm...though, Bryer is coming to pick me up as his date, I'm not sure how I'll explain you to him. He's already aware that I know almost no one here."

"Nay worry thee, I shalt arrive at thy ball alone and wilt...mangle...I think thee call it."

"Mingle! That's mingle, Erda." Amy burst into laughter. "Please don't mangle the townsfolk." Amy snorted.

"Aye, mingle." Erda said unfazed.

Amy chuckled as she sat and took a careful sip of her hot drink.

"Samhain was a'ways celebrated by thy family, a veil between thy dead and livin' is weaker for a'time. 'Tis a'time to honour thy ancestors and be placing food on'table a'fore them."

"Samhain?" Amy shook her head and sipped her hot chocolate.

"Aye, 'tis the old name for All Hallow's Eve or as thou saith, Hallowe'en."

"I didn't know that, I guess there's a lot you could teach me."

"Aye, mayhaps. Pray tell, why doth people of thy time nay celebrate on thy thirty and first day of October?"

"Oh, we do, well, usually. It's just that Hallowe'en is next Wednesday and nobody wants to party on a weekday, not when they have work in the morning. So we generally move big parties to the nearest weekend."

"Thy people art odd, thou canst nay move when the veil is thinner."

"True, very true." Amy said but didn't like to tell Erda that Hallowe'en had become utterly commercialized and was now more about costumes and monsters, parties and scary food than it was about the thinning of the veil, to most people anyway. Amy hoped Erda had seen some of it before, in her four hundred years of wandering, otherwise tonight's party would be quite a shock. Hmm...maybe this wasn't such a good idea after all, she thought and was a little worried how Erda would react.

*

With the chime of the mantel clock and in the darkness of the night, there came a knock on the door.

Amy gave herself one last check in the mirror and rushed to the door. Before she opened it, she took a deep breath and steadied herself. "Not too eager, play it cool." She said to herself and then opened the door.

Bryer's hand was raised as if he was going to knock again. "Good evening." He smiled, took off his hat and bowed in a gentlemanly gesture suitable for his costume. He was dressed as a Victorian gentleman, in top hat and tails. "I remembered you said Dracula was your favourite movie and especially the Gary Oldman version of Dracula, with him being a 'sexy', I think you called it, Count in Victorian society. So I got as near as I could to that costume."

"Oh, how wonderful that you remembered. You look awesome by the way, very snazzy." She grinned, a silly happiness fluttered around inside her.

"Snazzy? Not sure what that means, you and your British words, but I'll take it." He laughed. "You, however, look incredible." He looked her up and down.

Amy stood in the doorway dressed as Morticia Addams, in a long black, low cut dress that flared at the bottom, a long black wig and pale but stunning makeup. She smiled the most alluring and evil smile she could muster.

Bryer laughed. "You are so beautiful. Pale and mysterious. Cara mia." He quoted from one of the Addams Family movies.

Delighted that he could quote it, Amy said, "Nice one, you smooth talker."

"Always." He said and winked. "Have you had any Trick or Treaters yet?"

"No, but then I am rather far out of town to be convenient."

"I've had loads tonight, I wasn't sure they were going to let me escape." He grinned.

"The whole Trick or Treat thing is done a lot less in the UK. Don't know why though, I think it's lots of fun for the kids."

"Yeah, I loved it as a child, we made some great memories, my brother and I." He said and a swift glimpse of sadness crossed his eyes but was quickly replaced by his normal mischievous sparkle. "Are you ready to go?"

"Yup." Amy threw her jacket around her shoulders, stepped through the doorway and locked the door behind her. Although rain was forecast, it hadn't started yet, thankfully, and the night sky was bright and clear, the stars glittered and the glowing full moon beamed down on them as they climbed into his truck and set off for town and the party of the season.

*

Music and laughter could be heard from the parking lot as Amy and Bryer closed the truck doors and walked across the tarmac. Many of the other costumed guests were arriving at the same time and they were all walking quickly towards the town hall, trying to get inside as soon as possible and out of the cold.

The town hall was a beautiful two story red brick building and a remnant of the colonial days. The front was symmetrical in design with four white columns reaching up to the second floor. Above the columns sat the white clock tower with the massive clock face that had been looking down on the townspeople since sometime in the 1860's. Across the four columns was a brightly coloured banner decorated with ghosts and jack-o-lanterns, with large orange letters announcing that the Pumpkin Ball was that very night.

Amy glanced up at the banner as they walked under it, and returned her eyes to the entrance and the few white steps before it. She was delighted to see the town made an effort when it came to parties.

The doorway into the town hall was filled with pumpkins of all shapes and sizes, some were carved with gruesome faces and had lanterns in them, while others sat on straw bales next to the skeletons, black cauldrons and illuminated skulls. The whole display had real, multicoloured autumn leaves spread all over it and pumpkin lantern fairy lights were covering the doorway and the side windows.

They could hear that the live band had started as they walked through the outer door and showed their tickets to the fully wrapped mummy who stood there, it said, 'Mmmmm.'' And took their tickets.

Bryer laughed and took Amy's coat from her and passed it over to Frankenstein's bride in the cloakroom, pocketing the coat ticket as he did so. Taking Amy's arm in his, he escorted her down the short but highly decorated hallway to 'The Woodland', as the blood dripping sign stated, or, as it was usually called, the ballroom.

The doors were swept open by two gorillas and Amy and Bryer entered the festooned hall. The band was playing at the far end of it and up on a stage that was decorated like a woodland but it also included a huge cauldron centre stage with dry ice bubbling out of it and a fake fire made from coloured lights underneath it. The band members were all dressed as zombies and were doing a cover of the Monster Mash at that moment.

Amy looked around her at the many different, and, in some cases amazing, costumes and they made for a strange mixture of dance partners on the dance floor, which was situated directly in front of the band. Amy noticed there was a cowboy dancing with a witch, a pirate dancing with Cleopatra and so many other unusual mixes that she smiled to herself, pleased to see that the townsfolk of Morton Creek embraced the costume party idea wholeheartedly. Around the dance floor were several tables, which had lovely flower arrangements on them and six chairs at each. All the flowers were orange in colour and even small pumpkins were included in the designs, every single one of the arrangements had cobwebs draped over them and small battery operated candles which gave each table a wonderfully spooky glow.

A huge decorated buffet lined the left hand wall of the room, where people had already started to help themselves. On the opposite side of the room was a long bar and even that had been decorated, it had subdued lighting so as to not spoil the effect of the other party lights. All the staff at the bar and those working at the buffet were dressed as devils in black clothing, with red horns and tails that glowed in the dim light. It was hard to see the ballroom's real decorations as it was thoroughly buried under the copious amounts of sheer gauze, spooky lighting, spider webs and silver painted trees that shone in the multicoloured flashing lights from the stage.

Bryer guided her to the nearest empty table and waited for her to sit, he leant forward towards her.

"What do you think? Small town, big party." He grinned.

"Wow, this is great." She said into Bryer's ear as the music was a little too loud to talk normally.

"I know, right?" He straightened up but didn't sit down. "What can I get you to drink?"

"Um...I'd love a red wine, please."

"Okay, I'll be right back."

Amy watched him head toward the bar thinking how good he looked tonight, when a cool hand brushed her shoulder. She looked up to see Erda looking down at her with a huge smile on her face.

"Greetings." Erda said.

"Hello, having fun?"

"Oh yes, thy parties art a'wonder. I see thy people nay do worship upon this night, mayhaps 'tis good, for a'right time is on thy thirty and first day of October." Erda nodded and looked around at the fun people were having. "'Tis a night of frolic nay worship."

"Yes, I wondered if that would bother you."

"Nay, I hath seen many a'party on a celebration night and nay honours tha' night. 'Tis nay different for this."

"Hello there!" A familiar voice came from behind Amy.

Amy turned to her other side and there stood Maggie from the book shop, she was dressed as a corpse bride, face all blue and dead looking while wearing a tatty brides outfit. She placed her glass, of something red with a disturbingly real looking finger floating in it, on the table.

Maggie sat down next to Amy. "How are you, Amy?" She said and looked from Amy to Erda.

"I'm very well thanks. Oh, sorry, this is Erda, apparently she is here on holiday from England, can you believe? She heard my accent and came over to introduce herself." Amy looked at Erda and hoped she got the idea and would go along with it.

"Hi, I'm Maggie, I run the local bookstore here in town. How long are you here on holiday for?"

"Nay long, I wilt return to my home upon the morrow." She said.

Amy cringed when she heard Erda's strange 17th century language. Oh God, that will definitely give the game away, she thought.

"That's just awesome, staying in character like that, good for you." Maggie laughed.

Amy breathed out a breath she hadn't realised she'd been holding.

"Well, I hope you've had fun in Canada." Maggie said.

"Aye, 'tis a loverly place, thou art lucky to live here."

"Yeah, I think so too." Maggie smiled. "Oh, look there's Annabeth, from the cafe."

Amy looked in the direction where Maggie was pointing to see Annabeth, who was dressed as an 18th century lady in a hoop skirt and a very high wig. What was it she had with big hair, Amy wondered.

"Have you met Annabeth yet?" Maggie said.

"Not this time around but I remember her from when I was here before. We never did get along, even as children."

"Yeah, she can be a bit difficult, her hair is almost as big as her ego." Maggie said and looked directly at Amy with a huge smile on her face.

Amy couldn't help but laugh, it was exactly how she felt about Annabeth too. "You are bad, you know that right?"

"Yup but always truthful." Maggie nodded happily and took a sip from her bizarre drink.

"Ladies." Bryer said from behind them.

"Bryer, well don't you look handsome tonight." Maggie said as she shamelessly eyed him up and down.

"Thanks, Mags. Looking pretty good yourself, you here with a date tonight then?"

"Yup. Talking of which, I'd better get back to him." She stood and picked up her glass. "Amy I have a spot in two weeks when we could do a signing, shall I put you in it?"

"Sure, I'd love to."

"Great, how about we have lunch tomorrow and we can hammer out the details."

"That would be great, I'll ring you in the morning."

"Okay, then. Well, you two have fun tonight." Maggie said, winking at Amy.

"You too." Amy said.

"See ya, Mags." Bryer said as he sat down next to Amy passing her a glass of red wine. "Who was the other woman that was here? I couldn't see her well enough through the crowd to recognise her."

"Thanks." She said as she took the glass. Amy hadn't realised that Erda had moved on from their table. "Oh, just someone who is on holiday in the area. We spoke briefly but that was all." She stuck as near to the truth as possible because she hated to lie, but what else could she say?

"Oh, right." He took a sip from his glass of orange juice and placed it back on the table as he looked around the room at the people and listened to the music. The band was now doing a cover of the Time Warp and it had brought many people up to the dance floor. "Look, there's Cy and Kath." Bryer nodded over to the buffet table.

Amy looked but couldn't spot them in the crowd of costumes. "Where? What are they wearing?"

"Just there, near the end on the right, the ones dressed as Bonnie and Clyde." He pointed to a couple in 1930's clothing.

"Oh yeah, how on earth did you know it was them?"

"Cy told me what their costumes were when I spoke to him yesterday."

"Oh, that's cheating. I thought you were being rather clever." She smirked at him.

"Nope, although, on second thought, perhaps I should not have told you I spoke to him and just looked smart." He grinned, rose from his chair and held out his hand. "Want to get some food?"

"Sure, will it be okay if I leave my drink here?"

"Yup, I'll leave mine too, they can claim these seats for us." Taking her hand, Bryer led the way across the room and towards the massive buffet.

Amy liked the feel of his warm hand in hers and when they got to the end of the buffet tables, where the plates and cutlery were, she was sad when he had to let go to pass her a plate and napkin. Taking them from him, she looked at all the wonderful food, there was almost every kind of buffet food she could think of and enough diversity for all dietary requirements and taste buds. The entire length of the food tables were beautifully decorated with small squashes and various skulls, fake leaves and spiders, they even had large candle sticks with artificial candles lit in them.

Amy and Bryer were only a few people behind Cy and Kath as they got their food, when they were all finished they chatted for a while and then went to their separate tables to eat. Apparently, Cy and

Kath were here with friends from their Mah-jong group and they had bought two entire tables for the night, seeing as the money from the ball tickets was going to a local charity, they were more than happy to come as a large group.

Although another couple had sat at their table, Amy and Bryer were able to enjoy an intimate date. Much to Amy's delight, there was much laughter between them and Bryer even turned out to be an excellent dancer, they were on the dance floor many times throughout the night and that included all of the long, slow, sexy ones.

The party continued until one o'clock in the morning and as Amy and Bryer were leaving, she felt so happy that she kissed him briefly on the cheek when he leant forward to wrap her coat around her. He seemed startled but very pleased, as a huge smile spread across his face. He offered to fetch his truck while she stayed dry in the warm foyer because, as predicted, it was now raining heavily.

The drive home was a comfortable and cosy one, the heater was keeping them both warm while the rain lashed viscously at the windscreen outside. Bryer was a good driver and Amy felt safe as they chatted pleasantly all the way home in the storm. By the time they pulled up outside Amy's cottage, the storm had gotten quite violent as branches flew around and the rain, coming with the wind off the lake, was almost horizontal in the truck's headlights.

Bryer parked as near as he could to Amy's path. "Give me your key and I'll open your front door, so you can make a run for it." He said as he took off his long tailed coat and placed it on the back seat with his top hat.

Amy passed him her keys and before she could say 'thank you' he leapt out of the truck and ran up the path getting utterly soaked in the process. Amy could only just make out his shape as he tried to unlock the door in the howling storm, the only light he had was from his truck lights and she noticed they kept making odd shadows on the roof of the cottage with the moving trees.

Bryer reappeared at her door with an umbrella, which he had opened and held over his head with some difficulty, he quickly opened the door. "If you cuddle up with me under this and we run, you may not get too soaked."

Amy could have fallen in love with him on the spot, she smiled at him and climbed out of the truck. Doing as he asked, she cuddled up close to him under the meagre protection of her umbrella and they ran for the door, which he had left just slightly ajar.

Gasping and laughing they tumbled into her hallway, they were only just slightly less wet than if they'd had no protection at all.

"Well, that was fun." She said. "And I don't just mean the run to the house, I had a great night tonight, thank you, Bryer."

"Yeah, so did I." He said and pushed back his dripping hair. "Perhaps we could do it again sometime, if you would like."

"I would love to, but perhaps we could do something a bit quieter next time, don't get me wrong I loved it but it would be nice to be able to talk without having to shout in your ear." She said.

"I agree. How about I cook you dinner at my place? Are you free on Monday night?"

"Yes, I am and that would be great, we could also look at the photos together too. Do you want me to bring anything?"

"Nope, just yourself." He smiled at her and took a step towards the door.

Amy followed him. "Well, thanks again." She said as a nervous, awkward feeling grew within her.

Bryer turned back and took a step closer to her. "You're welcome and thank you for agreeing to come with me." He reached his hand up and stroked her damp cheek.

Amy's heart beat faster as she felt his warm, damp touch. She was looking deep into his eyes as he leaned forward and kissed her gently on the mouth. She responded in kind as he placed one hand on the side of her neck pulling her towards him and his other hand slid around her waist and firmly held her against him. Their kiss became quite passionate and his hand moved up her back to between her shoulders as she wrapped both of her arms around his neck and her hands felt his warm back through his wet shirt. The kiss ended and they finally broke apart, both of them breathless and surprised by their instant passion, there was definitely some strong chemistry between them.

Bryer smiled that glorious smile that made Amy want to undress him on the spot. He inclined his head and kissed her again, this time it was slower and more gentle, he lingering on her lips for just a moment longer and then he stepped back, turned and, without a single word more, walked out of the door into the dark night and the raging storm.

Amy stood there in her damp costume, hair dripping down her chest but not feeling anything except her own storm raging inside her as the door closed and the date ended.

Chapter Nineteen

Amy found herself staring off into space, remembering all the fun she'd had last night at the Pumpkin Ball. It was quite a party and she'd had a wonderful time dancing the night away and especially spending the evening with Bryer as her date. A smug, happy smile spread across her face.

"I know what you are thinking about." Maggie said and she leant back in her chair while the waitress placed two bowls of steaming pumpkin soup, and a large plate of garlic bread, on the table in front of them.

"Thanks." Amy said to the waitress.

"Oh yes, indeed I do." Maggie nodded knowingly.

"Oh, and what would that be?" Amy said as she looked back towards Maggie. She was thoroughly enjoying her company and it was as if they had known each other for years not days.

"A certain tall, blue eyed, handsome photographer that you were out with last night." Maggie didn't miss a thing.

"He is rather yummy, isn't he?" Amy said.

"Not my type, but he did look great in that costume last night, I'll give him that."

"So what is your type, Miss Maggie Moon? By the way, I have to ask, is that your real name or are you undercover or perhaps in witness protection." Amy giggled.

"Oh, very funny. Nope, it's my real name. Although those other lives do sound exciting, perhaps I should try one. You writers, always coming up with the crazy stories. I think you're the crazy kids of the world." She grinned, tore off a piece of garlic bread and enthusiastically dipped it into the orange coloured soup, blew on it to cool it down and ate it. "Oh Goddess, that's really good." She said the second she tasted it.

Amy did the same with her bread, "Oh my, you're not wrong, it's bloody delicious."

"So, we're all set for your signing in two weeks, like we discussed last night. Surprisingly, after all those drinks, I did remember about it this morning and, before I came here, I went into the store and put you on the calendar before I did actually forget and I also placed an order for a few more of your books, so you'll have plenty to sign, you best-selling author you." Maggie grinned.

"That's right, you just remember who is the famous one here." Amy tried to make a stern face but burst out laughing, "Seriously, thanks for setting it up, I think it will be fun."

Maggie laughed and shook her head. "Not sure how many people you will get but I'm guessing it will be less than you're used to, this is a small town after all and not some glamorous signing in some smart place in London."

"Hush now, you're only jealous." Amy loved how they had the same sense of humour and could so easily joke with each other.

"Yup." Maggie nodded and ate her soup with a cheeky look in her eye.

"Not to worry, a change of pace will be good and I'm sure we will still have fun." Amy truly meant it.

"No doubt."

"Oh yeah, Kath said last night, that you are trying to sell your parents' cottage. How's that going?"

"Nothing yet but I'm sure someone will want it, well, the land anyway. There are some people in town who think a buyer may just want the land and they'll tear down the cottage, which I think will be such a shame, really, it's lovely, I've quite grown to like it."

"So don't let them." Maggie said between mouthfuls.

"How can I stop them if they buy it?"

"Don't sell it."

Amy's spoon stopped halfway to her mouth, "What?"

"Simple, if you want to know for sure that the cottage will still be standing when you're old and grey, do your ancestors a favour and don't sell it."

"I...well, what would I do with it then?"

"You could rent it, or perhaps keep it as a vacation home or even..." Maggie paused and put a large piece of garlic bread in her mouth and sat looking at Amy pointedly while chewing it.

"Or even what?"

Maggie wiped the garlic butter from her lips on the napkin and said, "You could live in it."

"What? Don't be daft, I live in London, my life is there." Amy's eyebrows rose to her hairline.

"So? Lives can be moved. Just a thought."

"Yeah, huh. I guess they can, but, still, everything and everyone I know is in the UK."

"Not everyone." Maggie said, smiled and pointed to herself, "We also have tall blue eyes, the handsome photographer here."

"Shut up, smart ass." Amy said and then burst into laughter.

Maggie blew her a kiss in defiance and laughed too.

The rest of lunch was filled with laughter and putting the world to rights as only good friends can.

*

Amy had decided to stop by the grocery store on the way home and spend a few minutes catching up with Aunt Kath and Uncle Cy. She was now, however, absentmindedly grabbing the grocery bags from her truck to carry into the house, when she felt that weird creepy feeling you get when you know someone is behind you. She spun round to find Erda looking at her expectantly.

"I do wish you wouldn't do that, you're gonna give me a heart attack one of these days. Anyway, where have you been? I've not seen you since the ball, I was beginning to think I'd dreamt you up."

"Around I hath been, giving thee...how does thy time say...ah, yes, 'space'." Erda said with a mischievous look in her eyes and an overly sweet smile.

Amy walked up the path with her groceries, sat them on the path and opened her front door. "Space? Really? That's the word you're going for?" She said as she picked up the bags again, walked through her open front door and couldn't help laughing at Erda's choice of words.

"Aye."

"Space for what? I've been busy going to the ball with you in tow, I might add, and now out for lunch and doing grocery shopping. What do I need space for exactly?"

"I knowest thy dost, aye. I am canny to such ways."

Amy put the bags on the kitchen counter and looked at Erda with suspicion on her face, "What?"

"Perchance thy hath a suitor." Erda smiled gently at Amy and watched her blush.

"I...erm...stop that. He's a friend." Amy stammered and turned away from Erda's eyes so she wouldn't see the hope in her own. Perhaps Erda had seen the kiss last night, after the ball, when he had dropped me back home, she thought. Amy began unpacking the groceries like nothing else mattered on the planet and busied herself by putting the shopping away, she then filled the kettle and clicked it on, all the while not looking Erda directly in the eye. Although she could feel Erda watching her as she did all these things, her eyes felt like lasers burning into the back of Amy's head. In fact, Amy was trying so hard not to think about Bryer that when the kettle boiled, she almost jumped out of her skin.

"What dost thou know about Warding?" Erda said.

Amy finally turned round and sat down at the kitchen table with her newly made mug of tea. She was more than a little pleased about the change in conversation topic, even if she didn't know what the new topic was. "Never heard of it, what is it?"

"Hallowing?"

"Nope, not a clue. What are they?" Amy put her elbows on the table, leaned forward intrigued and rested her face on her hands.

"They art a'same. 'Tis old way of protection for thy people and thy things. I want thee to Ward thy cottage."

"Why? What's wrong?" Amy looked alarmed and looked around her expecting some danger to leap out and attack at any second.

"Naught is wrong, a'sense of an evil eye is upon me."

"An evil eye?" Amy's eyebrow raised.

"Aye, a premonition, if thou wilt, of wrong doing."

"Oh." Amy wasn't quite sure what to think of that piece of information. "How do I Ward?"

"I can teach thee a'way but 'twill be less strugglesome if thee allows I to show thee." Erda said. 'Thou wilt need charcoal or something to draw with. Mayhaps a fountain pen, they art for drawing art they?"

"Well, writing actually. What are we drawing on? Kinda makes a difference to what we can use."

"Thy thoroughfares, thy doors and windows, and hearths too."

"Oh, erm...wait a minute, I think I might have something we can use." Amy rushed off to search through one of the boxes of her parents' things and was back in the kitchen in moments. "How about this?" She said holding up a bottle of clear nail varnish, "It will dry clear but your ward will still be there, kinda invisible. Will that work?"

Erda looked surprised, "A grand magic indeed." She peered at the clear liquid in the bottle. "A lit taper is also needed."

"Taper?"

"Aye, candle?"

"Ah, right hang on." Amy rummaged behind the cleaning bottles in a kitchen cupboard below the sink and came out with a fat, pink candle that had lost it's 'rose' scent during all the years it had lived in the dark cupboard. "This do?"

"Aye, be it lit and follow me."

Amy struck a match and lit the candle, she dripped some of the melted wax onto a saucer and placed the candle in the hot wax, securing it in place. "Where do we start?" She said feeling a sudden surge of excitement.

"Thy main thoroughfare is as good a'place as any." Erda walked out of the kitchen, followed by Amy, and headed down the hallway directly to the front door.

"What now?" Amy said as she felt the excitement rise to new heights in her body because she knew she was about to do something actually,

and truly, magical. Her inner child was delighted, she
had always known deep down that magic was real, it
was one of the things she loved to write about in her
children's book series.

"Hold thy pot aloft and ready, giveth me thy
hand." Erda held out her hand to Amy.

As their hands met, a strange cold tingle went
through Amy's arm, it wasn't unpleasant, ,just
surprising, but before Amy could verbalise the
feeling, Erda was guiding her hand towards the
wooden door frame and, with a flourish, she painted
something with the varnish and began to say:

"Fire I carry round thy frith-stead,
and bid men to keep thy peace.
Light I carry for enclosing,
and bid ill wights flee away.

Thunor wéoh,
Thunor wéoh,
Thunor hallow this holy stead.

Fire I carry round thy frith-stead,
and bid men to keep thy peace.
Light I carry for enclosing,
and bid outlaws flee away.

Thunor wéoh,
Thunor wéoh,
Thunor hallow this holy stead.

Thunor wéoh,
Thunor wéoh,
Thunor hallow this holy stead. I

When it was done, Amy couldn't see what was painted on the door frame as Erda had painted it too quickly, it could have been a word or a symbol but it was way too fast for Amy's eyes to follow. She peered closely at the drying nail varnish on the wooden frame and moved her head from one side to the other, trying to catch the light on it but still she couldn't quite make out what it was.

"'Tis good." Erda said.

"What did we draw?"

"'Tis a Sign of Forfend, a protection sign for thee and thine." Erda said as she moved towards the living room and its deep set window, still holding Amy's hand.

"Can you do it slower this time so I can see what you draw?"

"Aye." Erda, as good as her word, drew the symbol more slowly on the wide window ledge, in the clear nail varnish, and said the words once again.

Amy had never seen the symbol before but somehow it was familiar to her. She followed Erda around the cottage as they, hand in hand, repeated the symbol, and the words of Warding, on every entrance to her home, even the attic windows and the fireplace, all the while Erda holding her hand and drawing the symbol with it. When at last they came to the final window in the main bedroom, next to the front door, which completed their circuit, Amy asked, "May I do this one? Would it work if I do it?"

"Aye, thy hath a gift."

Amy cocked an eyebrow at that comment but decided to concentrate on the Warding, for now at least and she stored the comment away for another day.

Carefully, she drew the image which consisted of a strangely wiggly 'S' with two circles and a weird looking eye with a three pronged fork in the middle.

Once the symbol was drawn, Erda began to say the words of the Warding and paused after each line so Amy could say it, after the first verse Amy tripped up on the pronunciation.

"Thunor wéoh." Erda repeated.

"Thuno Weeahh." Amy said.

"Nay, Thoo-nor vey-oh."

"Thoo-nor vey-oh."

"Aye." Erda nodded her approval.

Amy continued with the words of the Warding and felt decidedly accomplished when she finished it, she stood back and admired it even if she didn't truly understand how it all worked.   Amy's stomach rumbled loudly and, taking it as a sign that it was time to start dinner, Amy turned and walked out of the bedroom heading back toward the kitchen.

"'Tis a fine thing done, aye." Erda said, nodded to herself and followed Amy back to the kitchen.

Amy grabbed several items out of the fridge and put them out on the counter and gathered together the various things she would need to make dinner. She put a raw chicken breast on a board and began cutting it up for the stir fry, then, on another board, she began to chop vegetables. These simple tasks gave Amy's mind a chance to think about what they had just done together. "How is it you know these things, Erda?" She turned to look at her, knife in hand. "These magical things, I mean."

"Amma taught me her Galdr's from a'time I was upon her knee, she was a Völva just as her dame was and her dame's dame was a'fore her."

"Amma? That's a name?"

"Nay, lass, ye'd call it...um...grandmother."

"Oh, right. I didn't understand the other words either, Völva was it? And Galdor?"

"Galdr and Völva, aye, Galdr's be spells and incantations, Völva be...'tis a seeress or wisewoman, of a sort. Amma's blood came from folk of the old country, thou knowest as Danes."

"Danes, as in Vikings? Cool."

"Amma taught me much of charms, herb law and magics. Perchance, I can teach thee?" Erda looked hopeful.

"Oh, yes, teach away, I'd find it all extremely interesting." She said as she stirred the chicken in the hot pan.

"'Twould be a happiness to tutor thee." Erda smiled a truly sincere and happy smile.

"Good that's settled then." Amy said as she pushed the chopped vegetables off the chopping board and into the hot pan, with the almost cooked chicken and a satisfying sizzle. "Tell me about the symbol we just used."

"'Tis a Sign of Forfend as I saith a'fore, 'tis a crosshopple of tway symbols, one of protection and t'other to stop unbound Souls a'visiting."

Amy washed her hands, dried them and grabbed a pencil and paper. She redrew the symbol they had used on it, "Which parts belong to which?"

Erda took the pen from Amy's hand and drew the two separate symbols on the paper.

Amy instantly recognised one of them. "I knew it! I have seen that symbol before but it was slightly different. Which one is that?" Amy pointed to the image with the two circles and the wiggly 'S'.

"'Tis to stop unbound Souls a'visiting." Erda looked at her, surprise written all over her face. "Take time to pause...is thee sure?"

"Yes, positive, except the one I saw had the big circle at the top, not the bottom, but yes it was definitely that symbol." Amy turned back to the cooker. "Is that important, that I saw it, I mean?" She said as she stirred the vegetables and chicken mixture.

"Prithee, where didst thou see it?" Erda came and stood next to her, placing her cool hand on Amy's arm gaining her full attention.

Amy could feel a cold area on her arm but not the actual pressure of a hand, how odd she thought and looked at Erda who seemed a little less distinct than usual. "I...well, I accidentally saw some crime photos the other day." Amy said and paused a moment trying not to see all those awful images in her mind again.

Forcing her brain to think only about the meal she was cooking, she enthusiastically added Worcestershire Sauce and a little Soy to the hot pan.

"I nay understand thy meaning." Erda said.

"Um..." Amy tried to think of a way to reword her sentence, "I saw images of murders today and that symbol was amongst them, I'm sure of it."

"Oh, spite!" Erda looked away and chewed her nails.

Amy watched her and thought it was a very odd thing for a Spirit to do. "What's wrong?"

"Perchance naught but by day's approach I shalt knowest." Erda looked thoughtful, "I must leave thee a'while." She said and vanished.

Amy shuddered, "Okay...but I'll never get used to that." She said to the empty room. At last, she spooned the cooked vegetables and chicken onto her plate and she placed her dinner, along with a bottle of wine and a glass, on a tray and walked out of the kitchen wondering where Erda had gone off to in such a rush.

Amy decided to have her dinner in the living room that night and sit by the fire to eat it. Within moments she had the fire lit, opened the bottle of wine and poured herself a glass.

She turned on the classical music station on the old radio and then, snuggling down on the sofa with a cover over her and her tray on her lap. She realised she was really beginning to enjoy the cottage and the simplicity of life here, even if the October air was beginning to turn cold.

This room needed a good room heater or something, just to take the edge off when the fire wasn't lit, she thought as she ate her dinner and enjoyed the music.

Erda had returned by the time Amy was on her second glass of wine, dinner long finished. She gradually began to emerge in the chair next to the fire, slowly and surely she became more visible until she seemed solid again.

Watching this happen, Amy decided she much preferred this way of appearing, instead of the instant appearance next to her, which always made her jump and she was beginning to get twitchy because of it. "That's much better, when you appear like that, it doesn't scare the crap out of me like the other way."

"Aye." Erda said as she stared into the flames of the fire.

"Everything alright?"

"Mayhaps."

"Want to talk about it?"

"Nay, nay 'till I am certes."

"Okay." Amy took 'certes' to mean certain and she felt instinctively that something was very wrong but she didn't know how she knew such a thing. She felt the need to talk, talk about anything just to feel safe. "What's it like?"

Erda looked at Amy.

"I mean, what's it like being a Spirit? What does it feel like?" Amy said as she snuggled further into the blanket and the sofa.

"'Tis naught as living, but naught as I thought a'fore. 'Tis a'lonely and too, too cold as a winter's brook."

Amy watched Erda as she continued to watch the fire.

"'Tis my lot so I endure. Giveth devil his due, John's destruction of my body...he a'freed my Soul and alloweth me to a'wander time and places unknown to me a'fore."

"You must have seen some wonderful things."

"Wondrous and foul, I conceived 'twould be other than 'tis. I hoped for a world of carefree ease and strange enticements but I find nary a thing but conflict and war, greed and plague."

"But you said wondrous too."

"Aye, some. Forgive my rambling, 'tis a dark mood upon me this night."

Amy felt she could offer no consoling words without truly knowing what was going on. "I'm sure you will feel better tomorrow." She said hopefully and rather uselessly.

Erda straightened her skirts absentmindedly and said, "Dost thou knowest where I might attain a horse head hereabouts?"

Amy was about to take a sip of her wine and stopped. "A what?"

"Horse head...a head of horse."

"What the hell do you want that for?" Amy sat up more on the sofa and frowned at her.

"Needs must I make more of thy protection."

"What has that got to do with the head of a horse?"

"'Tis an old charm Amma showed me, I ken it's making but hath nary done it a'fore."

"I don't think you can get horse's heads around here so we had better make do without one."

Amy couldn't believe the conversation she was having. She was talking about horse heads for protection with a 17th century Spirit in her living room. Life was more than a little strange at times, she thought to herself.

"Aye, shame. Certes 'twould helped."

"What's going on, Erda? You are starting to scare me."

"On a'morrow, after ye rest and ye hath broken thy fast, we wilt need to a'wander in past as Spirits again." Erda said matter-of-factly.

A cold shiver slid its way down Amy's spine unbidden, she did not like the sound of that.

Chapter Twenty

The Voice stared out of the Host's eyes and, through the misted up car window, out into the pouring rain and at the yellow house. It was a nice ordinary house, in the middle of suburban America, in the small town of Evans Mills, NY. The street was lined with trees showing off their beautiful autumn colours despite the rain and all the other houses in the street were also painted cheerful colours, they all had neat front gardens with perfectly cut grass and lovingly tended bushes and flower beds. It was the sort of street where children could happily play outside together in safety, where neighbours watched over each other's properties and were friendly and invited each other over for barbecues and parties.

"We hath travelled far and at great speed, thou art sure of thy location?" The Voice said in the Host's head.

"Absolutely, I have not let you down yet, have I?" The Host said, smug in the knowledge that they were right.

"How is it thy Sigil doth nay work here? Wherefore canst we nay translocation ourselves within as a'fore?"

"I'm not sure, unless the Sigil did not reach the hands of someone within. Unfortunately, I think we are going to have to do this one the old fashioned way or maybe I should say new fashioned way." The Host laughed at their own cleverness.

"I nay understand what thy means."

"Just trust me and go with whatever I do." The Host climbed out of the vehicle, stretched from the long journey and crossed the road, heading towards the yellow house through the cold rain. Once at the black painted door, the Host knocked loudly and listened. A television could be heard from inside the house and it sounded like it was playing a children's programme. The Host heard footsteps coming toward the door.

The door opened and a red-haired woman cautiously smiled and said "Hello?"

"Gina Cartwright?" The Host said and smiled their most innocent and helpful smile.

"Yes, can I help you?" The woman looked at the visitor and wondered what they wanted, especially as they held a small cooler in one hand. She frowned defensively at the Host, almost as if her instinct were screaming at her to shut and bolt the door that very second.

"I'm here about..." The Host began.

Gina began to listen to her instincts, and before the Host could finish their sentence, Gina was pushing the door closed. "No, thanks." She said to the stranger.

With one great shove the Host forced the door open and managed to make Gina stagger backwards, the Host quickly walked into the house and locked the door securely behind them.

Surprised by the intruder's strength, Gina took a moment to gather her wits but once she did she cried out for help and stepped backwards and away from the intruder. She remembered the safety of her child and ran for the living room where her son was watching the TV, but she was not quick enough. The intruder was already in the room, kneeling down and talking calmly to the child.

The intruder seemed to have unnatural strength and speed that Gina couldn't account for.

She stopped in her tracks and watched wide-eyed as the intruder tried to persuade the small boy to go upstairs to his room and wait there until Mommy came to get him. Her heart beat insanely in her chest and the only words that went through her mind were, don't hurt him, please don't hurt him.

"You can do that for Mommy, can't you, little one? You can go to your room all by yourself, can't you?"

The boy looked at his Mommy for confirmation, she nodded vigorously and then he grabbed a stuffed dinosaur and ran up the stairs.

"What the hel…" Gina began.

The Host held up their index finger and waited until they heard the boy's bedroom door click shut, the Host then turned towards Gina.

"What the hell is going on? Who are you? What do you want?" Gina's voice came out slightly higher than normal because of the deep, cold fear she could feel lurking in the pit of her stomach. "Answer me right now, or I'm calling the Police."

"You are Gina Cartwright, grandchild of Arthur and Amelia Cartwright lastly of St. Ives in Cornwall, England?"

"Yes, but I don't see what that has to do with anything. Are you one of those Mormons who get all excited about family trees? Whatever you want, it doesn't excuse you from forcing your way into my home like this." Gina said, putting her hands on her hips, feeling a little more secure and in charge.

Before Gina could utter another word about the matter, the Host flew across the room, faster than the eye could follow, and deeply plunged a knife several times into Gina's neck. Then, as the Host wrenched the knife out, a great arterial spray hosed the sofa and the curtains behind. Gina gurgled and squeaked as she tried to use her ravaged throat but to no avail. She quickly dropped to the floor with a sickening crack, as her head hit the once immaculate hardwood floor. The blood, and her life, steadily pumped out of her throat making a darker puddle on the already dark flooring.

"Thy must hurry, her life force is leaving her." The Voice said.

"I know, I know." The Host put on a protective coverall, surgical gloves and quickly got to their knees next to Gina and began using the knife to pry out the eyes of the woman. One by one they popped out and the Host immediately severed the connecting tissue, placing the still warm eyes inside the waiting Ziploc bag full of ice. This time, instead of taking just one part from the body, the Host turned back towards Gina, opened the mouth wide and cut away inside it and through the hole in her throat, to remove the tongue. Bagging the limp, but still warm and wet, tongue in another large Ziploc bag, again full of ice. The Host then pulled off the protective wear and sealed it all into an even larger plastic bag. The Host carefully packed everything back in the cooler, which they had brought with them just for this moment.

"There, we now have everything we need." The Host said triumphantly, stood up straight and picked up the cooler.

"Nay all, there be but one last component." The Voice said.

"I know but that's different, I meant, it is the last of these types of things that we needed to do."

"Verily thou speaketh truth." The Voice said with a hint of crazy joy to its voice. "What of the child? He hath seen thy face."

"He is too young to remember me clearly."

"Mayhaps, though a witness to thy deed he still is."

"I will not hurt an innocent child that was not part of our deal." The Host said and walked away from the desecrated body.

"'Twill be nay fault of mine if thy art caught for thy deeds out of fear of killing a mere babe."

"Enough, I will not talk about this any longer." The Host said and began checking the room for self-incriminating evidence and started wiping fingerprints from anything they had touched. They left the house closing the big black door behind them and sauntered along the path towards the road as if nothing had happened except a nice visit. The Host quickened their step as lightning flashed and thunder roared making it obvious that the storm was settling in for a spell.

After they had put the organ filled cooler in the trunk, the Host sat back in the car and felt the need for a towel and a warm shower due to the rain having soaked through their jacket and the water dripping off their hair. The Host grabbed the travel mug that sat in a cup holder on the vehicle's central column, and drank the remains of the somewhat cooled coffee, they turned the key to start the car and pulled away from the curb.

The Host had decided to only drive part of the way home, as it was some distance and the rainstorm was worsening. They decided to spend the rest of the night in a local motel, the organs would be safe in the cool box until tomorrow as long as the ice was replaced.

*

The motel was drab and dreary but you truly get what you pay for these days and, as this place was a cash only motel, it was exactly what the Host wanted and perfect for not being traced by the authorities or anybody else for that matter.

When the Host climbed into the motel room's lumpy bed, after they'd eaten a pizza delivery and had a very hot shower, an ecstatic smile spread across their face, the dark deeds of the last few years were finally over and their purpose was almost complete, soon they would have everything they desired. They were so close to their goal, so close that they could almost taste it.

The Voice within laughed with joy too, it almost had what it wanted as well and it had waited a very long time indeed.

The Host sighed contentedly and fell into a deep, peaceful sleep knowing the deal they'd made with the Voice was nearly at its fruition and nothing would ever be the same again.

A promise is a promise, after all.

Chapter Twenty One

July, 1628, London, England.

Amy could see light through her eyes, it made them a bright red colour. She opened her eyes and once again felt the strange disorientation and slight dizziness that came with Spirit travel. Although, she was pleased to find that this disconcerting feeling was substantially less each time she travelled in Spirit form. She blinked, adjusted her eyes to the dim light and looked around her. She found herself laying on a rough, wooden bench near the wooden panelled outside wall of a building and it sounded like there was a party going on inside.

Erda stood over her looking concerned. "Dost thee fare well?"

"Yeah, where are we? And when?" Amy sat up, her head throbbed a little but she was none the worse for the travelling, she was definitely getting used to it. Just a few more trips and it probably won't bother me at all, she thought.

"'Tis London, in the Year of Our Lord 1628."

Amy looked around her, the bench was at the entrance of a dark, dirty alley and a dim light shone on her from the oil lamp above her head. It seemed that the old lamp was apparently attached to the wall of a very rowdy public house. Across the dirty street was a wooden side of a building. "How can you tell? And how can you go anywhere, in any time?"

"Tis as I saith a'fore, I think of a'place, a'time and arrive, 'tis how it works. Now come, we must nay tarry." Erda grabbed Amy's hand, hauled her off the bench and rushed down the road past the pub, past the pasty shops and tailors that were closed for the day, past people who had spilt out of the bars and were standing in the streets talking and past a huge round building.

"Wait...oh my God!" Amy skidded to a halt and freed herself from Erda's grasp, she stood staring up at the majestic building in front of her. Her mouth hung open in surprise. "Holy crap!" She said as her eyes roved hungrily over the impressive structure.

"What ails thee?" Erda said.

She rushed back to Amy's side and stared in the same direction uncomprehendingly.

"That...that is The Globe Theatre, I mean the original one, where Shakespeare's plays were actually performed, amongst others. Wow."

"'Tis not the original, 'twas burnt down over there." Erda pointed to the other side of the Thames, "It be rebuilt hereabouts after a fire."

"Oh, I didn't know that. But, still, it's not the one now in London. What an honour it is to see it." Amy stared at the round building. It was three stories high and had a small tiled roof that only partially covered the structure, very much like a modern day football stadium.

"Come, we must nay tarry."

"Okay, okay." Amy forced her eyes to stop looking at such a historical site and she regrettably turned away.

Erda grabbed Amy's hand again and they rushed through the dirty, foul smelling streets. They were careful to side step the horse manure and the open drain that ran down the middle of the dark streets, as it was full of human waste and rats scuttling around it. In the distance, they could hear shouting and as they drew closer they saw a large group of people begin to dissipate. The mood of the crowd seemed to have changed abruptly, a strange silence came over them. Amy could hear an occasional outburst of nervous laughter followed by shushing noises and murmurs.

"What's happening?" Amy whispered to Erda, forgetting that no one could see or hear them.

A horrible stench of voided bowels assaulted Amy's nostrils as they got nearer to the few remaining people. Amy's mind faltered at the intense smell and she instinctively put a hand over her nose, but Erda seemed not to notice.

Where the large crowd had once stood, there were now only two grey-haired women, who stood clutching each other and facing a stone wall. Amy noticed from a distance that they were both dressed like Erda, but she couldn't see past their long skirts to get a glimpse of what they were looking at.

Amy and Erda arrived at their side in moments, just as one of the women spoke.

"'Tis good a'devil hath gone but nay one deserve to rot in a'gutter." One said to the other.

"Aye. Come away, Mildred. We'll fetch a boy to his house to come collect his remains." Said the other woman.

"Aye, Cissy." Mildred nodded in agreement.

Amy watched the two women walk away arm in arm and turned back to look at the crumpled confused heap on the floor. It took a moment for Amy's brain to make sense of it and for her to realise what she was looking at.

It was a body.

A dead and extremely crushed body laying in a heap of gore, clothing and rocks.

It was a body that was barely recognisable as a man.

"Oh dear God!" Amy said, shuddered and quickly looked away with revulsion.

"A'moment he hath died my Soul become free upon this world in Spirit." Erda said dispassionately.

"You mean that..." Amy pointed at the oozing, stinking corpse at their feet, "that is...John?"

"Aye." Erda said with no emotion on her face.

Amy studied Erda's face and body language and guessed that, after knowing this had happened for more than four hundred years, it really didn't cause an emotional reaction in her any longer.

"Now we wait." Erda said.

"Wait for what, I'd say we missed the show." A nervous laugh erupted from Amy's lips and she quickly cleared her throat, "Why in God's name are we here? Looking at..."

"We a'wait to knowest for certes where his body went."

"Why?"

"If 'twas destroyed with fire then I am wronged on 't'other matter, but if naught 'tis burned and 'tis buried in a tomb..."

"Yes?"

Erda didn't answer, in fact she spoke very little as they waited and waited. Eventually, they saw a light swaying in the distance. As it came closer they saw it was a horse and cart, it pulled up next to the body and a large man climbed down, walked to the back of the cart and hefted down a large trunk.

"Baldwin." Erda said and looked at him with immense distaste.

"I recognise him from your...from when we were here before." Amy said carefully.

"Aye, Baldwin's John's man servant, he be a'one who beat me whence John tired of it and bound me." Erda looked directly at him. "Thou art a burly-boned doghearted lout."

Amy couldn't help but grin to herself, she had to admit she liked the way Erda insulted him.

They stood watching as Baldwin put the trunk on the ground, opened it and went back to the cart. This time he came back with an oddly shaped shovel and began the unpleasant job of trying to pick up his former master from the dirty street. It was a messy process, whenever he lifted a solid piece of the corpse another less solid and slippery piece would squeeze out and slip to the ground making a horrid 'plop' sound, it sounded like a dead fish falling on to a wet stone. Eventually, he got all the large pieces in the trunk and proceeded to scoop up the wibbly, juicy bits from the ground with the spade and slop them into the trunk very unceremoniously.

Erda grabbed Amy's arm and pulled her towards the cart.

"Where are we going now?"

"Needs must we knowest where he lay." Erda said as she picked up her skirts and climbed into the back of the cart.

Amy followed behind and quickly scrambled up into the cart and sat down on its roughly hewn boards.

Baldwin hefted, with some difficulty, the even heavier trunk back on to the cart, which made the cart rock perilously. He then threw the sticky, wet spade in after it. Amy couldn't help but flinch from the spade even though she knew, deep down, she could not get any of the stinking mess actually on her. Baldwin climbed aboard at the front and snapped the reins against the horse's back, with a jerk the cart rumbled forward. The lamp swayed dramatically casting a strange moving light onto the cobbled, dirty streets and their odd assortment of houses that stood cheek by jowl along the road.

Amy watched as the world of 1628 London passed steadily by. It was surreal, almost like she was in a moving exhibition at a London museum or something. The ride, however, was far bumpier and more uncomfortable than if it were an attraction and the stench wafting off the River Thames with the light breeze was entirely too realistic and made her hold her hand over her nose. They jostled their way through the seedier parts of London where she saw many a pub or tavern, as they were known then, and past the whores with their breasts out showing their rouged nipples while they cat-called for customers. At last, they were out into open fields and the fresh air. Amy tried to work out where they were but what landmarks there were, were difficult to make out in the dim light and everything had changed so much over the next four hundred years.

Eventually, after what seemed like hours by today's travel, but probably wasn't, they drew up in front of a large house set back from the road and, although she had only seen it from the back previously, she knew this was where Dr John Lambe had lived. The house was reasonably large and made mostly from timber except for some layers of small bricks, this was all Amy could see of the structure and its grounds as they bumped their way down the drive, past the front of the house and round towards the back. Very little could be seen of the surrounding land and buildings as the night had now fully closed in on them and their sight was restricted to within the little circle of pale yellow light from the cart's lamp. The cart came to a jerky stop near the ornate wooden door at the rear of the house, where a woman and an old man appeared. The woman had obviously been crying and was presently mopping her face with a cloth. The old man, Amy recognised from her last visit here, when he had come out to talk to John while Erda was tied to the pyre and waiting to die.

"Dost ye 'ave 'im?" The woman said, anxiously twisting the cloth in her hands.

"Aye, Mistress." Baldwin said.

"Henceforth to kitchen with 'im, thy Master left instructions." She said

Baldwin nodded and climbed down from the cart to retrieve the trunk full of his Master. With the help of the other man, Baldwin struggled to get the trunk indoors as the woman led the way with a candle. Amy and Erda followed the trunk until it came to rest upon the stone floor of the large kitchen.

The woman stood at a long oak table, she had already set out all sorts of ingredients upon it and was consulting a book and holding a letter. "Put 'is bits in't two boilers." The woman pointed to two large iron cauldrons sitting on the floor next to the huge fireplace, which contained a massive roaring fire.

With a nod and a grunt, the men transposed parts of John's body as directed, trying, and failing, to contain all of John's viscera without spilling it on the flagstone floor.

"Careful, thou dumb-witted clots!" The woman shouted, her face turning red with anger.

"Apologises, Mistress." Baldwin said as he cowered before her.

"Who is she?" Amy asked as she watched the drama unfold like some kind of demonic comedy show.

"It be Agnes Langley, she be John's huswife and she be his magical student too."

"What's she doing with...well, him?"

"Looks as she be making to preserve his bones and boiling off flesh." Erda said as she moved around Agnes to take a look at the book and the letter that now rested on the table. "Aye, 'tis as I thought. 'Tis a charm for preservation of bones so thy Soul can take them up again when called."

"Oh, God, he's coming back?" Amy stared at Erda in horror.

"Mayhap, if he comes back as Spirit he wilt be harder than a'devil to kill."

"You think?!"

"Aye."

"Can we stop it?"

"Nary know how, anon mayhaps." Erda looked worried, very worried indeed.

A short, stout woman appeared at the doorway of the kitchen and stopped in her tracks. "What be a'foot hither, prithee?" She said with a light Scottish accent.

"Nary thy concern, Molly. Thou be minding thy charge." Agnes said.

"'Tis why I come, Abigail hath a'nother nightmare, I come to thee for a wee potion for the lassie."

Agnes grabbed a few dried leaves from a bottle on a shelf and stuffed them hurriedly in Molly's hand, "Make thy charge sup a draught with this." Agnes immediately turned her back on Molly dismissing her and continued preparing the mixture of herbs, carefully checking each of the instructions in the book and every now and then checking the letter as she measured out her ingredients.

"Abigail? Is that your daughter? I thought she was safely away from here."

"Aye, I believed 'twas such. I a'visited with her later in her life and she was safe. I nay knowest she hath been hereabouts."

"Is it possible we have changed things?"

"Nay, nary a chance, I've tried many a'time. Nay, we art but shadows watching."

"Good to know."

"Aye, in some cases, aye."

"If we are just shadows as you say, how come you can touch and move things then?"

"Whence first I become Spirit I canst, but over a' time and with much forbearance, I am able."

"So I can't?"

"Nay, thy needs practice, remember thee how many years I hath been Spirit."

"But if you move things, aren't you changing things?"

"Aye, but naught that matters, we canst nay change a'portant things."

"Hmm..." Amy wasn't convinced.

Amy and Erda continued to watch as Agnes ordered the men to put the two large cauldrons on the metal hooks over the blazing fire, while she added the herbal liquid and muttered a chant, which Amy could barely hear over the sound of the crackling fire.

"Toil she art upon wilt take much a'time, come." Erda held out her hand to Amy.

"Where are we going?"

"Foreward a'time."

As Amy clasped her hand in Erda's, the room faded a little and she watched as Agnes scurried around the kitchen topping up the liquid in the boiling cauldrons periodically. She also prepared and ate a small, cold meal with the two men at the big oak table while waiting for her boiling concoction to finish cooking. It was like watching a TV program on fast forward, Amy thought as she watched utterly amazed. Erda released Amy's hand and the fast movement ceased immediately.

"Whoa." Amy felt a little dizzy, she blinked and stared at Erda, "Well, that was different."

"'Tis as I saith, I think of a'place, a'time and arrive."

"Yeah, I see that now. It's kinda cool though."

"Thou hast nay body, how canst thou be cold?"

"That's not what I meant. Oh, never mind." Amy knew Erda would never understand that particular expression.

Agnes now ordered the men to remove the cauldrons from the fire and put them on the stone hearth. With a large bowl under her arm, Agnes ladled out large globs of cooked flesh, which looked remarkably like boiled pork. Setting the flesh aside in the bowl, she took tongs and plucked the bones out one by one from the human based stock. She carefully and reverently placed each of the bones on a white sheet, which she had already spread out on the table. It took some time to collect all the bones, but she was determined and very careful. Once all the bones lay in a pile on the cloth, she placed a small bronze amulet with them and wrapped them together in the sheet creating a human bone parcel.

"Now we shalt see." Erda said with a tinge of excitement in her voice.

Amy was feeling somewhat pale and nauseous and she had decided she would never, ever, be able to eat pork again and probably never be able to even look at cooked pork ever again.

"Baldwin? BALDWIN!" Agnes shouted.

The large man appeared quickly in the kitchen doorway. "Aye, Mistress?"

"Tis time. Get thy cart. Hast thou done all I saith?"

"Aye, Mistress."

Amy and Erda followed Agnes, who lit the way out to the yard with a lamp, while Baldwin carried the wrapped bundle of bones. Placing the human parcel reverently upon the ground, he hurried around the corner of the building and soon returned with the horse and cart, both he and Agnes climbed up and sat at the front with their precious cargo between them. Again, Amy and Erda quickly climbed in the back of the cart just as they set off into the dark landscape surrounding the house.

Within a few minutes they had stopped near the woods at the edge of the property, Agnes climbed down, unhooked the lamp and began to walk into the dark woods.

Baldwin followed behind carrying his Master.

Amy and Erda followed behind him.

The bizarre group stopped at a small outcrop of rocks, which had some kind of opening. Everyone followed Agnes, who had already made her way inside the cave's entrance, the path was narrow and only just big enough for Baldwin to enter. By the time they had all gotten inside, Agnes had lit two other lamps from hers and set hers on the ground. They all found themselves in a small, damp cave and at its centre was a low, flat top rock with a metal chest on it and next to the chest was a large glass, wide mouthed bottle. To the left was a cauldron of something boiling violently, which was hanging over a small fire. The cave was filled with sweet yet somewhat acrid smoke.

Amy and Erda wrinkled their noses at the smell, neither of them recognised it and were instantly curious of the cauldron's contents.

"Thou hast done well, Baldwin. Thy Master is pleased with thee." Agnes said.

Amy didn't like that Agnes used the present tense when talking about her dead Master. She involuntarily shuddered and felt decidedly creeped out by the whole thing. Amy watched as Agnes carefully placed the glass bottle within the metal box. "I bet that was expensive to buy during this time." She said, referring to the large glass bottle.

"Aye, I hath nary seen such a'wonder." Erda said as she looked more closely at the bottle that fitted perfectly into the metal box.

"Place 'im within, Baldwin." Agnes said.

Baldwin did as he was bid, this time he handled his master's bones with a lot more reverence than he had shown before. He unwrapped the bones and placed each and every one of them in the glass bottle, they only just fit in it. He then placed the amulet, which had been wrapped with the bones, into the metal box between it and the bottle. As he did all this he kept glancing at the bones, he seemed afraid of them and looked relieved when the job was done.

Perhaps, he didn't like the way Agnes talked about their Master as if he was still alive either, Amy thought.

"Now pour thy liquid upon 'im." Agnes said as she began to chant under her breath.

Again, Baldwin did as he was bid.

Agnes continued to chant, her voice was so low that Amy didn't recognise the words, it could have been in another language as far as she could tell.

Finally, Agnes had finished her chant.

Baldwin poured water upon the small fire extinguishing the flame and creating a lot of steam.

"Good." Agnes said and placed a huge stopper in the bottle. She melted some wax in the flame of a lamp and began to spread it around the bottle to seal it shut. When the deed was done, she picked up her lamp from the ground, blew out the two cave lamps and made her way out of the cave into the fresh night air.

Baldwin, Amy and Erda followed Agnes outside, leaving Dr. John Lambe, hopefully forever, in his silent grave.

Amy was pleased to be out of the cramped cave and happy to breathe the clean air again, even when she knew she wasn't actually breathing it.

"Seal it closed with thy stone." Agnes said.

Baldwin placed many heavy boulders over the entranceway, while Agnes and the two Spirits stood and watched.

Agnes said yet another chant, but a shorter one this time and, with a vial of what looked like blood, she painted, using her fingers, a protection symbol on the largest rock, sealing the doorway closed.

Amy recognised the symbol, it was exactly the same symbol Amy and Erda had used on the cottage, the Sign of Forfend.

"Enough I hath seen." Erda said and before Amy could agree she was waking up in her bedroom at the cottage and back in her own time.

Amy shuddered.

Although she wasn't actually cold, the shiver that went down her spine had come from the dark deeds she had witnessed that night in London, in 1628.

Chapter Twenty Two

October, present day, Canada

Detective Inspector Andy stared at the white board and he couldn't believe his eyes.

He had scoured every case similar to his recent murder cases from the rest of Canada, the US and the UK. His colleagues had sent him their files and he had put the details up on the huge white board. There were crime scene photos, names, arrows and comments written in his own hand. He had finally finished getting it all up and was now just standing back looking at it, coffee in hand.

"Fuck." He said as the he realised he was right, they were all linked. All the murders had been done by the same person or persons over the last seventeen years. He had a major serial killer or killers on his hands. The clinching piece of evidence had come from his 'techno whiz kid' partner and now three things had become abundantly clear: all the victims had body parts missing. There was absolutely no trace evidence at each crime scene, which could not be explained. And, probably the most important thing of all...all the victims were related to each other, yes, every single one of the fourteen victims were members of the same family. Some were more closely related than the others but still, related they were.

"Fuck." Andy said again just as Mitch walked into Andy's office.

"What you found, boss?" Mitch said and leant against the desk looking at the white board too.

Andy relayed what he had found to his partner.

"Shit." Mitch said.

"Exactly."

"How are we going to catch him with no evidence and no leads?"

"No idea." Andy took a sip of his coffee, deeply wishing it was a shot of good, expensive scotch. "How's your research going?" Andy noticed a file in Mitch's hand for the first time.

"I have something which may help, if we're lucky." He said with a satisfied smile on his face.

Amy glanced at the clock on the kitchen wall from her seat at the table. If she didn't hurry, she was going to be late for dinner with Bryer. It was already six thirty-five and she was supposed to be there by seven o'clock. Although her body had laid dormant most of the day while she travelled with Erda to the past, she felt tired and sluggish. She had hoped a long bubble bath would have helped but it hadn't, hence why she was now running late. She just couldn't find the energy to rush about while getting ready. She had, however, made an effort with her appearance, she had put on a deep blue coloured top and light grey cotton trousers, she had teamed them with a nice pair of heels and done her hair and makeup carefully. She was amazed to feel butterflies in her stomach, she was really rather excited by the thought of this evening. She finished applying her lipstick, put in her favourite earrings and took a deep calming breath. Yes, this was a date but it was their third, so why did she feel so nervous? She began to pack away her cosmetics into their little bag and placed it to one side of the kitchen table.

"Dost thou hath to thy hand thy invisible paint?" Erda said from the sink where she was leaning and watching Amy's preparations.

"The clear nail varnish you mean?" Amy looked into her makeup bag. "Yeah, I knew I'd put it somewhere useful. Here you go." She said as she passed it over and forgot Erda could touch things and quite expected it to fall to the floor just after she released it, but Erda took it in one smooth movement as if she were still alive. "You must teach me how to do that when I'm in Spirit form."

"Aye." Erda smiled. "Canst I taketh thy pendant?"

"Sure." Amy said, took it off and held it out to her, wondering what Erda wanted it for.

"Lay it on thy table."

Erda moved forward and drew the protection symbol on the back of the necklace with the clear nail varnish.

"It's not a special necklace you know. It's just a pretty stone that caught my eye at a gem store a couple of years ago. It's not so important to me that you have to protect it."

"'Tis naught the pendant I protect, 'tis thy wearer."

"Oh, right. I see." Amy was a little surprised that she needed personal protection. "Thanks." Amy blew on the symbol to dry the varnish more quickly. "I really must be going." She stood up, grabbed her truck keys and her bag.

"Ensure thy wears it 'til thee comes home."

"I will, once it's dried, I promise." Amy said as she reached the front door and then turned back, "One thing..."

"Aye."

"Why did you do it, the necklace I mean. Surely I could have painted it on?"

"Aye, 'tis calming to me to knowest thou wilt be protected by my hand."

"Oh, um...right." Amy blinked, smiled then waved goodbye as she rushed out of the cottage and headed for her truck. She climbed in, started the engine and turned on the heat. True to her word, Amy put the necklace on and sent a quick text to Bryer to say she was running a little late and would be there as soon as possible. As she drove towards town, she couldn't help but feel amazed at how quickly she had gotten used to having Erda around, even if she did talk strangely and was a Spirit, at least she no longer scared her. She felt an odd connection to her, almost as if she were a sister, which was a lovely feeling considering she had never had one.

As she pulled up to the curb, outside Bryer's photography store, her lights shone on a small figure waving at her from across the road. "Hello, how are you, Ms Carpenter?" Amy said as she climbed out of the truck.

"Very well, thank you Miss Grey. I was just closing up, when I saw your vehicle and wanted to catch you." She called as she crossed the road to meet her.

"Oh? Something you need?" Amy locked her truck.

"Two things actually, I was going to telephone you in the morning but I might as well tell you now. I have had an offer on your property." She smiled triumphantly.

"Already? That was fast."

"Yes, well, I did say the land was somewhat sought after. Anyway, the gentleman wants a surveyor to look at the property to see if it's worth saving or if he will need to demolish it and build anew."

"Oh, I see." Amy's heart sank at the thought of the lovely cottage being destroyed.

"It just so happens that Mr. Owens, my surveyor, is in town tomorrow doing another property. Would it be convenient for him to call on you?"

"Of course, morning or afternoon?"

"Well, let me see now." Ms Carpenter opened her handbag and withdrew her diary. She opened it to tomorrow's date and said, "He is with the Millers at eleven o'clock, so first thing after lunch, would one o'clock be alright with you?"

"Yes, that's fine."

"Good." She said as she snapped the diary closed and placed it back in her bag. "If you could pop into the office sometime after he has left, I would be grateful as there are a couple of forms you need to sign and then we can get the ball rolling, as it were." Ms Carpenter smiled sweetly.

"Yes, I can do that. I'm sorry, I'm afraid I have to go, I'm running a bit late. I'll see you tomorrow then?"

"Marvellous, thank you, Miss Grey." Ms Carpenter raised her hand as a goodbye gesture and began walking back across the road and towards her car, which was parked directly outside her office.

"Funny, I never noticed her office was open so late before." Amy said to herself as she turned. She paused to add the two appointments into her phone's calendar and then walked towards Bryer's building. She knocked on the store's front door and tried the door handle, pleased to find it was open, as he said it would be, she let herself in.

"Hello? Bryer?"

"Up here." Came the faint voice from the back of the store.

Amy, closing the door behind her, made her way to the corridor at the back of the store and up the stairs to Bryer's apartment. It looked quite different at night with no light streaming in from the huge windows which now had the drapes drawn, but there were soft lights lit around the apartment making the place seem really rather cosy and warm. He even had a real fire roaring in the fireplace, which Amy had previously thought was only for decoration.

"I do love your apartment." She said as she took a couple of steps into the room.

"You said that before and I'm happy you do. Come in and relax. Dinner is almost ready." He said as he held out a glass of white wine for her.

"Thanks." Amy said as she took a glass from him and watched him return to his kitchen, seemingly very comfortable cooking unlike some men. "Do you like cooking?"

"Yes, love it. It's my way of relaxing. I hope you like fish?"

"I love fish."

"Good, I thought you had mentioned you did and I know you'll enjoy dinner tonight then." He said and smiled at her.

Amy could feel her heart race as she looked at that wonderful smile, she looked away quickly, so she wouldn't be caught staring, only to find her eyes looking down at his chest and the green cotton shirt he was wearing, she had to admit his chest looked muscular and shapely. Shocked that she was indeed staring, she tried to tear her eyes away but they had a life of their own and they looked directly at his crotch. Blushing and horrified at her body's betrayal of all things decent, and hoping he hadn't noticed, she forced herself to turn away from him and walk around the apartment admiring the photos on the walls. She sipped her wine and tried really hard not to think of him naked. She failed, utterly.

After a stern talk with her libido and when she felt she could trust herself again, she turned back to watch him putting plates and cutlery on the table. He had really made a big effort. There were lit candles on the table and place mats with material napkins set out for them both. "Is there anything I can do?"

"No, just relax. Dinner will be ready any minute." He grinned at her and turned back to the kitchen counter.

"What are we having, exactly? It smells great." She was dying to know and felt even more intrigued by this man who seemed so comfortable in a kitchen cooking away.

Bryer took something out of the oven and placed the steaming dish on the mat at the centre of the table. "Please, sit down." He walked around the table and pulled out a chair for her to sit down. He poured more wine into both of their glasses and sat down on the opposite side of the table.

"Thank you." She said, thinking how much she liked a man to be a gentleman and peered at the dish of steaming food.

Bryer smiled proudly at her, "We'll start with mushroom caps stuffed with crab meat, that's followed by garlic butter poached haddock with brown rice and asparagus. Then for dessert there's a wild berry cobbler with a crispy oatmeal topping. I hope you are hungry tonight."

"Wow, that sounds lovely. And, yes, I'm very hungry." Amy said, utterly impressed.

"I'm glad you approve." He passed her the plate of large, stuffed mushrooms.

Helping herself she said, "Where did you learn to cook?"

"My grandmother taught me, she was one of those ladies who loved to cook anything and everything from scratch. I remember, when I was growing up she always had something that smelt delicious in her kitchen. Also, my ex-wife hated cooking so I had to do it all. Grandma's lessons served me well then and have done to this day."

"I didn't realise you were married before." She said taking a bite of the mushroom, "Oh God, this is wonderful."

"Thanks, I'm happy you like it." He said and took a bite of his own and nodded in agreement, it was indeed good. "Yeah, we were married for only three years, it didn't work out."

"I see." Amy wasn't sure what she should say so she went with something safe. "I'm glad your Grandma taught you so well, this is lovely and it's so nice to have someone else cook for me. I get sick of cooking for myself."

They cleared their plates of the first course quickly and Bryer soon went back to the kitchen to collect the next one. Sitting back at the table, after placing the dish on it, he said, "So what about you?"

"What about me?" Amy said as she dished herself some of the yummy garlic smelling haddock.

"Have you ever been married?" Bryer said as he spooned some of the brown rice onto his plate.

"Nope, although I would like to one day. I'd like children too." Amy stopped talking, and spooning the food onto her plate, horrified she would scare him off and refused to look him in the eye. She quickly recovered and managed to serve herself some asparagus while mentally kicking herself.

"Yeah, me too. I've always wanted children." He said as if he wasn't the least bit daunted by her remark and he continued to make easy conversation, much to Amy's relief, during the rest of their meal.

Amy surveyed the table, every scrap of food had been eaten and it was utterly delicious. "Well, I think I could let you cook for me again, it was bloody delicious...all of it." Amy looked at Bryer with a cheeky look on her face.

"Oh you will, will you?" He laughed as he reached out over the table and placed his hand over hers, "I'd be more than happy to, it's actually nice to have someone who appreciates it."

"Glad to hear it." She said as her stomach filled with butterflies from his warm touch.

Bryer smiled, released her hand and began to stack the plates. "Coffee? Oh, no, you would prefer tea, right?" Bryer said as he raised from the table his hands full of empty dishes.

"Actually yes, that would be great. Would you like a hand with the clean-up?"

"No, no. I'm just going to load the dishwasher while the kettle boils. You go and relax."

"Okay, thanks." Amy picked up her half-empty wine glass and began to wander over to one of the large, comfortable sofas. It had been a wonderful meal, he really was a good cook. I could get used to this, she thought to herself on the way. She decided to remain standing to stretch her legs out.

She smelt his musky scent before she felt him.

Bryer had followed her over to the sofas and stood closely behind her. A ripple of excitement found its way out of her stomach and radiated outwards wrapping its tendrils around her limbs, making her weak and shaky. She felt her breath come faster and she swallowed hard.

Bryer gently placed his hands on her upper arms and slowly moved them up to her shoulders, he pulled her back against him and held her there for a moment. He then moved his hands down her arms to her hands, which now hung loosely by her sides. He removed the wine glass from her hand and placed it on the coffee table. Reaching up he moved her hair away from the back of her neck exposing the warm flesh and gently began kissing it.

Amy stretched out her neck and allowed him full access as a ripple of goosebumps found their way around her body to her nipples and other deeper places. She felt his hands come round the front and brush past the side of her breasts, his touch, even over her clothing made her breath come faster.

He kissed her neck harder with little nibbles making her gently groan, he could feel himself pressing against her, achy with need. He moved his hands onto her breasts, cupping them, feeling the sensual weight of them, and he could feel her nipples were erect through the material of her top. He lowered his hands to the bottom of her top and pulled it up over her head. He caressed her warm, bare flesh of her stomach feeling the skin tremble, with their shared excitement, beneath his hands. He withdrew his hands and stroked her back, kissing it as he went and eventually he undid her bra, letting it fall to the floor. Taking his hands off her for just a moment, he then quickly removed his own shirt.

Amy felt his bare chest against her back, the delicious warm flesh pressed against her naked skin.

His warm hands were back on her skin but this time they moved toward her breasts, leaving a hot trail behind where he had touched her. She could feel herself wanting him, she wasn't surprised to realise that it was a need she had been repressing for some time now.

Together, locked in this embrace they slowly moved forward several steps until they were at the edge of his bed. He gradually turned her around and looked into her eyes, silently looking for permission to continue. With the merest nod of her head, he kissed her on the mouth, gently at first and then with growing passion, his need obvious against her.

She began to remove the rest of his clothes for him, until he stood naked before her. Her eyes roamed hungrily over his lovely body, it was obvious he worked out and kept himself fit. She looked at the tattoo just above his left nipple, it was of a raven flying through an open window, she hadn't known he had one until this moment and she really rather liked it.

He smiled and began taking the rest of her clothes off, greedily returning his hands back to her warm skin.

Amy was amazed at how utterly and totally unselfconscious she felt, whenever she had thought about this moment, and, she admitted to herself, that she had enthusiastically thought of it several times recently, she had thought she would be at least a little shy, but no, she felt brave and strong and above all, very sexy.

Bryer ran his hands down her back and over her bottom, gently squeezing as he did.

Amy encircled him with her arms, enjoying the feel of his muscular back under her hands as she felt his front pressed against her.

Guiding her fully onto the bed, he lay next to her gently caressing her body, as she did his. Theirs was a mutual joy in discovering new found lands.

Their passion built as their touches became more intimate and when they could hold back no longer, they did what nature had intended all along. As they moved in time, they fit together like a flesh jigsaw puzzle, perfectly matched as they became one.

It wasn't long before she could feel that delicious urge within build and she allowed herself to completely let go, losing all sense of time or place, no longer feeling the bed beneath her as they moved ever nearer to bone melting bliss.

*

Afterwards, he breathlessly lay against her, sweat glistening on their bodies.

She lifted her head, brushed her hair out of her eyes and smiled a deeply satisfied smile. It was the kind of smile that one can only find after good sex. She kissed him slowly and sexily, her passion growing again. Just kissing him turned her on and it had the same effect on him. She ran her hands over his smooth skin and muscles of his chest and then downward, exploring and playing with all of him.

There was just something so incredibly sexy about him, and when she came back up the bed, she kissed him on the lips again, passionately and deeply. Eventually, she broke away and relaxed next to him. She could feel their sweat was beginning to cool on her skin so she pulled up the discarded covers over them both and snuggled down next to him, their bodies tangled together.

When he managed to catch his breath, he said, "That was...a lot of fun, think we can do that again soon?" He said with a naughty smile on his face as his fingers played with her nipple.

"Definitely." She said huskily.

He turned more towards her and kissed her hard, making her breathless again with need.

"Glad you enjoyed it." She gasped and smiled smugly, gently stroking his chest with her hand as she cuddled up against him. Before long she felt the boneless tiredness creep up on her and she floated happily off to sleep, safe and warm in his arms.

Their sleep was broken by the shrill sound of a phone ringing. Jumping out of bed, and not covering his nakedness, Bryer crossed the room to his phone and answered it. Amy watched, admiring the view of his wonderful body. Yes, she could definitely get used to this, she thought.

Ending the call Bryer said, "I'm sorry, there's been a traffic accident and they need me to take some photos. You could stay in bed until I get back, if you like. I'll only be an hour or so."

"Nah, I'll go home and get some sleep. I'm not sure I'll get much more if I stay." She smiled at him and absolutely knew there would be no hope if she did stay.

He returned to the bed and kissed her long and hard, breathlessly he said, "No, you're right, you wouldn't."

Chapter Twenty Three

Wednesday, 31st October

Amy lay in bed, her mind was half awake and her body half asleep and thought about the excellent sex she'd had the night before. She stretched out languidly in her bed, opening her eyes, looked at her surroundings and smiled a deeply satisfied smile. For the first time in a rather long time, she felt truly relaxed, safe and comfortable in the place she found herself, both physically and mentally. She'd had a wonderful evening the night before with Bryer and she was, despite being in the process of selling it, feeling very much at home in this lovely old cottage.

At last, she gathered her thoughts and directed them towards the day ahead of her. She leapt out of bed feeling full of energy and threw on her dressing gown, she slipped her feet into her warm, furry slippers and headed to the kitchen for some tea and toast. On the way past her bedroom window, she opened the curtains to find the garden covered in frost making the plants look like they had been painted with white frost paint and there was a deep, white mist completely blocking her view of the woods. She looked at it for a while and rather liked the feeling of being enclosed in her own little secretive world. She smiled to herself contentedly as she wandered into the warm kitchen. Thank goodness she had remembered to switch on the heating timer of the oil fuelled AGA, it made such a lovely difference to the early mornings.

Erda was sitting at the kitchen table and she watched Amy enter the room. "Mornin'." She said and smiled a knowing smile at Amy.

"Morning, Erda." Amy said and then saw her face, "You can take that look off your face." Amy grabbed the kettle, filled it and placed it back on its stand and switched it on with a loud click.

"'Tis naught to be ashamed of, thy hath been tupping, 'tis nature's way."

"I...erm...okay." Amy busied herself by making toast and decided to add some scrambled eggs to it, all the while trying not to think of Bryer's hands on her body and daydreaming about the things they had done together, she began to blush with excitement.

Amy's stomach growled and distracted her mind from Bryer back to what she was doing as she finally plated up her breakfast and poured the hot water into a mug with a tea bag in it. "I really must get a teapot." She said to herself and sat down with her breakfast at the table and began to eat it enthusiastically.

Erda just watched her and said nothing.

"I was wondering..." Amy said between bites. "Do you sleep at all?"

"Sleep, nay."

"Oh, so what do you do when I sleep?"

"I rest and ponder."

"Where?"

"I go to my bottle, I think, 'tis a'place of rest... 'tis hard to tell thee but feels like sleeping but my mind thinks while my Soul rests." Erda frowned, it was obviously difficult to put into words.

"I see." Amy said, though actually she wasn't sure she did at all. A funny thought came into Amy's mind and she had to stifle a giggle, she imagined Erda to be like a genie with a bottle full of big cushions where she lounged whenever she went in there.

"I nay canst tell thee more." Erda said looking puzzled, like she had never really thought about it before now.

Nodding at Erda and pushing the amusing genie thought aside, Amy continued to eat her breakfast, which seemed to be vanishing quite quickly. She appeared to have a healthy appetite after last night, not surprising really. She smiled knowingly to herself but then wondered how on earth could she think straight with so many wonderful yet weird things happening in her life right now. When she stopped to actually think about it, her mind flitted from one thing to another...from the sadness that was the reason for her visit in the first place and the duty she was performing that came with it, then to the wonder that was Erda and all her involvement entailed and meant, and then to being back in a place from her happy childhood and, finally, to the surprise and delight that was Bryer. It was all so much to deal with that Amy thought she might like to take a walk, if the mist cleared, perhaps down to the lake, and hopefully relax, maybe even calm her whizzing mind a little. The more she thought about it and finding a bit of peace, the more she liked the idea.

Erda sat silently but she looked a little perturbed about something.

Amy brought her thoughts back to her food and finished it, she leant back in her chair and sipped her tea. She eyed Erda over the top of her mug. "Everything alright?"

"I hath a'thing I must tell thee."

"Oh?"

"Come." Erda stood and led the way into the living room.

The room had turned rather chilly overnight probably because it was the only room that was not part of the heating system, due to the now cold, large fireplace that was usually used to heat it.

This room really needs a heater, Amy thought, not for the first time. She set her mug down on the coffee table and quickly rebuilt and lit the fire. She glanced out of the deep set window and saw the pale blue beautiful sky beginning to emerge out of the early morning mist. She shivered, the autumn days were really beginning to turn cold even if they were still bright and sunny. She saw Erda sit in her usual chair by the fire looking thoughtful. Amy picked up her mug again and sat down on the sofa, curling her feet up under her and spread a blanket around her. "Okay, what's up?"

Erda looked up at the ceiling.

"No, I mean what's the matter with you?" Amy tried not to laugh, sometimes talking to Erda was like talking to a child who took everything she said quite literally.

"Hast thou found scripts of thy family?"

Amy frowned, "Scripts?"

'Aye, scripts...writings?"

"Um...letters and such?"

"Nay, thy branches."

"Branches?" Amy searched her brain and wondered what Erda could mean, when a thought came to her. "Oh, you mean family tree branches? Yeah, I saw some of that stuff in a drawer of the desk. You want me to get it out?"

"Aye." Erda said as she turned to watch her from her armchair.

Amy went over to the desk and collected the various pieces of paper and notebooks, she then spread them out on the coffee table. "Oh, there's something else too." She left the living room and went to the spare room, where she had begun to make a pile of things on the bed that she was going to keep, and quickly returned to the sofa holding the roll of wallpaper.

Erda looked up at Amy when she entered the room with a strange object in her hands.

"There's this, is this what you're after?" Amy unrolled the hideously flowery wallpaper and flipped it around to show the writing on the other side. As she unrolled it she revealed a massive, hand drawn family tree. "It must have taken my Dad a long time to do all this." She had immediately recognised her father's handwriting. She continued to unroll it until there was no more writing and the whole tree stretched out about four feet, she laid it on the coffee table, but it was so long it's ends dangled off the table and onto the floor.

"Aye, 'tis what I a'wanted." Erda peered at the writing at the top, it said: Nathaniel Blackmoor m. 1693 Sarah Goodman, Par. St Michael's, London. "Dost thou knowest these names?" She said and pointed to the top names.

"No, never heard of them but from looking at this they are my ancestors on my father's side. Why? Did you know them?" Amy looked surprised.

"Aye, Nathaniel is my great, great grandchild."

Amy, who had sat back on the sofa and was drinking her tea, nearly choked, "What?" She looked at Erda and then at the family tree as her eyes followed it all the way down to the bottom where her name sat in black ink. "You mean?"

"Aye, he is Abigail's great grandson...thou art my family." Erda said and smiled nervously at Amy.

"I...um...well, that's nice." Amy said, her brain had utterly lost the ability to think and the words just fell out of her mouth with no real meaning.

"I thought thou hath guessed why I am here and nay elsewhere."

"No...I..."

"Thy knowest I'm a'watching my family over many years."

"I know but I just...well, I just thought you were here because that's where your bottle ended up. I never thought...well, that you...and me...." Amy stared at Erda and realised she was looking at her own Grandmother with many, many greats ahead of the name. "Hello, Grandma."

Erda laughed, it was a pleasant relaxed sound and Amy enjoyed it. She knew it was the first time she had heard it and it was nice to see her enjoying a measure of happiness in a life so full of tragedy.

"Erda wilt be fine for thy calling me."

"Erda it is then." Amy smiled warmly and, all of a sudden, the Spirit of the woman sitting in front of her seemed more interesting and important. "Wow...I think you just blew my mind."

"I nay knowest thy meaning."

"It's just a saying, it means I'm amazed by the news."

Erda nodded and continued to look at the family tree, a look of pride came over her face. "Our family hath spread and prospered, 'tis good to see."

"Yes, I guess we have." Amy sat up more so she could read the rest of the tree. It was fascinating to see how the family had multiplied and spread out from England to Europe, the Americas and even Australia. Her father had really put a lot of hard work into the research, it must have taken up a lot of his time finding all these family members and their various bits of information, their children and all of their birth, marriage and death dates. It was quite an impressive feat to say the least.

"I was wondering, I know you said you had watched some of the family over the years, but did you try to contact any of them or show yourself to them, like you have with me?"

"Aye, a few over a'time but it nay went well for several, after one lost her voice from being a'feared and 'twas placed in an asylum, I nary wanted for many years."

"Oh, that's terrible." Amy paused from sipping her tea. "What made you contact me, then? How did you know I wouldn't go crazy too?"

"When thy slept by thy fire upon thy arrival, I spoke to thee and thee heard me. It hath nay been as easy a'fore."

Amy tried to remember her first night in the cottage. "I don't remember that, but okay."

Erda seemed a little more relaxed and talkative now that she'd shared the family connection with Amy, it had obviously been weighing greatly on her mind.

For the rest of the morning and over lunch, which was just a quick sandwich, Amy sorted through more of her parents' belongings and decided what would be thrown away, given to charity or taken back to the UK with her. Sometimes it was a sad, tedious task, and other times it was a fun exploration of her family memories.

Erda sat and watched her work through cupboard after cupboard, and they chatted easily about all manner of things, just as a family should.

*

Amy had just moved another 'charity' box by the front door when a knock sounded on it making her jump. Glancing at her watch, she realised it must be the surveyor. She opened the door and looked at

the middle-aged, ruddy-faced man who was bundled
up with a scarf and hat against the cold.

"Hello?" Amy said.

"Miss Grey? I'm William Owens, the surveyor
for Carpenter's Realty."

"Ah, yes, I was expecting you. Do come in.
That wind off the lake is getting rather cold, isn't
it?" Amy said as she shivered and moved out of the
doorway to let him in, then quickly shut the door
behind him, blocking out the cold wind.

"Thank you. Yes, I think we'll have an early
snow this year." He said while removing his hat and
scarf.

"Oh, really?" Amy admitted to herself that
she would rather enjoy a bit of snow, it rarely snowed
in the UK, at least in the part she was from. She
looked at Mr Owens expectant face. "So what do you
need from me?"

"Nothing, Miss Grey. If you will just leave me
to it, I should be done in about an hour."

"Okay, just shout if you need anything. Would
you like a warm drink first, though?"

"No, I'm good." He said as he removed his
coat, passed it over to Amy's outstretched hand,
extracted a file from his bag and then began his
work.

Amy took his coat, hat and scarf and hung them by the front door, and she then returned to the living room. Sitting down, she decided she needed a break from all the sorting and she picked up a book she'd bought at the lovely local bookstore, and began reading it as she happily snuggled up on the sofa, in front of the fire. Erda was nowhere to be seen, perhaps she was watching over Mr Owens, thought Amy.

True to his word, Mr Owens' checking and measuring took no longer than an hour and he'd saved the living room for last. When he'd finished with the living room, he said, "Well, I believe that's everything I need, Miss Grey."

"How did the old place do?" Amy asked looking up as she put down her book.

"Surprisingly good actually, whoever did the renovations several years ago did a good job. There are a few changes to code that need sorting but nothing major, they also put in substantial insulation so the place should be listed as a four season home instead of a three season one."

"Oh, well, that's good, isn't it?" Amy said not being sure. In England, almost every home was a place to live all year round but then, in England, they didn't get extremely cold winters like this part of Canada.

"Yes, very good. It will improve your chances of getting the amount you want for the place. You will be getting a full report, of course, through Ms Carpenter, your realtor, in the next couple of days." With that he packed up his belongings, wrapped himself against the cold weather and left with a cheery goodbye as he headed out the door.

"Well, that was easy." Amy said to herself as she pondered what it would be like to live in this cottage throughout the really cold winter months.

The phone burst into life and made Amy jump, forcing her thoughts to rush back to the here and now, she picked up the phone and sat back on the sofa to answer it.

"Hello?"

"Amy? It's Bryer."

"Oh, hello, Bryer." She said while trying to ignore the excited butterflies in her stomach and the silly smile on her face. "How are you?"

"Good. I just had a booking cancel this afternoon for a family sitting due to illness, can you tell it's the start of flu season? Anyway, I thought you might like a ride out to the falls with me I was going to take some photos of the autumn leaves with the falls as a backdrop before this wind blows them all off the trees." He laughed.

Amy's bones just melted at the sound of his warm, infectious laugh. "Oh, that sounds great. I just have to pop into the realtor's to sign some papers and then I'll meet you at your place. That okay?"

"Sure, we could get some dinner on the way back, if you like. I know a great little restaurant near the falls."

"That would be lovely. I shouldn't be more than an hour."

"Okay, see you later."

"Bye." Amy pressed 'end call' and smiled at the phone, she thought, and not for the first time, she was really beginning to enjoy her stay here.

*

Pushing open the door, Amy heard a bell ring somewhere deeper in the realtor's office but there was no one sitting at either of the two front desks. "Hello?"

"Miss Grey?" A voice came from a room at the back.

"Yes, Ms Carpenter? I'm here to sign those forms." Amy said, pleased the old lady hadn't forgotten she was coming to the office.

"Yes, yes, dear...do come through."

Amy unzipped her coat, removed her gloves and rubbed her hands together to warm them up, she followed the woman's voice past the two empty desks, down the brightly wallpapered hallway, which had lovely photographs of old houses, Bryer's work, Amy presumed, to a larger office at the back. This was obviously Ms Carpenter's office, as the owner of the business she had the much larger and more fancy desk.

Ms Carpenter rose from her chair as Amy entered. "Sorry about that, the Moltby twins, my assistants, are both out with the flu. Do be seated." She said and gestured to a chair.

"Ah...I heard it was going around." Amy said as she sat in the chair directly in front of Ms Carpenter's desk.

"Yes, well, such things happen at this time of year when the weather turns chilly." Ms Carpenter said. She was, as usual, perfectly turned out in a floral print dress and a Chanel style jacket. Sitting back down, she searched through a pile of grey files in her desk tray, "Here we are, now as I said, you've had an offer on your cottage and land, conditional to the survey, of course, for your full asking price."

"Really? The full price, isn't that unusual?"

"Not at all, especially on the properties surrounding the lake, they are usually snapped up as soon as they go on the market. Buyers don't tend to quibble about the price unless it's ridiculously high and yours was priced perfectly for the market, of course." She said proudly.

"Of course." Amy said, trying not to be annoyed by the attitude of the woman.

"I need you to sign these documents provisionally giving me permission to make the sale on your behalf and then as soon as the buyer goes ahead, after the survey and, well, that will be that as they say. Also, as he wants to pay with cash and has no house to sell himself, the rest of the sale will go through very quickly." She said and handed Amy the two documents.

"I see." Amy took the documents from her and noticed she had to sign in four places, two page markers marked the areas on paperwork. Amy leaned forward and took the pen also offered by Ms Carpenter's outstretched hand. Ms Carpenter seemed to be in a little too much of a hurry to complete the sale, Amy thought. And, as she held the pen over the dotted line where she was supposed to sign, she hesitated for a moment.

"Is there a problem?" Ms Carpenter asked, looking concerned.

"No, not at all." Amy's hand still held the pen over paper and it didn't move. "Yes, actually, perhaps there is."

"Oh?"

"May I take these home and read through them? I want to make sure I understand the process thoroughly." Amy said. She knew she was making an excuse and stalling but her instincts were screaming at her to stop and reconsider.

"Of course, my dear, just make sure they are back to me and signed by tomorrow afternoon, because that's when I'm calling the buyer with the results of the survey, and I know he wants to get the sale completed quickly."

"I will, thank you, Ms Carpenter." Amy rose with the documents in her hand. She felt instinctively protective of the cottage and needed more time to think about what she was going to do with her family's legacy. Amy said her goodbyes and left the large office. She folded the paperwork, put it in her bag and began to wrap herself up warm against the cold as she made her own way out through the rest of the realtor's office.

Outside, the cold wind bit at her neck and face, she quickly pulled up the collar of her coat closer around her neck and headed back to her truck and the warmth it provided. It seemed everyone was avoiding the cold snap as the street was deserted, Amy noticed.

The last thing she heard was footsteps coming up quickly behind her and something foul-smelling being put over her nose and mouth. She didn't have time to panic or struggle as she breathed in the stink of the chemicals on the cloth and she soon succumbed to its fumes and passed out.

Chapter Twenty Four

Detective Inspector Andy looked at the contents of the file that his partner, Mitch, had just handed him. For a moment, he let his eyes pass over the information while his brain was trying to take it all in. When he had finished reading every word he turned to Mitch with a look of pure amazement on his face.

Mitch nodded.

"Fuck me. Are you sure, you've double and triple checked this data? Right?"

"Yup" Mitch said proudly, knowing full well the effect it was having on his boss because he'd experienced exactly the same reaction just a short while ago when he'd made the discovery.

"It can't be a coincidence, can it? Surely, it's not." Andy looked back down at the file and reread the entire thing again.

"I definitely don't think so but if it is, it's the craziest one I've ever heard of."

"Yeah, but fuck, I mean.... Jesus Christ. What are the chances?" Andy, who had been leaning on his desk, stood up. "You know what this means, of course? Do we have any contact information at all? Or are we running blind here?"

"I found an old address and phone number, but that's all I've got so far. Unfortunately, I can't find anything more recent." Mitch said as he held out a single sheet of paper to Andy.

"Have you tried the number yet?"

"No, I wanted to wait for you to read the file."

"Okay." Andy took the offered piece of paper with the contact details on and walked round his desk, picking up his phone, he punched in the numbers from the paper. He stood waiting for the call to be picked up but there was no answer.

"Anything?" Mitch said.

"No, not even an answering machine. Right, well, I guess a visit is very much in order then." Andy grabbed his jacket off the back of his chair. As he put the jacket on he shook his head. "Holy fuck, who would have bet on those odds?"

"I know, right?" Mitch looked at his senior, "How do you want to do this? Hard and noisy or soft and quiet?"

"Let's take the soft approach for now, don't want anyone to get spooked." Andy said as they walked out of his office, he stopped at the doorway to turn off the lights and closed the door behind him.

*

The icy wind, which blew off the lake, outside of town, and off the river, at the end of main street, made for a very chilly wind tunnel effect down Main Street at this time of the year. Many of the local inhabitants tried to avoid shopping at such times and so the side street was empty except for one man.

Bryer, standing outside and wrapped up against the cold wind, had just finished stowing all his photography equipment safely on the backseat of his truck when his phone rang. He pulled off his right hand glove, stuffed his hand in his jeans pocket and yanked out the phone. He looked at the number calling and had expected it to be Amy, probably saying she was on the way, but it was Detective Inspector Andy Withers' number.

Bryer cringed, he sincerely hoped they didn't need him for a case right now because he was looking forward to spending some time with Amy, out by the waterfalls and afterwards for a good steak dinner at 'Randy's'. However, the detective only usually phoned when it was about a murder case and Bryer didn't hold out much hope for his late afternoon and evening plans. Sighing, but hoping for the best, he pressed 'answer' on his phone. "Hello, Detective Inspector Withers." He said as he sat down in his truck's front seat and closed the door, to stop the wind making a noise in the phone. He reached over to turn on the engine and start the heating, expecting to have to rush off at any moment to a new crime scene.

"Bryer, did you mention to Mitch the other day that you knew that English woman, the one who is visiting in Morton Creek? A Miss Amy Grey, I believe?" Andy said, straight to the point as usual.

"Yes, I do, why?" Bryer sat utterly still, the detective had his complete and undivided attention.

"I've been trying to call her for the last twenty minutes but there is no answer at her home.

Do you have any idea where she might be?" Andy said in a calm and carefully measured voice.

"She should be on the way to meet me, actually, we're going out to the falls to take some photos." Bryer somehow felt the need to explain himself to the detective. "Why? Is there something wrong, Andy?" He said. There was obviously no crime scene that needed his attention or he would have led with that, Bryer thought. At least, he hoped there wasn't, especially if Amy was involved somehow.

"There is a possibility, however slight, that she may be in danger, but we need to talk to her to confirm some of the information we have. Can you keep her there with you, when she arrives? We are on the way out to Morton Creek as we speak."

"What? Oh, shit, really? I need to know more right now, what the hell is going on?"

"Just keep her there and I'll fill you in on the details when we arrive. Okay?"

"Okay...yeah, sure. I'll keep her at my place until you arrive, I can do that. How serious is this threat? Tell me honestly, Andy." Bryer said and he could feel his heart pounding.

"Thanks, we'll be with you very shortly." Andy said, without answering the question, and abruptly ended the call.

Bryer stared at his phone and quickly tapped on Amy's phone number in his contacts list and waited, but it just went straight to her new voicemail. He didn't leave a message, not wanting to scare her, and ended the call. He quickly climbed out of the truck, closed the truck door behind him and locked it. Due to his mounting panic about Amy and her safety, he almost ran back inside his apartment, where it was considerably warmer, to wait for her and keep trying her phone.

As the minutes slowly ticked by, he found himself walking around impatiently. Eventually, he forced himself to sit down before he wore either his shoes or the floor out with his pacing. He sat on the edge of the sofa tapping his fingers on his knees, he was so agitated he couldn't think straight.

With a loud knock on the door, Bryer jumped up and rushed downstairs relieved that Amy had finally arrived and was safe, but when he opened the door he found Detectives Andy and Mitch standing on his doorstep.

"Is she here?" Andy said.

"No, not yet." Bryer said, worry clouding his face and making him frown. "Come in."

"Thanks." The Detectives both said in unison and stepped into the foyer of the store, closing the door and thankfully leaving the late afternoon's cold weather behind them.

"I've been trying to call her phone but it just goes straight to voicemail." Bryer said, looking to them for advice. "I don't know what else to do."

"Okay, keep doing that. We'll head out to her home and check the place out, you stay here in case she turns up. Call me, immediately, if you hear from her, got that?" Andy said.

"Sure. Of course. But what's really going on?"

"We are not certain, yet, but it's possible the serial murderer could be after her next. I need to know she's safe, and then maybe she could help us stop this fucker." Andy said as he grabbed the door knob.

"What?" Bryer stared at Andy in horror. "Fuck me." He said and ran a hand over his face and back through his hair, "I'll keep trying her phone. Let me know what you find when you get out there, will ya?"

"Will do, you just keep trying her. Okay?" Andy said and didn't wait for Bryer's answer as he and Mitch quickly left the store. They climbed in their car, pulled out with a screech of tires and headed down Main Street and out of town towards Amy's cottage.

"Shit, Amy, where are you?" Bryer said to himself as he accessed his contacts list on his phone and tried her number again. Yet again, it went straight to voicemail. He looked around him feeling utterly useless, there was absolutely nothing he could do but wait and keep trying her phone. Frustrated, he climbed back up the stairs to his apartment and began to make himself a drink. Opening the cupboard door to grab the coffee grounds, he saw the packet of tea he'd bought for Amy and, thinking the Brits use tea to calm their nerves, he made himself a cup.

He blew on the hot liquid to cool it faster and took a sip, blew on it some more and took another, "Ugh, why do they drink this crap?" He said and put down the mug on the coffee table with a shudder. Once again he tried Amy's phone and got the same response, voicemail. He wanted to throw the damned phone across the room but knew he couldn't in case she called, so he stuffed it deep into his jeans pocket and started pacing the room again.

Eventually, he thought of watching for her out of the windows facing the road, he was actually hoping to see her drive up in her father's truck any moment, she would be perfectly safe and well, with some normal excuse of why she was late. As his eyes scanned the road, he was startled to see Amy's truck already parked further up on Main Street. A wave of pure happiness and relief burst through his chest and radiated around his body making him smile with joy.

"Oh, thank God!" He said utterly relieved. She was safe and in town already, her phone must be off and she must be doing an errand before she arrives, he thought rationally and he began to relax a little. Sitting on the sofa, he grabbed a photography magazine off his coffee table and started to, admittedly half-heartedly, flick through the glossy pages while he waited for Amy to finally arrive.

Bryer could barely concentrate and the articles and images became a blur, he too quickly got to the end of the magazine, so he picked up another, but with the same result. Annoyed, he threw the magazines back onto the table, his interest in them completely lost. His instincts were now shouting at him, telling him there was something very wrong. He checked his watch, Amy was now an hour overdue, which was not like her in his admittedly limited experience. He remembered she had sent him a text before, when she was just going to be ten minutes late. Taking that as her normal behaviour, she would probably have sent him several texts by now, that was, if there was nothing wrong, of course. He quickly made up his mind, threw on his jacket, ran downstairs and out into the street towards her truck and he saw it was parked outside Carpenter's Realty.

"Of course!" He said to himself when he remembered she'd told him she had an appointment with Emily before coming to see him. He took a deep breath, let it out slowly and walked towards the realtor's office. It was empty but the lights were on and the door was unlocked, so he knew the place was open. "Hello? Emily, are you here? It's Bryer." He said as he stuck his head inside the door.

"Come through, Bryer, I'm in my office." Emily's genteel voice floated down the office corridor.

Bryer walked past the two empty desks and down the short hallway to Emily's office, praying that Amy would be sitting in there with her and everything would be okay.

Unfortunately, Emily was alone.

"What can I do for you, Bryer? I'm afraid I don't have any work for you at present." Emily said as she sat forward and clasped her hands together on her desk, she was all business as usual.

"Oh, no, I'm not here about that. Have you seen Amy? I mean Miss Grey?"

"Yes, we had a meeting a little while ago, why?"

"When did she leave? Do you know where she went?" He noticed his voice was starting to have a desperate edge to it and the disappointment of not finding her, happily sitting there, began to make him feel edgy again.

"She was only here a few minutes and then she left, I'm afraid we didn't discuss where she was going next. What is this all about, Bryer?" She frowned at him.

"I...we...believe she may be missing."

"What? Oh, my goodness, missing? Why? What happened? Is she in any danger?" The concern was written all over her aged face.

"Yes, but I don't have time to explain now. Wait, you said she left, but her truck is still outside." He said in a slightly more forceful tone, his eyes began to narrow, fear making him suspicious of everything and everyone.

Emily stood up abruptly. "I don't like your tone, young man. As I said, we had a meeting and she left. Perhaps she has popped into one of the other stores. Really, Bryer, I'm sure she is just fine."

"I hope so." He said and without another word, Bryer turned and left the office. He decided he would go and check all the other stores along Main Street, he knew that only a few of them would still be open this late in the afternoon. In and out of store after store he went, asking after Amy, but to no avail, she was nowhere in sight and none of the staff had seen her at all that day. It was as if she had just vanished into thin air. Reluctantly, with the dimming light and his dimming hope, Bryer returned to his apartment. He immediately phoned Andy and told him he'd found Amy's truck but unfortunately not her. He was trying very hard not to panic, but it didn't help when Andy said that he and Mitch would turn around and come straight back to town and a full search of the town's buildings would have to be initiated.

Bryer flopped down on his sofa and put his head in his hands, he had no idea what to do next. He had never felt so useless in his entire life and he hated the feeling with a passion.

As he sat and tried not to think of all the horrible things that could have happened to Amy, a strange feeling of goosebumps began to creep over his skin. It was almost like he was getting a cold virus or a fever, it was a kind of shudder and a skin crawling sensation all at the same time. He suddenly had the distinct feeling someone was watching him, in fact, it felt like someone was standing directly behind him. Quickly, he spun his head round to the right and to the left but saw absolutely nothing out of place, he was utterly alone.

Shaking his head, he tried Amy's phone again, "Come on, come on...answer the fucking phone." Again his call was met with her voicemail. "Shit." He slammed his phone on the coffee table and leaned back on the sofa, propping his head on the back of it and shutting his eyes. Not usually one to pray, his building fear told him it might be a good time to start.

Another cold shiver went down Bryer's spine and he could feel someone in the room with him, his eyes shot open and he stood up quickly and spun round as he did so. He looked in every direction but still he saw nothing unusual or out of place. The feeling of not being alone was now so very intense that, by instinct, he backed up against a wall as his eyes looked wildly around the room searching for something, anything, which would explain this horribly creepy feeling and make it go away. His heart raced like an over revved engine in his chest, his breath became shallow and fast, as a deep immobilizing fear grew inside of him. He began to feel a cold sweat coat his skin and it trickled down his neck and shoulders, his hands had become damp and slippery from it.

Something moved just outside of his field of vision, it made his eyes dart forward and settle on the area just a foot or so in front of him where the air seemed to vibrate and where a shape began to emerge. It was fuzzy and blurred but it was a human shape, of that he was sure. Then all he could hear, apart from his own heart beating frantically in his ears, was a muffled sound in his head, the noise began to sound like his name as it was repeated over and over again. Until it became unmistakably clear and his name rang in his head loudly, like a huge bell being struck right next to him making him jump.

The last thing he was even vaguely conscious of, was his body moving towards the impossible blurred thing without either his consent nor his control, he was undeniably drawn to it by the voice in his head.

He screamed and screamed in terror, but his screams were only in his head, because his body would no longer obey him.

Chapter Twenty Five

The banging which Amy could hear, she had begun to realize, was the blood in her head pounding against her skull. She struggled to open her eyes and, when she finally got her eyelids to cooperate, they felt restricted in their movement and there was nothing, absolutely nothing to see or to tell her where she was or what had happened to her.

There was just a solid blackness from the blindfold she could now feel had been tied tightly around her head, which, of course, stopped her from opening her eyes properly.

Across her mouth there was some sort of cloth tied as a gag, it tasted old and dirty and she forced herself not to think about what she might be tasting.

Fear gripped her with its icy fingers and she started to breathe rapidly as the panic began to set in. She could hear no noises and the only other useful sense, rather than touch, she had was her sense of smell and all that told her was that the air smelled musty. And even that sense was tainted by the chemical smell still lingering in her nose from whatever had been used to knock her out. Who the hell would do that? And why? She wondered. As her brain became more alert, she could work out that she was sitting on a chair and her hands and ankles felt tied to the legs of it. She couldn't move them at all, but could feel the roughness of, what she presumed to be rope, tight on her skin.

Time ticked away, as it does, but there was nothing for Amy to measure it by, no sight, no sound, just empty blackness, she had no idea how long she had been sitting there or how long she had been unconscious for.

She strived to stop the growing panic building up inside of her body and mind, but failed utterly. She began to wonder, what if the person who had taken her, stood right in front of her now and she didn't even know it, and what if they were about to slice her throat with a knife at any second?

A deep, dark fear crawled up her spine, and she broke out in a cold sweat, in her panic she roughly tugged at the ropes restraining her, but all that did was make her skin burn and arms and legs ache more.

She was trapped and she knew it, she had no clue what would happen next, nor how long she would live for. Scenarios of different kinds of deaths forced their way into her terrified mind making her pant and whimper in fear.

Trying to take a deep breath, she made an enormous effort to calm herself down and tried to think more clearly and rationally. She resigned herself to just listening and still she could hear nothing, amazingly there was not a single sound to be heard, which was creepy in itself. She continued to listen for so long that she wondered if it was day or night now, when, at last, she heard a faint creak.

She strained to hear more and she became sure there was someone walking on a squeaky wooden floor above her, as that's where the noise seemed to be coming from. Amy tried to scream and shout through her gag, but just a muffled sound came out. She even tried to rock the chair, so the legs would bang on the floor, and hopefully attract someone to help her.

Amy heard a door creak open and heard a light being switched on, the diffuse red light glowed through her blindfold but it did not help her, it gave her no sense of where she was at all. Footfalls could be heard on what sounded like wooden steps and they came closer. Amy continued to shout for help despite the revolting gag.

Amy was blinded by the bright light as her blindfold was suddenly ripped off, pulling some of her hair out from the back of her head with it. She winced, blinked, and tried to focus her pupils, which reacted sluggishly from the drug, slowly a blurred image began to coalesce as her vision cleared.

"There is no point making all that fuss, no one can hear you."

Amy stared at the person before her, unable to believe her eyes, nor contemplate the truth of it.

Emily Carpenter stood over Amy, all five foot three inches of her, she was, and looked like, a frail old woman well past retirement age. Her grey hair was neatly coiffed as she stood in her pretty floral dress with her Chanel style jacket over it.

Amy just gaped at her unbelievingly.

Emily grinned and Amy felt a cold shiver of fear run rampant down her spine. It was the most frighteningly evil smile Amy had ever seen, it was the smile of a psychopath. Emily took a step closer and yanked the foul gag away.

"Help! Help me, someone!" Amy shouted as soon as her mouth was free.

The hard slap, that made Amy's face sting and her eyes water, came from Emily so fast that Amy just didn't see it coming.

"I told you no one can hear you, so stop making that horrendous noise and have some dignity." She said as she walked behind Amy.

Amy looked around her, at last she was now able to see where she was being held, she was obviously in a basement, which was full of the usual items, old paint cans, buckets and shelves full of old toys, tools, storm lamps and preserves. She twisted in the chair but could not see what Emily was doing behind her. There were noises as if she was opening packages and, more unnervingly, she was quietly talking to herself.

Although Amy knew deep down that the old woman had definitely gone insane, she tried to listen to what she was saying, maybe she could use the woman's delusions to become part of the story and use that to her advantage. Possibly even make Emily make a mistake and she would get a chance to escape, like she'd seen characters do in TV dramas. She knew she was grasping at straws but she had to do something and she had no other ideas or options.

"Yes, I know...soon now, as I promised. Just let me prepare everything. Yes, yes...of course, I remembered." Emily said to herself. "There now, see?

Almost done...just two more and we shall have it. Patience, that's what's needed now. Yes, indeed, some patience."

Amy tried to inch her chair around to see what was happening behind her and perhaps see what her fate would be, but she could barely budge the chair at all. She did, however, spot her bag against the far wall as if it had been thrown there and utterly discarded.

She remembered her phone was in the bag.

Maybe, while Emily was busy, doing whatever her crazy head was doing, maybe, Amy could get to her phone and call for help. Well, she would if she could get out of these bloody ropes, she thought.

Once again, Amy tried to wriggle free of her bonds, but she only succeeded in creating more painful rope burns on her wrists. Tears ran down her face from the effort, pain and frustration.

"Tears? Really, and I thought you were made of stronger stuff than that." Emily watched her captive dispassionately and shook her head in disgust.

"Fuck you." Amy said through clenched teeth.

"Charming. Rude language is the result of an insufficient intelligence, I'll have you know." She said imperiously.

"Kidnapping someone and talking to yourself is the result of insanity." Amy snapped back at her captor.

"On the contrary, my dear, it is a sign of industriousness and mental fortitude, obviously." Emily walked away talking to herself again. "I am, a few moments will make no difference. Hush, I'm finishing it now."

Amy listened, and Emily stopped talking to herself for several minutes, which seemed to last an eternity and, although Amy could still hear sounds of Emily doing something behind her, she had no other clue as to what the old woman was up to.

Eventually, the silence was broken.

"There now, see? Just as glorious as we thought it would be." Emily said and let out a big breath as if she had been holding it for a long time, and said, "Yes, alright, it is time."

Emily appeared in front of Amy, she had on an apron and rubber gloves, both of which were smeared with blood and other fluids, neither of which Amy wanted to think about right at that moment. The icy cold fear found Amy's spine once again, and, clutching it tightly, it trickled its way down...all the way down into her Soul.

"Time to give you a front row seat, I think." Emily said as she dragged Amy's chair round to face the opposite direction, making a horrendous wood on cement scraping noise as she did so.

Amy's eyes nervously swivelled as the chair moved round, deep in her heart, she expected to see instruments of torture and pain, but what she really saw stalled her mind so completely that it could no longer function properly. Her drowning mind only decided to fixate itself on the fact that the old woman was much, much stranger than she should have been, almost inhumanly so.

"There, what do you think of our masterpiece, quite beautiful, isn't it?" Emily said, her voice strong and proud.

Finally, Amy's mind clicked back on and she realised what she was looking at.

In front of her, on an old wooden table was a skinned, dead body.

It was also a body that had been opened up to expose all of its internal organs. As the smells of both the body and the chemicals, combined with the horrific sight overloaded her senses, she instantly vomited on the floor, narrowly missing her right shoe. Amy spat the last of the vomit away and looked back up, sadly her eyes couldn't help but refocus on the hideous thing before her. She could see that each of its organs had been stitched into place, however, and what made this image worse, was the glaring fact that the body had no skin on it, not a single piece, it was just muscles, bones and the new organs. Amy shuddered and wondered if she was going to vomit again.

"This has been my life's work, and, although it's taken several years to collect the parts from the various sources, my final creation is a thing of beauty, is it not?" Emily gloated over her repulsive creation with the look of an old master appreciating their latest painting or sculpture.

"Fuck me, you are insane." Amy said, now comprehending the enormity of her crimes, she knew now that many people must have lost their lives for this monstrosity worthy of Frankenstein himself, and, what made it even more revolting was that Emily was talking about it as if she has just restored an old car from parts found at a junkyard.

"Of course I'm not." Emily said, "No insane person could accomplish all this." Emily gestured with her hands towards the gruesome thing that resembled a body. She walked back to an old bench that sat beside the table where the body lay, and moved around some boxes, jars and Ziploc bags until she found what she wanted.

Amy's pulse raced, was this it? Was this her death, her fate at the hands of a mad old woman in a foreign country, thousands of miles away from home?

"And now for the finale." Emily said and her face broke into that crazed smile again that could freeze the marrow in the bones of the strongest person.

A terrified scream built in Amy's throat and released itself with such a powerful force that her voice cracked and broke mid-scream. Amy coughed and began to scream again, a pure primal and instinctual scream that would have hurt the ears of anyone listening, maybe even cracked glass. And perhaps it would have, if Emily hadn't quickly stepped forward and cut the scream off mid flow by grabbing Amy's throat with one extremely strong hand and squeezed it shut. With the other hand, Emily put an oxygen mask over Amy's face and, although Amy's vision began to blur and darken from the lack of air to her lungs, she saw the mask was attached to a strange valve and a glass jar. As soon as the mask was in place, the hand let go of its choke hold and Amy involuntarily breathed in and out.

Just as quickly as the attack had begun, it ended, and Emily pulled the mask away from Amy's face and released her. Amy coughed and gasped for air, her throat hurting from the powerful assault.

Emily walked away with the jar and placed it carefully on the bench. She began lighting candles, burning incense, and making strange mixtures of herbs and liquids, muttering to herself the whole time. Soon the room was filled with pungent smoke that made Amy's eyes water and her throat more dry than it already was.

The door at the top of the stairs, behind Amy, opened and closed, and footsteps could be heard coming down the wooden staircase. Again, Amy couldn't twist round enough to see who was behind her.

"They know it's you and they will soon be here."

Amy heard a monotone voice from some distance behind, presumably from the stairs. It was a voice Amy knew only too well, even if it sounded lifeless and without emotion.

"Thank you." Emily said and went back to her dark deeds.

The person walked a little more forward, away from the stairs, and Amy could finally see their face as she stretched round in her chair as far as she could, to look at the traitor, the deceiver. "You complete and utter bastard!" Amy spat out as a boiling rage exploded inside her.

Bryer just looked at her uncomprehendingly and then back at Emily.

"Ah, yes, the lovers...a lover's reunion, how sweet." She grinned nastily.

"Fuck you!" Amy shouted as tears of anger streamed down her face.

"So you've said, my dear. Really, you should try to expand your vocabulary. People are so lazy these days, no one wants to work on self improvement at all." Emily tutted and shook her head.

Amy looked from Emily to Bryer. Five minutes ago she would have called him her lover but no longer. How could he have betrayed her like this after...after.... Amy's anger devolved into deep wrenching sobs and she gasped out between them, "You. Fucking. Shit."

"Oh, don't you go blaming the handsome guy, now. No, he's under a spell and doesn't even know what he is doing. It's a very simple spell really, men's minds are so easily swayed."

"What? A spell, are you saying you're a Witch now?" Amy's eyebrows raised at the added absurdity of this new revelation.

"That's one name for it, but not one I would use." Disinterested in further conversation, Emily looked away and began chanting something over the gruesome corpse.

Out of the corner of her eye, Amy saw Bryer move slowly away from their position. He quietly went to what appeared to be a blacked out window and turned his back on them both for just a moment, and then quickly turned back. Emily never even noticed him move, she was so intent on what she was doing and so disinterested in him, as he was entirely in her control.

Glancing at Bryer with hatred, she saw him wink back at her and shake his head a little as if to say 'keep quiet, do nothing.' Amy stared at him in astonishment, was he tricking her or was he actually trying to help? How could she ever trust him again?

A groan drew Amy's attention back to Emily and her weird ritual, or whatever it was, around the corpse. She was no longer chanting, and a low groaning emanated from her lips, then she began to violently shake. Amy had no clue what was happening as she watched horrified, wondering if Emily was having a fit of some sort. Finally, the shaking stopped and Emily panted, desperately out of breath, and clutched the edge of the table for support. She recovered her breath slowly and hobbled around the table to the bench, she picked up the strange glass jar, the one with the mask attached.

Amy noticed that Emily was trembling now, her hands shook and she didn't look as strong as she had just moments ago, even her walking was more laboured.

Emily clutched the jar to her breast like a prized possession and watched the corpse intently, and, although her face looked tired and haggard, the look of absolute awe on it was unmistakable.

At first, Amy couldn't see what Emily was looking at, as she was seated and had less of a view, she glanced up again at Bryer, who stood rooted to the spot with a look of pure shock on his face. Looking back at the corpse, Amy could now see what had shocked him to the core. In front of their eyes, the corpse of patchwork organs began to knit together, literally. Incredibly, the incisions and sutures vanished one by one as the body sealed them together, as if they had never been separate items. Then, Amy watched in horror as the body began to grow its own skin.

Bryer suddenly lurched forward and went to attack Emily with an old baseball bat he'd grabbed from the pile of junk, but her reaction was too quick and she pulled a gun from the pocket in her Chanel style jacket and, without hesitation, shot him from about two feet away. The bullet hit Bryer in the upper chest and he staggered backwards with a look of disbelief on his face, he tripped over the old paint cans, and, as he went down, he hit his head hard on the metal shelving with a loud, sickening crack.

"NO! Bryer!" Amy screamed but he lay on the floor motionless, and the wound on his chest bled heavily down his t-shirt. She turned back to Emily, "You bitch."

"Oh, please, you hardly know him. Anyway, I wouldn't worry yourself, he looks dead to me and there's nothing you can do about it now. Priorities, young lady, you must consider your priorities. It is the only way to succeed in life, you know."

Amy couldn't believe the callousness of her words, looking back at Bryer her heart ached for him. She could only hope he wasn't dead yet, but how could she help him? And if he was still alive, how long would it be before he did die? Especially when he was losing so much blood.

Emily looked at her imperiously for a moment as if waiting for more conversation.

Amy began to wonder, perhaps if she could annoy Emily she would react and do something stupid, and she would finally get a chance to break free. "A gun? Seriously? I thought you were a

Witch." Amy sneered at her, while silently praying her tactic would work.

"My dear, real life is not like Harry Potter, you know. There are no wands that shoot lightning at your enemies here." Emily's eyes went back to watching the body grow its skin, having completely lost all interest in Amy.

Amy now knew deep down that she couldn't bait Emily into doing something stupid after all, she was way too interested in the changing corpse. A terrible feeling crept over Amy, what would happen when it had all of its skin? And, by the looks of it, that wouldn't be long now, as the skin had grown over most of the body except for the chest area and the face.

The skin on the face began to grow over the red muscles and the white bones, Emily leaned forward and pressed the mask to the newly formed lips and nose.

With a click of the valve, a hissing noise could be heard, and then what sounded very much like a sharp intake of breath by the corpse. Emily took the mask away and was smiling a most wondrous smile, "Welcome, my friend." She said as the corpse began to breathe deeply and noisily.

Amy's brain stalled again due to her utter shock at this new development. How could it be breathing? It was a corpse, she thought and she just stared at the abomination in front of her eyes.

At that moment, Erda appeared silently next to Amy and watched the events unfold with her.

After a few noisy breaths, the re-animated corpse sat up and looked around the room and at the people with a gleeful, maniacal look upon its face.

Chapter Twenty Six

The newly reanimated corpse turned its handsome head and looked around the room, firstly it looked at Emily, then at Amy and finally at Erda, its eyes lingered for several moments on Erda. Although, it seemed to have no real interest in Bryer who was still laying on the floor bleeding.

There was complete silence in the basement, not a single word was uttered, and no one moved an inch.

The naked body on the table then did the last thing anyone ever expected, it burst into laughter. It was the deep, rich, joyous laughter of the insane, and Emily joined in as if the corpse had just told a remarkably funny joke that only they understood.

Amy and Erda looked at each other horrified.

"Holy shit." Amy said. It was the only thing her stunned mind could think of to say.

At last, the corpse stopped laughing and just sat there on the table with a huge, satisfied grin on its rather attractive face.

For several more moments, every one continued to look at each other and they still said nothing. It was as if time had stopped entirely, as if the universe itself had refused to continue with such a grotesque miscreation within it.

Finally, the corpse, which was no longer a corpse, looked back at Erda, again it smiled but this smile was a cruel and evil one, and it said, "Thy curse is finally broken, thy ruttish hedge-born scut!"

"Thy mouth is still as foul as thy corpse, John." Erda said, seemingly now unmoved by the whole bizarre event, as if all the clues and strange warnings from her instincts had now clicked into place in her head.

"It's about time you bloody showed up." Amy was able to say at last, and somewhat angrily to Erda.

Erda looked deep into Amy's eyes but said nothing to her.

Amy looked again at the once-corpse-now-alive-man who had managed to climb easily off the old table as if he had known and used this new body his entire life. He, apparently, didn't mind being utterly naked in front of everyone as he showed no inhibitions nor embarrassment, in the least. Amy realised, with a shock so great that another frisson of fear ran through her tired body, she was now actually looking at Dr. John Lambe, Erda's former lover, murderer and also Amy's own, many times over great, grandfather. Amy's mouth dried up as she looked from person to person trying to reconcile what she was indeed seeing. Was this all real? Or am I dreaming? She wondered.

"Thy hex nay longer corrupts me, many years I doth but try inhabit others. Alas whence I take full control, a'body withered thereupon rotted as thy curse foretold. Thence a kindly thought bid me welcome whereupon our search began a'new." He held out his hand to Emily and, taking hers in his, he kissed it gently.

Emily smiled sweetly, as if to a lover, and passed him a man's pair of trousers and a shirt. She seemed uncomfortable with his nakedness, even if he wasn't. "Remember, your promise, John." She said as he took the clothing from her.

"Aye, Mistress Emily, we shalt come to thee." He said and stroked her cheek gently with an indulgent smile upon his face.

It would have been a nice scene between lovers, if it hadn't been so nauseatingly disgusting, Amy thought.

John examined the clothing and put it on slowly as if he didn't have a care in the world. However, the zip on the trousers puzzled him for a while, until Emily reminded him how it worked. They had obviously shared many things together over the years and modern fastenings must have been one of them.

"You, you are the killer of all those people!" Amy blurted out, horrified as the thought dawned on her. She wasn't sure whether she spoke to John or Emily or both.

John looked over at her, "Aye, whilst my abode 'twas within Emily, we hath achieved many things of such a wondrous nature."

"What hath thy truly done, John?" Erda said, frowning at him.

"Thou shalt be proud by my cleverness, 'tis all to do with blood." He said with an imperious wave of the hand and paused, as if his brilliance needed to be coaxed from him by fervent acolytes waiting upon his every word.

"May I?" Emily said.

John thought for a moment, "Of course, my loverly." He said, convinced she would make him sound even more impressive and he could then listen to her words and bask in his own glory.

"The illustrious Dr. Lambe could not, unfortunately, hold himself in another body and push out their Soul, without the body decaying as he said, and, when he chose me, that glorious February day many years ago in England, he found I had some knowledge of the arcane arts too. Between us we worked out that, although he was trying to be whole, he was going about it the wrong way. We formed a partnership and began our heroic search."

"Thy saith thy searched a'fore, what pray tell dost thou search for?" Erda said, unfazed by the ridiculous hubris.

"Search for what?" Amy said at the same time as Erda and frowned, she felt rather puzzled by all.

"For blood, my dear." Emily said to Amy and smiled at her in a kind way, as if she were a young child asking the simplest of questions. "You see, when his Soul possessed the other bodies, they essentially became him again and the curse was triggered, but we came upon a better idea. What if the blood was Erda's? Would the curse then refuse to be triggered because she was the one who had created it in the first place and she had certainly not directed it at herself, of course. So, we decided we would use parts of her bloodline to build a body of her DNA, and, if it was pure enough, his Soul would mix with her blood and the curse would not touch him. He would then live to carry on his glorious and very important work."

"Wait? What?" Amy stared at Emily.

"These devils hath killed members of my family, thy family, Amy, just so he couldst return."

"A little succinct but essentially, yes." Emily said, nodding.

"Holy fuck! You killed members of my family just for the spare parts? To build...you?" Amy stared at John, "Jesus Christ! They were your family too, Abigail was your daughter, do you not feel anything, you bastard?"

"Sweet child, thou art too sentimental. I needed, so I took, 'twas always such." John said as he moved closer to Amy and took her face roughly in his hand. "Thou art lovely, thy sweet breath giveth mine life, gratitude." He swiftly closed the distance between them and kissed her hard on the mouth.

Amy struggled to pull her face away, both sickened and revolted by him and his touch.

Erda stepped forward, she was ready to do something, anything, if he hurt Amy.

John released Amy as quickly as he had grabbed her and he stood by her with a smug grin on his face.

Amy turned her face away from him, not wanting to see the evil that lived in his eyes.

From behind her, Amy could hear a low groan and realised Bryer was indeed still alive, he must have only been knocked unconscious by the blow to the head. However, she also knew he would still be bleeding from the gunshot wound and he wouldn't be able to last too much longer. He needed medical help right now, but what could she do to help him? Or any of them?

Emily also heard the groan and pulled out the gun from her pocket again and raised it in Bryer's direction once more.

"No!" Amy screamed.

John spun round and took a step nearer to Emily, he quickly and easily knocked the gun from her shaking, gnarled hand.

It startled her and she blinked at him. "But John..." Emily said.

"I shalt complete my own bidding now, dost thou comprehend?" He took a step closer to Emily, "'Tis time for thy due, come hither, my loverly."

"Oh, yes. Yes, please, make me young and beautiful, take away this aged, painful body and the wrinkles, just as you promised." She said as she came into his arms, her voice rising in pitch as her excitement and ecstasy grew.

John held her close and caressed her grey hair, whispering sweet things in her ear and promising many delights of the flesh. All of a sudden, he grabbed her hair and pulled her head back and she glared at him, suddenly frightened by his strength. Placing a single hand on her throat, he squeezed it hard until the life fled her body and he dropped her to the ground like an unwanted rag doll. He looked down at her vaguely, and then his eyes quickly flicked away, his interest now permanently lost.

Amy screamed in fright. This was the second time she'd seen someone killed in front of her and both of them by him, the last one being Erda, and it was not something she ever expected nor wanted to see again. Amy closed her eyes, unable to watch the horror that was happening around her any further.

Bryer began to groan more as he started to regain consciousness.

Erda stood completely still, she said and did absolutely nothing except watch John rather intently.

Amy tried to calm herself and took some deep breaths, she gulped the air in quickly but all that did was make her slightly dizzy. She opened her eyes again and looked at Erda, "Do something for God's sake." She couldn't believe she was just going to stand there and watch, would she watch while he murdered her and Bryer too?

"I am." She said simply.

"Naught thou canst do, Erda. I am upon thy earth again, whole, thy blood hath healed me. Thou are but Spirit, thou canst achieve naught." He said, realising he had the upper hand at long last.

Erda moved forward and walked around the other side of John, forcing him to turn around to watch her. Her eyes flicked to Amy and back at John, while she asked him what he planned to do next. He was more than happy to boast about his plans. In fact, he explained in great detail how he would find acolytes to teach the arcane arts to and then he'd make more children for his grand legacy to continue, of course gaining wealth and prestige as he went through the years. He had obviously thought this through, plotting away, long and hard, while living inside Emily.

Without warning, Amy felt the ropes on her wrists loosen and finally they were free. She glanced over her shoulder to see Bryer nodding at her indicating to the right hand side of her seat, she looked over in that direction and saw the gun laying on the cement floor. Bryer also untied her legs from the back legs of the chair and then, as quietly as he could, laid back down on the ground, and he couldn't help but groan again when he did so, he was evidently still in a lot of pain and he looked deathly pale.

Amy's arms and legs were entirely numb from being held in the same position for so long, and it was pure luck that she couldn't actually move them yet, when John glanced round to see what the groaning noise was behind him.

"Enough of thy useless chatter." John said to Erda as his attention snapped back to her, and he turned around to face her once more, now knowing nothing was amiss behind him.

All of a sudden, there was a great noise from above, as if someone had just kicked in a door. Much shouting and banging could be heard as footsteps of what sounded like several people, moved across the room above the basement, making the wooden floor boards creak and dust fall downward. Finally, it sounded like they were at the door of the basement, which they banged on and shouted through it, demanding the door be unlocked.

John immediately looked panicked, and he began looking around for the gun. He knew the power of it from when he was squatting inside Emily, and he liked the feel of it very much, it excited him in ways he hadn't known before.

Erda remained stock-still and continued to watch him carefully.

Amy, finally regaining the feeling back in her limbs, tried to leap for the gun at the same time John did. They struggled with it and the gun went off, narrowly missing Amy's upper arm by millimetres. John, being the stronger of the two, wrenched it away from her hands and pointed it directly at her.

Amy gasped and staggered back nearer to Bryer. She put her hands to her ears because of the painful ringing she was experiencing from having the gun fired so close to her.

The banging grew louder and more urgent on the basement door, and, now that whoever it was had heard a gunshot, their attack upon the door had intensified and the wood had begun to crack and splinter from the furious onslaught.

"Must needs I taketh my leave." John said as he turned and quickly moved aside a shelving rack to reveal a hidden old door, it was obviously Emily's emergency exit.

Amy crouched by Bryer and placed her hand over the bullet wound, pressing against it hard, trying to stop the bleeding, which made him groan more with pain.

Erda still remained unmoved and she continued to watch John.

"For God's sake Erda, don't let him get away." Amy cried, desperate for Erda to do something, anything.

John turned the doorknob but it was locked, he rushed back to Emily's cooling body and rummaged in her dress and jacket pockets, and, finding an old key, he stood and staggered, apparently dizzy for a moment.

Again Erda watched him without moving.

John shook his head and frowned, he was now having trouble seeing as well as standing. "What doth thou think thou hast done?" He said fear beginning to creep into his voice.

Erda watched silently.

"Thy foul-toothed devil's whore, what spell hast thy cast upon me?" He staggered over to Amy and Bryer and held the gun to Amy's head.

Amy froze as the barrel of the gun pressed into her flesh just behind her ear and she stared balefully at Erda, her heart pounding crazily in her chest. Surely Erda wouldn't let her die, would she? She was family, after all.

There was absolutely no sign of emotion on Erda's face, she seemed not to care in the least.

"Retract thy spell or lose thy child." John said.

Amy, terrified, looked up at John who now looked distinctly ill, the pallor of his skin had changed from a healthy pink to a sickly grey colour and he was sweating profusely.

Gripped by some mysterious pain, John abruptly collapsed to his knees, gasping. He waved the gun shakily in Amy's direction.

Amy held her breath as several things happened at once.

With a loud sound of wood breaking, the top panel of the door to the basement finally gave in and shouts could be heard from the top of the stairs.

John groaned in agony, dropped the gun and clutched his torso.

Amy watched as the gun skittered away in the opposite direction to her.

Erda, at last, moved. She came close to John and looked down upon him, "Thou ought to hath knowest, John. Thy way to remove a'curse 'tis to make the one who saith it, taketh it back. Thy killed me a'fore thou couldst do that."

"Saith now, I beg thee." John gasped out, pain creasing his face.

"Thou gave me no mercy nor my family, thy shalt have none." She stood and watched him writhe in agony.

Detective Inspector Andy finally got through the door and burst onto the stairs with his gun out, telling everyone to put their hands in the air and not move.

Erda watched her ex-lover squirm in agony and said, "Thy got it wrong, John. Yes, I hexed thy body but I also hexed thy rotten Soul." She said and smiled.

It was a smile of pure and utter revenge and it chilled Amy to the bone.

Swiftly, Detective Inspector Andy ran down the stairs and reached the basement, his gun pointing at the four people, out of five, he could see in the room. He quickly scanned, assessing the situation, all of them were on the floor, one appeared dead, Bryer had been shot but the woman next to him looked essentially unhurt and the other man looked injured in some way. Detective Mitch could be heard calling for backup and an ambulance from the top of the stairs.

John opened his mouth and a terrible, agonised scream burst out as his flesh began to ripple and rot and the outer skin slid off his body, like water off a duck's back.

Everyone in the room watched in horror as this now skinless man continued to scream and squirm in excruciating agony until, finally, they saw his stolen organs detach themselves and fall away.

With one final and terrible shudder, Dr. John Lambe's Soul was abruptly rejected from the monstrosity of a body, and the remains of his misappropriated body parts exploded violently, with the power of the hex, and splattered all nearby with warm, hideous gore. The remains of the corpse collapsed into a sinking, wet puddle of dripping body parts and vital fluids.

Chapter Twenty Seven

Thursday, 1st November, Canada.

Amy sat rather forlornly in a pale green, with geometric shapes on, faded hospital gown over her jeans. Her shirt was utterly ruined by the amount of blood and gore, which had covered her, from when John disintegrated before her eyes. She was completely exhausted and sat, barely able to move, in the surgical lounge at the hospital in Glendale, waiting for news on Bryer who was still in surgery. She had already been checked over by a doctor and, thankfully, had only suffered rope burns on her wrists and ankles and minor abrasions and bruising from the ordeal, and she had been cleared to go home. She was very aware just how incredibly lucky she was, it could have been so much worse. Bryer, on the other hand, had been shot and the wound had made him lose a lot of blood and he had been knocked unconscious by hitting his head on the metal shelving in the basement.

Detective Inspector Andy sat quietly next to her, staring into space. His clothes were also splattered with blood, but not to the same extent as Amy's had been. He had only spoken a few words since their arrival a couple of hours ago.

Amy didn't know what to say to him, in fact she really didn't feel like talking to anyone at that moment.

Every time the door to the operating theatres opened, Andy and Amy jumped up and stared at whoever came out, hoping for some news, but no one had come out with news about Bryer, yet.

Amy had tried looking at the women's magazines spread copiously around the sitting area but her mind couldn't take anything in and she gave up on them. Sighing, she looked around the room, it was a typical hospital room full of chairs, small tables and the piles of magazines, of course. The walls were a sickly sage colour with landscape prints screwed onto them, the lighting was way too bright, and it smelt strange, as all hospitals do.

A shimmer to the right of where she sat caught her eye, turning her head to focus on it more clearly she realised it was Erda slowly seeping into existence and materialising so she did not make Amy jump. Amy watched, endlessly fascinated by the process, as Erda's shape became more distinct and defined. Finally, she became whole again.

Erda smiled encouragingly at Amy.

Amy nodded toward the restroom, "I'm just off to the bathroom, come find me if there is any news." She said to Andy.

Andy simply nodded and continued to stare off into space.

Erda followed Amy across the room and into the ladies bathroom.

Amy checked all the stalls to make sure they were alone, the last thing she wanted was to be caught apparently talking to herself, in a hospital. They would lock her up.

"Where have you been?! You vanished as soon as the ambulances arrived." Amy said, still feeling angry with Erda for not doing anything during the whole nightmare.

"Thou was well enough, hence I followed Bryer to watch upon him, I thought thee would want it so." Erda said.

"Oh, right...erm...that was thoughtful of you, thanks." Amy felt ashamed for her quick anger. "How is he doing?"

"I nay knowest he be still attended by thy physic."

"Why didn't you do anything? With John, I mean. He could have killed us all and you just stood there completely unconcerned." Amy said as she hauled herself up on the countertop next to the sink because she was too tired to stand any longer, and her legs were feeling wobbly.

"I was a'waiting for my hex to work its true purchase upon him and my attending him wilt likely cause him to stay therefore nay hurt others."

"Never mind about others, what about us? Emily, and John, I suppose, nearly killed Bryer and John held a gun to my head!" Amy's anger boiled to the surface again and exploded with her words.

"Thy were nay in real danger..."

"Not in danger? Are you fucking kidding me?"

"Nay, I nay hath kids for thee.' Erda looked confused by Amy's words. "If he want to kill thee he 'twould done so and nay saved you for thy Breath of Life."

"The what? What's that?"

"'Twas the last part of his spell, he needed the Breath of Life from a family member to seal it. "

"Oh, lovely. So that's what that was."

"He hath other designs for thou tho', he saith he want children for his legacy."

"Oh my God, seriously? That's just disgusting."

"Aye, he be a warped devil. 'Tis truth."

Amy thought for a moment, "So you kept him talking while waiting for the hex to kick in."

"Kick in?"

"Yes, to work, to happen."

"Aye, I distracted him with his own pride."

"That was a dangerous risk."

"Nay 'twas not, I knowest him well, remember thee."

"Right." Amy wasn't truly convinced that he wouldn't have killed her had he not...he...she couldn't even bring herself to think about what had happened to him. "Remind me to never get on the wrong side of one of your nasty hexes, okay?"

"Thy hast naught to fear of me." Erda smiled, "Granddaughter of mine."

"Amy is just fine, thanks." A grim smile appeared on her face.

"Amy it shalt be."

Amy looked at Erda and had never wanted a reassuring hug more in her life but what would a hug from a Spirit feel like, she already knew Erda's touch was cold. Perhaps a hug from her wouldn't be comforting at all.

Amy climbed down off the counter and, with Erda following a few steps behind, she returned to the waiting room where Andy hadn't moved a muscle. Sitting down next to him again, Amy thought she had better talk to him as he didn't look like he was coping well with what he saw. "You okay?"

"Yeah...just not sure what the fuck I saw happen in that basement."

"Hmm..." Amy had no clue what to say to him that would explain it all, there was just no version of the truth that would work out well for everyone concerned.

Andy closed his eyes and blew out a long breath. "I'm pretty sure that...wasn't...normal. I mean he was alive and then he wasn't and he literally fell to pieces, how the fuck does that happen?" He looked directly at her.

In his eyes, Amy was shocked to see the horror and terror that deeply haunted his mind.

"I just don't fucking understand it." He said and turned away from her and went back to staring into space.

Amy's heart went out to him, what could she say or do that would explain it or even help him in the slightest? Telling him that she has been haunted by her ancestor, who was burned alive by an evil man but who managed to put a hex on him before her last breath. Then his Spirit returned, like hers, only he tried to be corporeal instead and destroyed many bodies in the process, only to find out later that his descendants bodies might withstand the hex, so he joined with a madwomen and killed his, their, family to take pieces of them so he could build himself a new body, which he then brought back to life with a spell. Only to die a horrible death when the hex eventually caught up with him. Oh yeah, if she told him that they would definitely lock her up and throw away the key.

The door to the operating theatres opened and a short woman in scrubs came out and looked around her. "Detective Inspector Withers?"

Andy's head snapped up at her. "Yes?" He stood and walked over to the woman.

Amy quickly followed him.

"Hello, I'm Dr. Warren, Bryer Burnett's surgeon." She said.

"How is he?" Andy said.

"Are you Mr Burnett's family?" The woman said to them both.

"No." Amy said.

"No, he doesn't have any, but the guy works with me for the Police." Andy said.

Amy was surprised, she hadn't known Bryer had no family.

"Ah, I see. Well, Bryer is doing well and out of surgery. He's in recovery, at present, we removed the bullet with very little damage to his shoulder. We did have to give him a transfusion because he had lost so much blood and he does have a concussion, but he is strong and will heal with no permanent damage."

"Oh, thank God." Amy said as she breathed a deep sigh of relief.

"Well, that is good news. Thank you, Doctor." Andy said as a smile appeared on his face.

It was the first time Amy had seen him smile, it completely transformed his face and showed just how handsome he truly was, even if it was in a penal code kind of way.

"Thank you, Doctor. Can we see him?" Amy said.

"Not yet, in a couple of hours when he has recovered from the anaesthetic. I suggest you both go home and get some rest." The doctor said and smiled, she turned and walked back through the swing doors and back into the operating wing.

"Right, I think I'll take her advice and go home, take a shower and maybe a nap. By the time I get back he should be awake." Amy said.

"I was thinking of doing the same, I'll give you a lift."

"Thanks, Detective Inspector Withers."

"Call me, Andy."

"Okay, Andy." She said wearily.

Andy nodded, escorted Amy out to his car and then drove her home almost in complete silence, which suited Amy, her mind was just as full as Andy's and she didn't feel like talking about any of it.

*

After taking a long, hot shower, she slept for a little while and then had the pleasure of putting on some nice, clean, fresh smelling clothing. Amy got a taxi into Morton Creek to collect her truck and then, good as her word, headed back to the hospital in Glendale to see how Bryer was doing.

Walking the hospital corridors, she felt much better now that she was rested and clean. It's amazing what gets taken for granted and, no longer seeing all that blood on her, which kept bringing all the horror back, she felt a lot more relaxed. Now, at least for a while, she could pretend it didn't happen, even if it was a temporary salve for her sanity.

Amy took the elevator to the fourth floor, and made her way to the nurse's station to get Bryer's room number, thankfully he had already told them she could visit, and they gave her the number without hesitation, once they had checked his visitation list. Well, at least that is a good sign, Amy thought as she felt a little nervous about visiting him, not really knowing if all these horrible things that happened had changed their relationship.

Bryer shared his room with a man who had broken his leg in two places and it was up in traction, the man was asleep when Amy entered their room. Bryer, whose bed was by the window had the head of his bed raised so he could sit up a little, he sat staring out at the rather grey first day of November, not really seeing it. His shoulder was bandaged and his arm immobilized to protect the wound, his gown was only covering the uninjured side of his body and he looked tired and pale.

"Hey there." Amy said as she cautiously approached the bed, "How are you doing?"

"Hey. Okay, I think. You?" He looked her up and down searching for injuries.

"I'm good, thanks. Just a few rope burns and bruises." She lingered by the end of the bed, "Mind if I sit?'

"Sure." He said and gestured to the seat, by his bed, with his good arm.

An awkward silence fell between them.

Amy desperately searched for something to say, "The doctor said you will make a full recovery so that's good news, isn't it? Does it hurt?"

"No, it's numb from all the pain killers."

"Ah, good."

More silence.

"I'm sorry." He said and looked her straight in the eye.

"What for? You freed me even though you had been shot. You were very brave and have nothing to be sorry about."

"You don't understand." He sighed and looked down at his hands.

"Understand what?"

"What I did." He turned away from her, looked out the window again and watched the rain begin to fall.

The silence was so complete that for a few moments only the rain could be heard tapping on the window, until the general hospital noise found its way back into the silence and made them look at each other again.

Something was definitely playing on his mind, she could see it in his eyes now.

Erda slowly appeared by Amy's side, "Tell her thy truth."

"I'm trying." Bryer said to Erda.

Amy looked from Erda to Bryer and back to Erda, "You can see her? You can see, Erda? When? How?"

"I first saw her that day I came to take photos of your cottage, but I didn't know what I was seeing then. It was just a glimpse and I thought it was the lack of sleep or too much coffee or something."

Amy's eyebrows raised, "Oh, you never said."

"Then she appeared to me at my apartment when I was going crazy looking for you. Scared the crap out of me."

"Yeah, I know that feeling well." Amy looked reproachfully at Erda.

Erda just smiled serenely.

"Wait, you were going crazy looking for me?" Amy's eyes shot round to focus back on him as she realised what he'd just said.

"Of course. Anyway, once I got past the shock of seeing a ghos...a Spirit." He corrected himself quickly.

Erda nodded approvingly.

"Erda explained that I had been under a spell for some time, can you believe it? Apparently, it was put on me by Emily who used me to inform her of the police progress on the various murders, allowing her to keep one step ahead. When Erda made me remember everything, I found out I had been helping her with phone calls and visits for some time. I had no idea I was doing it, that I was helping a serial killer. I didn't believe Erda or my eyes...at first." He looked embarrassed and ashamed.

"Nay fret thee lad, 'twas nay fault of thine."

"Yeah, well, feels like it." He took a sip of water from the plastic glass on the side table. "Apparently, Erda here was able to counteract the...spell...somehow, I don't know how it all works, and when Emily called me, I really heard her voice in my head by the way, it was as if she was...right there next to me...telling me to do whatever she wanted. She told me to come over and tell her exactly what Detective's Andy and Mitch were doing. I managed to fake it, to pretend she still had me under a...spell and, luckily, it got me in the door."

"That was brave of you." Amy said. "But it must have been horrible to find out what was happening to you. Thank goodness Erda could stop the spell, who knows what she would have had you do next."

"Yeah, I know. I had no clue how bad things really were until I was down there with you though."

Amy turned to Erda, "Why didn't you just come straight to the basement, instead of sending him into danger?"

"I couldst do naught, thy hag hath protected thy room same as we hath thy cottage. I couldst nay enter."

"Ah, so that's what you were doing at the window." Amy said, looking back at Bryer. "Did wonder at the time."

"I scratched off the symbol with my keys and broke the protection so Erda could come in."

"Nice." Amy nodded.

"Yeah, got shot for it though." He grinned.

"Oh, you'll live." Amy said and laughed, relieved to see some of his old self coming through.

"Thanks for the sympathy." Bryer said and they both laughed as the tension between them eased considerably.

The door swung open and Andy stepped into the room. Walking past the other patient who had now woken up because of the noise in the room, Andy arrived at the foot of Bryer's bed and nodded to Amy. "How are you doing?" He said to Bryer.

"I've been better, thanks."

"Yeah, I'm sure. Listen, we will need statements from you two, probably tomorrow when you've had time to...well, time to..."

"Get our stories straight?" Amy said and saw that haunted look on Andy's face again.

"Nothing to get straight, Andy. Amy was kidnapped by Emily who was as crazy as they come, and had been collecting trophies from her murderous spree. I went in to try to rescue her, got shot. Amy and Emily struggled and managed to spill the body parts on the floor in that struggle and Emily dropped down dead, probably from a heart attack or something, she was quite old after all. And that's when you burst in." Bryer said and looked at Andy.

Andy looked at Bryer, then at Amy who nodded her agreement and then he looked back at Bryer.

Amy waited and held her breath, whatever Andy thought and did now she knew it would affect them for the rest of their lives.

"Sounds about right, from what I saw." Said Andy as relief spread over his face, he felt that same relief settle over him entirely. Now that he had the events all tied up with a neat little bow, his mind finally had permission to forget whatever else he might or might not have seen and he could just go with the official story.

Amy breathed out heavily and she saw Bryer do the same.

"Right, I'll be off then, someone will come by to see you both tomorrow for the official statement. Take care of yourself, Bryer." Andy said and left without another word.

There was quiet in the room as everyone thought about the story, the silence was only punctuated by the sound of the patient in the other bed snoring again.

"Hmm...that was nicely done, Bryer." Amy said when Andy was out of earshot.

"Aye, thy storytelling skills art great." Erda said.

"Well, I'd had some time to think about it while laying here. I knew it would be difficult to explain the truth so I thought of a way around it without too much lying."

"One small problem..." Amy said and the other two looked at her, "Emily was strangled and didn't die of a heart attack."

"Ah...good point." Bryer said and sighed.

"Nay concern thy self, I wilt visit thy doctor of death and guide his hand whilst he writes his scripts."

'Oh...right." Amy said hoping it would be that simple and would work.

"You will do what?" Bryer said, confused by Erda's old fashioned language.

Amy lowered her voice, "She means she will visit the Coroner and help him write that Emily died of a heart attack on the forms...kind of guide his hand if you know what I mean."

Bryer looked at Erda, he was not sure if he agreed with this course of action, but what else could they do without either himself or Amy being blamed for Emily's murder? He looked at Amy and raised his eyebrows, questioning the move.

"Yeah, I think it's the best way forward." Amy said to Erda. "Just let's not think about it too much." She said to Bryer.

"I wilt leave thee now, unless thy hath needs of me?" Erda said.

Amy tried not to think about the Coroner who was about to be temporarily possessed by Erda, admittedly for the greater good of all concerned. Amy looked at Erda, "Wait, you will be coming back won't you? I kinda got used to having you around."

"Aye, lass, I wilt be a'round thee some more yet." Erda smiled and evaporated.

Amy and Bryer were quiet again.

"So that's your Grandma, huh?"

"Yeah, sort of, she's my many times great Grandmother actually, but yeah, she's family."

"And he...that...monster...John...was your x-times great Grandfather?"

"Yup." Amy nodded.

"Shit. Well, I guess it's true what they say."

"What do they say?"

"You can't choose the members of your family." He said with a grin.

Amy smiled too, "Nope, not even the dead ones."

Epilogue

The fire crackled and spat as the orange glow of it illuminated the room with a warm, cosy light. The lights from the Yule tree sparkled and shone on the ornaments and tinsel hanging from the tree's evergreen branches. The mantel over the fireplace was covered with the green branches that had been pruned off the tree and had several lit candles decorating it.

There was a delightful smell of a traditional Yule dinner cooking, which came wafting in from the kitchen. Amy had decided to cook it with all the trimmings for Bryer, to show him how the Brits celebrated Yule. She was thoroughly enjoying having someone special to share it with for a change. She was sitting on the sofa with her head on Bryer's shoulder and her slipper covered feet were up on the coffee table watching the flames of the warm fire. She was waiting for the cooker alarm to go off telling her the roast potatoes had finished cooking and it was time to serve, everything else was ready and keeping warm. She snuggled closer to him and into the blanket that covered them both, she sipped her eggnog slowly, enjoying every moment of the peace and quiet and continued to stroke Bilsby, her cat, who had recently arrived from the UK. She glanced out the window and big flakes of snow were softly falling to the ground making the already thick white carpet thicker.

"I love the winter here, it's how it should be...all white with snow, making everything look new, clean and fresh. We don't get much snow in the UK, at least the part I'm from." She said, feeling both happy and excited at the same time.

"Are you glad you decided to stay then?" He lifted her chin and kissed her gently on the lips.

"Oh, yes, it's the best decision I've ever made, love it here. I always wanted a place of my own, a cosy little place with a garden and a nice view and, of course, here I had it all along. You certainly can't find any of that in the middle of London."

"No, I guess you can't."

Quietly, Erda appeared in her usual seat by the fire, it had become her favourite spot. It was probably due to her need to feel warm again or perhaps it was a reminder of her gruesome death, she never had explained it.

"Happy Yuletide to thee." She said to them both with a smile.

"Oh Erda, it's lovely to see you, Happy Yule."

"Happy Christmas, Erda." Bryer said and went back to reading, now fully accustomed to her dropping into their lives.

"Where have you been this time? Paris? Rome? How about Prague, I hear that's lovely." Amy said, her mind thinking of all the places she'd like to visit one day.

"I hath found out why I didst nay knowest of Abigail being at John's house. I travelled back to look upon true happenings."

"Oh, so what happened?" Amy said.

"Nay long after his death, his house burnt down upon ground with a'many of his servants in. Abigail and her nurse were the only ones to escape a'burning. 'Twas whence John's sister took her and raised her up as her own."

"Wow, well that explains it. They were very lucky then." Amy said, pleased Erda now knew the truth of her child's younger years.

"Aye." Erda nodded and looked into the flames of the fire.

"Where else have you been? We've not seen you at all recently." Amy said, wondering what Erda had been up to for the last few days.

"I hath been down south in thy United States of America. Found a small town with some int'resting old magical books, I thought thee would like a'visit with me upon thy morrow or thy morrow's morrow."

"You mean visit as in not actually go there but still go there?" Amy laughed.

"Nay." Erda smiled.

"Oh?" Amy looked at her, surprise written all over her face.

"I fancy teaching thee a'nother way a'travel, 'tis how Emily and John...did their devil's deeds." Erda said.

Amy cringed at their names despite herself. "And what way is that, exactly?"

"'Tis a'way to be a'place quick but with thy body, nay just thy Spirit."

"Really?" Amy said as her eyebrows rose.

"Aye. 'Tis by use of a'nother Sigil, the one thee saw a'fore part of the Sign of Forfend."

"Oh, yes, I remember there were two combined and one I recognised from the crime photos Bryer had. Well, it sounds interesting, if you think it's safe then it's a date." Amy said, intrigued.

Bryer put down his book. "You'll have to show me how to do that one day, Erda." He said, thinking how useful that would be. "It could come in real handy sometimes."

"Aye, I wilt teach thee lad." She said and smiled, but her attention soon returned to the flames of the blazing fire, as it always did. After a while she turned back to look at Amy. "I hath a'need to teach thee, Amy, of plants and trees and magics."

"Oh, I would like that, Erda."

"Thou wilt need a place to dry and store 'em and to work such magics as I teach thee."

"Well, we could use the attic, I guess, perhaps get some counters in and some cabinets and drawers. What do you think to that idea?"

"'Twill be a grand scheme." Erda said and smiled.

The phone rang on Amy's desk by the window and made Amy and Bryer jump. Erda didn't even twitch, it was as if she knew it would ring right then.

"I wonder who that could be." Amy said as she flung back the blanket and grabbed the phone off the desk. "Hello?"

"Ah, Amy, darling, how the devil are you? Oh, and happy Yuletide, my darling."

"Felicity, how lovely to hear from you and happy Yule to you too."

"I do wish you weren't in the colonies for Yuletide, darling, you are missing so many supper parties." Felicity's voice was a little slurred as if she'd already had a few too many party cocktails.

"Now, you know very well I've moved here permanently, Felicity."

"I know you said that when you came back to sell your flat and pack up your adorable little things, my darling, but I do miss you."

"Well, we can always chat on Skype and we can stay in touch by phone or email, of course, and there will be more book tours too. We will see each other from time to time."

"Too true, my darling, too true. Do you truly like it there? With all that horrid snow?" Felicity said 'snow' as if it was a dirty word.

Amy turned and watched Bryer as he sat reading again, he was still snuggled under the warm blanket they'd shared. "I adore it here." She said with a very happy heart.

"Well then, who am I to stifle your happiness?" She paused, perhaps to take a drink of some exotic cocktail. "I just wanted to say, I read your new book proposal and the sample chapters you sent."

"Oh, yes? And what did you think?" Amy mentally crossed her fingers and hoped Felicity liked her book premise.

"Well, it's far, far outside of your normal genre, but I thoroughly enjoyed it, and I want you to send me the full manuscript, shall we say by summer, June, something that should do. I do rather believe we can sell it, darling."

"Oh, that's excellent news, Felicity." Amy's face lit up with a truly joyous smile.

Bryer and Erda both looked at Amy.

Amy made the thumbs up gesture to them both.

Bryer's face filled with pride and love and Erda smiled the biggest smile Amy had ever seen.

Felicity's voice pulled Amy back to the telephone conversation and she just heard the end of the sentence, "...and I simply love the title, however did you come up with it all? You are so adorably clever, my darling, I think it's exquisitely superb. 'Witch Bottle', what a title! It's wonderfully brilliant, darling."

Acknowledgements

Special mention goes out to Dan Fentiman for his editorial skills and marketing advice.

Also, my thanks go to Brynja Clark for all the research support both as a Chartered Herbalist and as an advisor of Northern European Traditions.

Finally, I am grateful to Sergeant P. Leon for his patience and assistance with all the Canadian police related information.

Source

I   The 'Anglo Saxon Hallowing Charm' is drawn from original Old English manuscripts and was translation to English by Galina Krasskova.
~ Adapted slightly by J.E. Marriott to fit the 17th century vocabulary.

The next instalment of the 'Witch Books':

Witch Tree

Find out what happens to Amy when she begins her lessons in the arcane arts, beginning with plants, trees and ancient magic. Will everything go smoothly with her first spells? More importantly, why are events changing around her, when Amy and Erda remember them quite differently?

Who is Cabot Tanner? And what does he really want?

With some of the town's people missing and some others who are appearing back from the dead, what is happening in Morton Creek?

All these questions, and many more, will be answered in 'Witch Tree', Book 2 of The Amy Grey Novels.

Witch Tree

History isn't safe when you can rewrite it.

About the Author

J.E. Marriott is an internationally acclaimed author of paranormal mysteries, supernatural thrillers and magically enchanted tales.

In 2008, she permanently moved from her home in Lincolnshire, in the UK, across the pond' to Canada where she has happily, and permanently, made her home in Brockville with her husband, two cats and is a full-time author.

She is a university accredited historian and avid reader of a wide spectrum of genres. She brings her unusual English lilt and humour to all of her writings, no matter the genre.